HIDDEN MICKEY

ADVENTURES 4

Revenge of the Wolf

Nancy Temple Rodrigue

Double R Books

HIDDEN MICKEY ADVENTURES 4
REVENGE OF THE WOLF

FOURTH NOVEL IN THE HIDDEN MICKEY ADVENTURES SERIES
SECOND EDITION PAPERBACK, VOLUME 4, JUNE 1, 2017
 ISBN 13: 978-1-9383193-3-4

DOUBLE R BOOKS
DOUBLE R BOOKS PUBLISHING
740 N. H STREET, SUITE # 170
LOMPOC, CALIFORNIA, 93436
 www.DOUBLERBOOKS.com
COVER CONCEPT BY NANCY RODRIGUE
 www.NANCY.RODRIGUE.org
COVER ARTWORK & COLOR BY CHRISNA RIBEIRO
 www.JUHANI.DEVIANTART.com
COVER COPYRIGHT © 2015 BY DOUBLE R BOOKS
 www.DOUBLERBOOKS.com

1ST EDITION eBOOK - JUNE 2015 - ISBN 13: 978-1-9383190-8-2
1ST EDITION PAPERBACK - JULY 2015 - ISBN 13: 978-1-9383190-7-5
1ST EDITION HARDCOVER - JULY 2015 - ISBN 13: 978-1-9383192-1-1
2ND EDITION PAPERBACK - JUNE 2017 - ISBN 13: 978-1-9383193-3-4

PRINTED IN THE UNITED STATES OF AMERICA

HIDDEN MICKEY ADVENTURES 4

The Fourth novel in this Action-Adventure Mystery series about
Walt Disney and Disneyland, written for Adults, teens, & tweens (9 and up).

From the author of the acclaimed HIDDEN MICKEY series.

TWO ADVERSARIES FINALLY FACE OFF

Unwillingly hurled into the past, Wolf must confront the mysterious Omah in a final showdown. What will they do when secrets are revealed? Will they be able to put the past behind them and work together?

PETER MUST GO TO NEW HEIGHTS TO FOLLOW THE CLUES

Armed with a new set of clues, Peter and Catie find themselves in parts of Disneyland they never expected to see. Wolf is still missing. Can Adam and Beth help see them to safety without Wolf?

WHO REALLY WROTE THE CLUES?

An old enemy is back. Determined to retrieve a cherished possession that has been lost for eons, she will stop at nothing to get it back—even if it means sacrificing Peter.

NOW IS THE TIME FOR REVENGE

Disneyland—then and now—is the backdrop for this exciting tale of revenge as the past and the present come crashing together. Revenge of the Wolf fits more pieces of the puzzle together as our friends and heroes fight to protect Walt Disney's legacy—and each other.

REVENGE OF THE WOLF

Dedication

To my husband Russ Rodrigue.
He has read every word I have written,
offered support every step of the way,
and has been there for almost every
book signing and appearance I have made.
His behind-the-scenes work
has been invaluable to me.
Thank you from the bottom of
my red diamond heart!

Nancy Temple Rodrigue

Disclaimer

Walt Disney Company Trademarks: *Hidden Mickey Adventures 4: Revenge of the Wolf* is in no way authorized by, endorsed by or affiliated with the Walt Disney Company, Inc., Disneyland Park, or WED. Disneyland Park is a registered trademark of the Walt Disney Company. Other trademarks include but are not limited to Adventureland, Bengal Barbecue, Buzz Lightyear, Disneyland Railroad, Fantasyland, Fowler's Harbor, Fowler's Inn, Frontierland, Haunted Mansion, Indiana Jones, It's a Small World, Jungle Cruise, Magic Kingdom, Main Street, Market House, Mark Twain, Mine Train Through Nature's Wonderland, Monorail, Motor Boat Cruise, New Orleans Square, Pirates of the Caribbean, Plaza Inn, Screamin', Sleeping Beauty Castle, *Snow White and the Seven Dwarfs*, Snow White Wishing Well and Grotto, Splash Mountain, Star Tours, Star Trek, Submarine Voyage, Tahitian Terrace, Tarzan's Treehouse, Tea Cups, Tomorrowland, Tom Sawyer Island, ToonTown, Walt Disney, and *Wonderful World of Color*. All references to such trademarked properties are used in accordance with the Fair Use Doctrine and are not meant to imply this book is a Disney product for advertising or other commercial purposes.

While some of the events and persons contained herein are historical facts and figures; other persons named and the events described are purely fictional and a product of the Author's imagination. Any resemblance to actual people is purely coincidental.

The actions depicted within the book are a result of fiction and imagination and are not to be attempted, reproduced or duplicated by the readers of this book. The Publisher and Author assume no responsibility or liability for damages resulting, or alleged to result, directly or indirectly from the use of the information contained herein.

ACKNOWLEDGEMENTS

I WOULD LIKE TO THANK THE FOLLOWING PEOPLE
FOR HELPING ME BRING THIS NOVEL TO LIFE:

SAM GENNAWEY, AUTHOR OF *THE DISNEYLAND STORY*
FOR HIS HELP WITH DISNEY TIMELINES

SUSAN HORKY
FOR HER VIDEO OF SNOW WHITE'S GROTTO

J. C. TREGARTHEN
FOR HIS HELP WITH THE ADVENTURELAND BUILDINGS

MY BETA READERS:

JESSICA COWGUR COLEMAN
TIMOTHY CRUMRINE
JENNIFER DUTROW
MARILYN JOHNSON
LAURA O'LACY
JEFF SMITH

THANKS AND ACKNOWLEDGEMENTS ALSO GO TO
OUR PROOFREADERS AND EDITORS:

ALYSSA COLODNY
KIMBERLEE KEELINE, ENGLISH, PH.D.
WWW.KEELINE.COM

Dear Readers,

Walt Disney once said: "Sheer animated fantasy is still my first and deepest production impulse. The fable is the best storytelling device ever conceived, and the screen is its best medium. And, of course, animal characters have always been the personnel of fable; animals through which the foibles as well as the virtues of humans can best and most hilariously be reflected."

In this adventurous, fun-filled novel, we delve deeper into Fantasy and find out more about Wolf's and Omah's pasts and how they came to be as we now know them. You will remember the exciting events in *Hidden Mickey 4 Wolf: Happily Ever After?* when Wolf was captured by Nimue, Merlin's apprentice. Do you recall what she said at that time? "I am known by many names." Now she is back to settle an old score and to retrieve something that has been lost to her for eons.

Will Wolf be able to fight this formidable foe once again? Or will it be too much for him to handle?

Hidden Mickey Adventures 4: Revenge of the Wolf begins where *Hidden Mickey Adventures 3: The Mermaid's Tale* left off when Peter and Catie were confronted one last time by the mysterious Omah. Wolf came to their rescue and suddenly disappeared with the woman after they tumbled over the railing of the old Motor Boat Cruise dock.

Peter and Catie are having troubles of their own when a new girl threatens Catie's friendship with Peter. As new clues are discovered, Peter finds himself becoming more involved in the search. What will happen when he finds a new room hidden deep in the Castle that holds a priceless artifact? What will he do when he has to make a future-altering decision?

I hope you enjoy the history of Disneyland and the new adventure,

Nancy Temple Rodrigue

Prologue

Disneyland

Kimberly's eyes grew wide as she pulled herself up the last rungs. If she hadn't known better, she would have sworn she was in Walt's apartment over the Fire Station, but that was on the other side of Main Street. They were above the Market House, having entered a door that was always locked. "This is amazing."

Peter and Catie ran from one piece of furniture to the next as they pulled off the covering sheets. In their excitement, Kimberly and Beth guessed they probably didn't even realize what had been uncovered.

"Slow down, you two! What do you make of this?"

"Mom, Walt left us an apartment just like his!" Peter happily threw himself onto the Victorian armchair set in the middle of a red, floral rug. His blonde hair was instantly haloed by dust, the swirling motes going in and out of the dusky light filtering in through the lace curtains.

Beth stifled a sneeze. "Hope Walt left a vacuum…. Hold on, you two. Let's take these covers off a little more slowly, please. Who knows how long they've been in place. Catie, help me with this one. It's pretty big."

The next piece that emerged from its shroud was a red velvet sofa flanked by two lovely antique tables. If the furniture did mirror what was in Walt's apartment, it would probably be a sleeper sofa.

Kimberly emerged from exploring the back of the apartment. "There's a tiny bathroom and shower back there. This really is an apartment!"

"And it's ours! We can stay overnight at Disneyland any time we want to!"

"Mom, can we…."

"No, it's a school night." Beth pulled open a set of white folding doors. "Here's a small kitchenette. Look, there's even a two-slice toaster. This is so…so cool!" She turned a full circle and compared what she was seeing to what she remembered about Walt's apartment. "This is really close to what Walt's place looks like. The furniture isn't exactly the same, though. Close, but I can tell these are reproductions while Walt's are true antiques."

"There aren't any pictures on the walls or any thingys on the tables like at home." Peter, finally pausing to take a breath, pointed at the bare, antique white walls.

"Hmm, you're right." Kimberly nodded as she looked around. "Probably because Walt figured whoever found it would want to decorate it themselves."

Catie called them over. "Hey, look at this! It was in the closet. It's heavy."

"What is it?"

Beth looked over their shoulders as Catie set the copper-colored item on the coffee table. "That looks like brass. Why would he leave a flower arrangement?"

"Remember, Beth? There used to be a flower market just a few steps from here on East Center Street."

Beth wasn't listening. Intent on the item and a piece of trivia in the back of her mind, she wanted to see the vase. "It's so oddly shaped. Would you mind if I take out the flowers?" Since Peter and Catie were the new owners of the apartment, she directed the question to them.

The two kids just shrugged. "I guess."

"Oh, my!" Beth's hand went to her mouth as the vase was completely revealed. "I heard about this years ago. I never thought I'd get to see it."

"It's a hat."

Beth had to smile at the unenthusiastic tone of Peter's voice. "Not just a hat. This was one of Walt's fedoras! Come sit on the sofa and I'll tell you about it." She saw the look exchanged by the kids. "Hey, it won't take that long. Come and sit."

"Well, I'm curious, even if they're not. What's the story, Beth?"

Happy to dig into her vast knowledge of Disney history, Beth ignored Peter's bored expression. "Walt and Lillian had a friendly, long-running argument over the hats Walt wore. He loved them all crumpled up and she didn't like the ones he always chose to wear. Once she even pulled his hat off his head and tossed it out of the convertible he was driving. Walt had to stop the car to run back and get it. He crammed it back on his head and they went on their way." Beth went back to the table and picked up the bronze hat. "Then, later, in 1941, Walt did something very special. He had the brim of a different hat—one that Lillian had tossed into a bull fight ring—shaped into a heart and had the whole thing bronzed. It was filled with violets and given to Lillian as a present. This is that present."

"Aww, that's so sweet."

Beth smiled at her daughter. "I thought you'd like it, Catie."

"Gosh, one more story like that and I'll cry."

Startled by the new voice, their heads jerked toward the ladder opening. Omah pulled herself into the room and looked around the apartment, ignoring the startled faces around her. "So this is what he did." Walt had never shown her the final prize. The muttering continued as she stalked over to the window and jerked it open. "So greedy to see what they got that they don't even let some fresh air in."

"What are you doing here!? You promised to stay away. How did you find us?"

The sharp blue eyes narrowed at Kimberly as Omah came to the center of the room. "So many questions. So few answers you deserve. If you don't want people to know you're going to Main Street, don't announce that you're going to Main Street."

"I don't care how you found us. Get out! Keep away from us!"

Her attention focused on the speaker, Beth. "Do not tell me what to do." She suddenly turned and pointed at Peter who took a step back. "And you! You ruined everything!"

They could see a glint of silver from her hand. Not knowing if the angry woman was armed, Beth stood in front of the children. "Get out and get out now. Wolf will be here any moment."

"Wolf." The word was almost spat out. "I've watched you ever since you got here. No sign of your precious Wolf." Her attention went back to the startled boy. "You had to butt in and spoil it. He... he said nothing mattered since you figured out the clue anyway. It didn't matter if I got the mermaid back or not! You ruined it!"

"Who are you talking about?" Kimberly's heart had started to pound in her chest. They all had assumed Wolf was watching from the shadows. She felt she needed to keep this woman talking so she couldn't act on what she obviously came to do. "Who said it didn't matter? Who are you talking about?"

"Wal…It's none of your business who I mean. I have a score to settle with the boy."

"You will not touch my son!"

The silver dropped lower and the edge of a blade was clearly visible. "I will do what I want."

"Get away from the boy!" Wolf's deep voice came from the opening in the floor.

Omah spun around to face the angry security guard as he jumped from the ladder into the room. "He ruined my life."

"He did nothing. This is your own doing, Omah. Drop the knife."

"That boy doesn't deserve this prize. I want that key so he can never come back here again."

"You get nothing." Wolf slowly walked toward the woman, his glare boring into her.

Eyes wide, she backed away, knowing the small blade in her hand would not stop him. It took only one look around the room to reveal how she would get away. Wolf had the access to the ladder blocked. That left only one other exit.

With a sudden, fluid movement, she flung herself out the open window. Knowing an awning was there—and her only way out— the tight green material over the stairs broke her fall. With a bounce and the agility of an acrobat, she grabbed the edge of the awning and swung down onto Main Street. A crowd of startled, gaping on- lookers scrambled out of her way.

Wolf flew down the ladder and quickly hit the hidden latch. As the door flew open, he ran out to the sidewalk. Looking both ways, unsure which way she had gone, Wolf was directed by several guests who pointed north on Main Street. As he took off, he finally spotted her close to the buildings, pushing people out of her way as she ran.

She knew he would follow, and she knew exactly where she was headed. Her breathing wasn't even labored as she rounded the Matterhorn to run past the Submarine Lagoon.

Wolf started to gain ground as he pursued the woman. She wasn't going to get away this time.

At the far end of the Motor Boat Cruise dock, Omah stopped running and turned to wait. It would be only moments before Wolf would reach her. With a sneering smile on her face, she knew exactly what she was going to do.

Expecting the dock to be empty, Wolf came to a skidding halt when he saw that Omah stood at the end. He could tell by her arrogant stance that she was waiting for him. There were a few people sitting on the benches in the shade provided by the overhead Monorail track. They had seen the woman race onto the dock and now, even more curiously, an extremely angry security guard just arrived. It took only a word from the guard to send them elsewhere, backward glances over their shoulders that showed they wondered at the drama that was apparently unfolding.

Once he made sure they were alone, Wolf slowly neared her position. "You aren't going to get away this time, Omah. You won't get past me again."

"Only a fool goes into a place with just one exit. And I am no fool. Do not think you have the upper hand, Wolf."

His blue eyes narrowed as he approached. It made him a little concerned that she was unafraid. People who think they are in complete control can be the most dangerous. He knew to proceed with caution. "I am always in control, Omah."

She gave a low, uncaring chuckle. "You have no idea what I can do, Wolf. No idea." She tilted her head to one side as she scrutinized him as if he was a bug under a glass. "You have this air about you. Tell me something, Wolf. What is your real name?"

That wasn't a question he expected. His pace slowed as he watched her. She made no move to get away or showed any anxiety that he was almost upon her. "That isn't important. This must end, Omah. You will not scare and threaten the children again."

Arms folded across her chest, she ignored his warning. "Tell me your name. Or shall I guess?"

"It doesn't matter what you do."

The words were hissed. "Sumanitu Taka? Is that right, Wolf?"

That stopped him in his tracks. No one outside of his closest friends knew his Lakota name. "So you are clever and figured out my heritage. So what? That doesn't change what will happen here."

"You have no authority over me, Wolf."

Her superior attitude finally got the better of him. "You will not be allowed to just walk away."

"Are you not even a little curious about *my* name? Omah is just part of it. Would you like to hear the rest?"

"I don't care what your name is." He was within a couple of feet from her. If they had both extended their hands they could have touched.

"My, how angry you are. I can feel your hands around my throat, squeezing."

"I haven't touched you!"

"Ah, but you would like to, wouldn't you? Are you that violent, Wolf? Is that what you have planned?"

She was attempting to goad him into action. He knew it, could feel it, but stood where he was, assessing his options.

She smiled at his silence. "Since you asked so nicely, I shall tell you." Sarcasm dripped from her words. "My name is Om-ahkapi'si."

It took a full minute for the word to register with him. His breath came more rapidly as he stared at her. "That's a Blackfoot word. It means…wolf."

Her eyes glared at him and the hidden knife dropped from her sleeve into her waiting hand. "Yes, it does. What are you going to do about it, Wolf?"

In a split second he saw the knife come straight at him. With the agility of his namesake, he jumped aside. When it was heard hitting the dock with a metallic clang, he gave a roar and leaped at the woman.

Eyes flashing in anger, she snarled at him, "So, you want to play rough, do you? I'll show you rough!"

With his arms around her slender frame, the adversaries fell over the protective blue railing of the dock. Wolf closed his eyes and held his breath, expecting to hit the water at any moment.

There was no water beneath them as they hit hard ground and

rolled over and over with the momentum.

With the awareness that came from centuries of travel, Wolf could feel the change come over him. It was the frantic, unwanted realization of the moment and then his transformation into a wolf was complete. Powerful legs still entwined around Omah, he refused to let go.

Wolf's eyes flew open when he heard an angry growl and felt hot breath on his face.

He was no longer wrapped around the body of a woman.

He stared into the eyes of a large, snapping red wolf.

CHAPTER 1

Disneyland

Their mouths slightly open, all of them equally stunned, Kimberly, Beth, Peter, and Catie stood in the middle of the small room above Main Street in Disneyland. The only movement came from the lacy curtains in the open window as they blew in the evening breeze. They had just witnessed Omah, the woman who had followed and threatened the kids since they found the mermaid hidden in the Haunted Mansion, jump out of that window. That frantic escape had been triggered by Wolf who had arrived just as she pulled a knife on Peter. The angry security guard had then disappeared down the ladder of the secret apartment to give chase. It had all happened in a matter of minutes, scarcely enough time for them to process the events that led to those dramatic exits, let alone react to them.

With the speed of youth, Peter Brentwood, age thirteen, and Cate Michaels, age eleven, recovered first.

"Whoa! Did you see that? That was so cool! She dove right out the window and had to have done a flip on the awning!"

"Peter, she pulled a knife on you again! What would we have done without Wolf?"

"Wish I could have seen her land! Wow, I'll bet Wolf didn't even use the stairs, Catie! I'll bet he just jumped straight down to Main Street!"

"Do you think he'll be okay?"

"Wolf? Ha! Nobody can hurt Wolf! I'll bet he already caught her and….uh…." A confused look briefly passed over Peter's face, his enthusiasm clouded. His gaze drifted toward the window. He wasn't sure what Wolf would do to the woman once he did catch her. Now curious, he hurried over to the open window, hoping he could spot them somewhere on Main Street and see the end of the drama.

Seeing his movement and coming to her senses, Kimberly quickly pulled him back, while resisting the urge to look down the Street herself. "Peter, you need to get away from the window. This apartment is supposed to be a secret." With slightly shaking hands, the window was closed and the lacy curtains pulled back into place. She wasn't sure what made her more nervous—that crazy woman's knife or Peter possibly following her out the window. With Peter's impetuousness, it was a possibility. "I didn't see anyone looking up at us. They still seemed to be focused on wherever it was that Wolf and that woman went. Let's just hope they think it's a new show or something." She looked over and noticed Beth had drawn her daughter into a tight, protective embrace. With a silent sigh, Kimberly knew Peter wouldn't appreciate the same public display of affection. *Why do they have to grow up so fast?* Putting her hand out, she lightly punched him on his arm. *That should be safe enough.* "You okay, honey?"

Not focused on what was going on inside the apartment, Peter still tried to peer through the lace. "What? Yeah, sure, Mom. Hey, at least she didn't stab me again!" A glance over his shoulder showed him that his mom's face had gone pale and he knew he needed to talk fast. "I mean, hey, she only nicked me with that fingernail file at Grandma Margaret's." As he rambled on, Peter's face turned thoughtful. "But, you know? I really don't think she meant to hurt me." Knowing his mom and Beth would instantly object, he held up a hand and kept talking. "I know she had a knife, but I…I don't think that was her plan. When she had me before, I think her mind was, like, somewhere else, you know? She got all soft and mushy-like when she had me on the Motor Boat Dock. She just wanted the mermaid. I don't think she wanted to hurt anyone." He could see the doubt written all over their faces. But, they hadn't heard her talk. He had. "Well," he amended with a half grin, "except for Uncle Wolf. I don't think she likes him very much."

With no desire to go through the same debate about Omah's intentions again, Kimberly conceded his point. "Well, you're right about that. She *definitely* does not like Wolf." She shot a look over to Beth and gave a slight tilt of her head toward the door.

Beth understood her silent question and finally released her death-grip on Catie. "Well, I think we've had enough excitement for one day. How about we head home and let your dads know about this super apartment?"

The expected chorus of no's came immediately.

"Home? How can we go home? It's still early!"

"But, mom, we haven't explored the whole apartment yet."

"Mom, can we spend the night?" Peter turned his green eyes on Kimberly and tried to pour on the charm. "Please? It was a gift from Walt! He said he wanted us to have a special place of our own!"

After years of being on the receiving end of that same imploring look coming from her husband Lance, Kimberly was quite immune to it. Still, it vastly amused her to see the identical look now used by their son. *My word, if he bats his eyelashes, I'll probably start laughing.* "Listen, you, we already went through this earlier. It's a school night. Maybe later." *Much, much later when I know for sure that Omah is gone from the picture for good.* The silent thought caused Kimberly to clutch her hands into fists. After she forced herself to relax, a calm smile was pasted on her face. "We need to let Lance and Adam know what happened." *And we need to get in touch with Wolf to find out exactly what happened out there….*

"And, I'm hungry," Beth added as she started shooing the kids toward the door. The promise of food usually did the job of distracting Brentwood men.

"Blue Bayou?"

Beth had to chuckle at the hopeful tone of his voice. "Nice try, Peter, but we're going home. Why don't you go down the ladder to ground level first and make sure Catie gets down all right. But don't open the outer door yet. We should all go out at the same time. Hopefully no one will question why a door that's always locked and apparently goes nowhere suddenly has four people coming out of it."

"I think there's a parade soon, so it might be getting crowded out there."

That reminder earned a groan. "I forgot about that. We'll see what we see."

"You first."

Beth hid her grin. Kimberly hated ladders.

Jostling for the best position on Main Street to view the parade, the former excitement of seeing someone jump out of an open window had been forgotten. No one seemed to give them a second look as the rusty-brown door of 106 Main Street clicked shut and locked.

No one, that is, except one woman who had drawn back from the crowd, hidden in the shadows beneath the brightly lit marquee of the Crystal Arcade. Directly across the crowded street from the secret apartment, the woman—like everyone else in the vicinity—had just seen someone fling herself out of a second-story window and swing down from the awning. A shocked look of recognition crossed her face as that person lightly landed on her feet and gave a contemptuous sneer at the people around her before running toward Fantasyland. "You!" The woman in the shadows sucked in a breath as her hand went to the reassuring green pendant that hung from her neck. "You! I…I got rid of you years ago. How did…." Her muttered tirade stopped short when a security guard suddenly burst out of the doorway, looked in both directions, and, aided by helpful guests, ran after the fleeing woman. "No! Not you, too. How could this have happened?"

As she stared after the rapidly-moving Wolf, another movement caught her sharp eyes. Her head swung back to the open window when a boy appeared, apparently to follow the action below. He was immediately pulled back by a blonde woman and the window was closed. "So, now, I see there are others involved in this little drama. How intriguing. And just how are all of you related?" The sharp cheekbones were pulled upward by what might have been called a smile. It was a cold, heartless smile, completely devoid of humor. "My, my, this has turned out to be an interesting day. It just might make the long journey worthwhile."

With patience borne out by eons of necessity, the woman waited and watched. She was rewarded when the door reopened and four people, including that boy and the blonde, emerged. Unlike the previous two, this group headed the opposite direction, possibly toward the exit. With the secure knowledge that she would be undetected in the crowd, she fell in step behind the small procession. Just before the entrance to the ornate Opera House, they were all stopped when a pretty brunette girl called out to them.

"Peter! Peter! Is that you? Oh, wow, hi! Imagine seeing you here!"

His mind on Wolf and the discovery of the apartment, Peter didn't see or hear the girl until he physically ran into her. "Oh, gosh, sorry…. Lisa? Uh, hi."

Lisa giggled at his discomfort and pushed her bangs behind her ears. "I guess you didn't see me." With eyes only for Peter, the girl ignored everyone else around him. "So, have you been having fun today? Wish I'd known you were here. We could have met up and had some fun together. You come here often? I have an annual pass. You want to go on Big Thunder with me?"

"Who's your friend, Peter?"

Barely able to keep up with Lisa's barrage, Peter gratefully looked back at his mom. "Oh, sorry. This is Lisa…." He couldn't recall her last name. "Uhm, we go to school together."

"OMG, we are, like, in just about every class together! We've been best friends forever! Is this your mom?" Lisa looked up at Kimberly and ignored Catie who hovered at Peter's elbow.

"Yeah, this is my mom, and this is Catie and her mom Beth who…."

"I'm so glad to meet you! I've known Peter, like, forever."

Three more girls came up and nodded hello to Peter. "Hey, Lisa, we've got to find a place to sit for the parade. You coming?"

Lisa looked back at Peter with a coy look. "You coming? My dad can drive you home later."

"Uhm, no, we're going home. We just found…." He broke off when Kimberly subtly jabbed him in the back. "Uhm, no, we're going home."

Lisa's mouth went into a small, well-practiced pout. "Oh, okay. I'll… I mean, we'll see you at school tomorrow. Then maybe we can make plans to come back and spend the day together." She gave him a quick hug before she ran off with her giggling friends.

"Yeah, sure. Tomorrow. Bye." Peter raised a hand as they walked off, slightly confused by the girl's actions, a dopey smile on his face.

"Just like his dad," Kimberly muttered to Beth, who nodded, as a big grin spread over her face.

The only one who wasn't smiling was Catie.

Just inside the door of the Mad Hatter shop, the silent woman looked back at the four girls as they headed into the crush of people on Main Street. Her eyes narrowed onto Lisa and she had her own secret grin as her attention returned to the retreating form of Peter. Long, graceful fingers mindlessly stroked the green pendant as she thought. She had been drawn to this Park to find something that was lost. She knew it was here, but just couldn't hone in on its exact location. It was…close, she knew that much. The boy—Peter he was called—had mentioned "Uncle Wolf" as they walked. *So, he knows Wolf.* Apparently well enough to call him Uncle. This boy might be worth keeping an eye on. He might be just what she needed.

Wolf… and Omah, too? She had to shake her head in disbelief. *How could they both be here? How was that possible? One thing at a time.* Well, they could wait. She had something more important to do first.

The pendant seemed to glow in the evening light as her fingers worked over and over it. It was a sharp, harsh green compared to the soft white glow of the hundreds of light bulbs that started to light up all the way down Main Street. Even the trees twinkled in the warm summer air. The woman didn't notice this enchanting sight any more than she had noticed the enticing aroma of vanilla that had been piped out of the vents of the Candy Palace.

Still worn out from the long journey from her ancient time period and a recent battle, she could focus on one thing and one thing only. At her bidding, two unseen bolts of green energy flew in different directions. As they snaked their way over the heads of the people, each unerringly found their mark.

One lightly settled on the girl Lisa, still wound up over seeing Peter. And the other twirled around Peter's face as it tickled his nose, causing him to swipe at the unseen disturbance.

Satisfied, she made an abrupt turn and stalked back to the locked door from which the families had emerged a short time ago. The light bulb, for some reason shaped like an acorn, flickered when she looked up at it and obligingly went out. The dark purple outfit she wore blended into the shadows as she mounted the steps at 106 Main Street. Her hand hovered over the brass door knob for just a moment before she turned it and stepped into the darkness within.

CHAPTER 2

The Great Northern Plains

Wolf's eyes flew open when he heard an angry growl and felt hot breath on his face.

He was no longer wrapped around the body of a woman.

He stared into the eyes of a large, snapping red wolf.

The agility of his quick reflexes was all that prevented her fangs from clamping down on his muzzle. The surprise that they didn't hit the water, along with the shock of Omah turning into a wolf, plus the unsettling knowledge that they were no longer in Disneyland, was instantly pushed aside as his survival instincts kicked in.

Omah's agile body twisted out of his grasp when her lunge at his nose failed. Her sides heaved with anger and anxiety as the two wolves circled each other, eyes unblinking, fangs bared. *He turned into a wolf! I don't believe it. How? How could this have happened? I…I just thought that was his name…some macho attempt at vanity.* Her mind continued to spin with unanswerable questions as she instinctively jumped aside to avoid his leap at her neck. The intense blue eyes narrowed as she studied him and looked for any opening to attack. Having no way of knowing that he, too, would turn into a wolf, she immediately realized it wouldn't be as easy to subdue him as she originally thought. The element of surprise had been lost. Plus, his actions so far revealed he obviously knew his way around a fight. Another detriment was that he outweighed her by at least fifty pounds. *He's just like me….*

Alert to every movement, Wolf saw her eyes go from being furious to being confused and knew he had an opportunity. He feinted to the left and rushed Omah's unprotected side. The momentary distraction was forgotten as her blinding rage set in again. The roars of the two opponents filled the dusty air as they twisted and turned, fangs dripping and snapping.

Omah sank her teeth into his hind leg and felt satisfaction when she tasted blood. Her tail whipped to the side, the wrong side as Wolf retaliated by catching it in his jaws. Before he could clamp down, she managed to jerk it free as she leaped away from him. To gain an advantage over his superior strength, Omah took off at a dead run toward a rise of wooded ground off to the west. Her face pulled into a wolf's version of a grin as she ran. Her den was there.

And the camp of her people would be close.

With a quick glance at the blood on his leg, Wolf overcame the surprise caused by her abrupt departure and, once again, took to the chase. *I've got to get some answers. This is getting old.*

Wolf's pace slowed as he neared the stand of pine trees. She could be behind any one of them, ready to leap on his back and bite into his spine. *There had to be a portal in Disneyland, but I didn't hear her call for the storm. How did she do it? And…where are we?* He knew he had to stop this mental questioning and allow his senses to take over. It wouldn't do him any good for her to catch him unaware. Eyes closed and nose up, his ears only heard the furtive movements of normal creatures in the woods. His nose, though, caught her scent over the crushed pine needles as strongly as if she stood right in front of him. She hadn't tried to lose him. There was a trail, and it was obviously leading him somewhere. But where?

Cautious, he stepped into the shade of the trees. Part of his mind registered welcome relief from the hot midday sun. *It wasn't this hot back home. It was also evening.* He shook off the nagging inconsistencies as he quietly padded deeper into the forest. The path she had made was a mixture of disturbed leaves, broken twigs, and hairs caught on low-hanging branches. No self-respecting wolf would ever leave behind a trail like this—unless it was done on pur-pose. Wolf knew he had to tread carefully.

Her path led Wolf round and round the trees and boulders. It was a long, winding, unnecessary course. With the knowledge that he was being played, Wolf had no choice but to follow if he was to have any hope of finding her ultimate destination. He didn't have long to wait. The forest began to thin as he neared the opening of a large cave. The ground in front of the cave was packed and scratched, evidence of much use. Coming to a stop, his head swung in each direction, searching, but her scent always brought him back to the cave. She was in there, waiting.

His eyes tried to pierce the darkness but he couldn't see far enough inside. It was too deep, too dark. A mocking, guttural growl came from the depths of the darkness. This was it. This was the invitation for him to come and fight, to end it once and for all.

Instead of a headfirst rush into the cave, Wolf paused. He had two options. Well, three, but he would not call a portal and try to find his way home. That wasn't his way. One, he could stay where he was, wait her out, and then stand his ground in the open. Or, two, he could go into the cave and fight on her turf. Either way, there would be a battle. He had to make sure she would never threaten the children again.

Her turning into a wolf—*just like me*—stumped him. There had to be more to it than what he could now see. She had not spoken a word since they fell over the railing of the old Motor Boat Cruise dock. Her reactions were purely wolf-like—both in her ways of attack and her intelligence of flight. He gave a low, frustrated growl. There were still too many questions and no easy answers. With a shake of his massive head he once again tried to clear his mind of unnecessary, distracting thoughts, all the while attempting to peer into the darkness in front of him.

Another taunting growl came from within. Now was the time for action.

I was supposed to take my uniforms to the dry cleaners today. Disgusted with himself, Wolf stamped his injured leg. The insignificant pain served as a reminder: *Keep this up and you will not make it home. Then who will protect Peter and Catie…and Walt? Focus.*

With a steadying breath, Wolf edged to the side of the cave's opening. There were no more sounds from within, not even the heavy breathing of a worried adversary. His nose swung side to side. There, on the right. That was where her scent was the strongest. *She's expecting a straight-on attack. I never do what's expected.*

Wolf knew he would need a couple of moments for his eyes to adjust to the darkness of the cave. Still outside, he closed his eyes from the glare of the sun and sprang into the left portion of the den where he then spun around.

He stumbled when his feet slipped on what felt like paper on the hard-packed floor. When his eyes flew open, a momentarily glance at his feet caused another shock to ripple through Wolf. Under him were pamphlets from Disneyland and photographs of Peter and Catie.

Reacting before his mind even registered the movement, he twisted to the right to avoid Omah's lunge. She had seen his distraction and attacked, her teeth snapping thin air where his foot had been. Wolf doubled back, his tail attempting to cover her eyes as he shouldered her legs to knock her down to the ground.

In a tumble they rolled across the dirty floor, biting and growling, unable to get a firm grip on anything. Bursting out of the cave and into the open, their bodies were still entwined. Their powerful heads jerked this way and that, snarling and snapping.

Wolf's superior fighting skill got the better of her and rolled her onto her back. Her muzzle was firmly in his jaws, his claws had her forelegs pinned to the ground. She fell limp under him knowing he could break her jaw with one bite.

When she suddenly stopped resisting, Wolf continued to hold his dominant position. A beaten wolf should slink away, never to come back to the pack. But, did she consider herself beaten? Or was she simply waiting for the next moment to strike back? His deliberation was cut short when he felt a nicking pain in his side. Not releasing Omah's nose, he turned his head as far as possible and his eyes widened. Now he could see that, as they fought, they had been surrounded by warriors, Blackfoot by their dress, their spears all pointing at Wolf. Once he had gotten the black wolf's attention, the nearest brave drew his arm back to hurl his spear into Wolf's side.

With a sharp bark, Omah gave the command for the warrior to relax his arm. Reluctant, the brave was slow to lower his weapon. It was still held ready and pointed at the intruder. With a mighty shove, she got out from under Wolf and slowly stalked around him. Now that her people were there to back her, Omah taunted her opponent as she snapped close to his face, her tail whipping back and forth in victory.

Unfazed by her show, Wolf didn't even flinch, but kept his eyes on the spear-bearer. Experience told him that, if he bested her again, the warriors wouldn't hesitate to attack.

Another of the Blackfoot warriors said something to Omah as they all turned to leave. She nudged the tense Wolf with her head, and pointed with her nose. Still loosely surrounded by armed warriors, Wolf had no choice but to follow.

Alert, angrier than he had ever been, Wolf kept his eyes constantly moving as they entered their camp. With no visual references he could identify, he was unable to determine where—or when—he was. A low growl of frustration earned him a soft nick in the shoulder from the spear-bearer. *Let me meet you face-to-face on the battlefield and then we will see who masters that spear.*

Omah glanced over her shoulder at the incident. A well-placed foot kicked a cloud of dust into the wolf's face. It was a reminder of who was in charge. The bared fangs that answered her showed he would not easily be cowed.

The two wolves were led to the Council of Chiefs to decide what should be done with the intruder. Omah sat on her haunches as she bowed her head in respect. Wolf looked each chief in the face and stood his ground, his head high, his tail straight. He was the son of the Shaman. They were equals. Ignoring the low, warning rumble from Omah, he likewise ignored her.

Unfamiliar with the Blackfoot tongue, Wolf could only wait. Since there was no need for the Plains sign language amongst their own people, he could only pick out a few words. As the talk dragged on and on, he was reminded of his long-winded father and gave a snort of amusement. When Omah's sharp ears caught the disrespectful noise, her head whipped in his direction. Wolf covered it with a cough and sneeze as he turned away from her.

With some time on his hands he tried to familiarize himself with the camp. They had entered from the south and were now in the center of a widespread gathering of buffalo hide tipis. These were much larger than the ones the Lakota used. Each tipi seemed to have a resident dog that Wolf knew would help pull the belongings on a travois. To the right was a loosely defined corral that held the tribe's horses, guarded by a handful of older boys.

Wolf knew that there were two kinds of Blackfoot people. One was a warrior tribe, and the other was more peaceful and strived to get along with their numerous neighbors. They both would fight, but the latter rarely fought to the death and would rather count coup by touching their enemy in battle without actually hurting him. So far Wolf had no idea which kind of people were now holding him. Thinking back over all of Omah's behavior, he still could gain no clear insight, even though she had never actually hurt Peter. He would just have to wait and see which way this was going to go.

As the talk continued, a small rock suddenly flew across Wolf's head and slammed into Omah's side. Eyes narrowed, she glared at the wolf next to her, but realized he hadn't done anything. Her eyes roamed the perimeter of the gathered tribe and stopped on a small group of children huddled together, armed with more rocks. With a snarl she sprang to her feet, fairly leaping over the watching Wolf.

Wolf found he was holding his breath as the group of children scattered. Omah leaped at the biggest boy. He shrieked as he scampered out of reach, and the others rushed in to jump on the wolf who somehow had lost her balance and stumbled. The shrieks became cries of laughter as the children fell on her in a pile, hands grabbing tufts of hair as she rolled over and pretended to bite at them. Dust filled the air as the melee continued, Omah's tail waving in the air as she leapt around with the children who were delighted to have her back playing with them. Their play was interrupted by a call from the Council as they motioned for Omah to come back to hear their decision.

Omah interrupted Wolf's contemplation on seeing a different, softer side of her when she slammed a shoulder into him to get him to move. The moment vanished. Not wanting her think she had the upper hand, Wolf snarled as he suddenly lunged at her unprotected throat. Caught unaware, she found herself in a precarious position. With no effort at all, she knew Wolf could bite through her jugular vein.

One of the braves sprang to her aid by whapping the shaft of his spear across Wolf's back. Wolf refused to let go. Omah understood the reason and reluctantly let out a light yelp. Dominance acknowledged, the pressure on her neck lessened. She backed away, eyes filled with anger and embarrassment.

Wolf was surprised when she merely walked past him, followed by the majority of the braves and chiefs. Knowing that he was expected to follow, with no other option, Wolf proudly kept his head up as he fell in behind her.

Still alert, it was obvious to Wolf that they were being taken to the far side of the camp, away from the horses. The tribe's horses would be used to Omah's scent just as his tribe's horses were used to him. The men would have to be concerned with a foreign wolf around their animals. A loss of a herd of horses would be devastating to a tribe who relied on them for hunting and traveling.

A large, loose circle was formed, leaving the two wolves alone in the middle. Wolf began to think he had his answer: This wouldn't be a rambunctious frolic with the children. The tribe apparently expected them to fight to the death. He knew he could take a stance by refusing to fight her, but figured the braves would then jump in to finish him off. A fight to the death wasn't his way and he desperately needed an alternate solution that would satisfy everyone. *I could partially maim her....*

With an angry roar, Omah did what was expected by her people and launched herself at him, effectively ending his speculations. There would be no time for deliberations. He had to fight.

He nimbly jumped aside and turned back to reach her throat again. Omah was no fool and had anticipated his move. He snapped thin air as she feinted to the left to bite at his unprotected, sore back leg.

Her fangs didn't have enough time to sink in all the way but still reopened the wounds she had inflicted only a short time ago. Wolf freed his leg and kicked dust into her eyes to momentarily blind her. It also gained him a moment to try to think of another option. Being surrounded in their circle, there was nowhere for him to run and escape to gain some time. Not knowing where he was or where to run made that choice unappealing. Omah had the definite advantage here.

While she was still disoriented with the dust, Wolf leaped on her back, his superior weight crushing her to the hard ground. With a loud yelp of pain, she tried in vain to wiggle out from under him, snapping at his paws, but unable to reach them.

Focused on only her, shifting his weight so she couldn't escape, Wolf didn't see the reaction of the crowd at her cry. One of the women, her elaborate deerskin dress decorated with porcupine quills and beads, grabbed the spear out of the hand of the warrior next to her. With a shrill yell, she rushed the huge black wolf and began beating his back with the spear. When that had no effect on the animal, she stuck the tip into the bleeding gash on his leg.

"OW!" *Oh, shoot. Rule one: Never talk.*

Omah's eyes immediately widened as she ceased to struggle under his suffocating pressure. "You can talk!"

Wolf's head jerked around to look down at her face. He had been about to grab the spear with his teeth and grind it into sawdust. "You can talk?"

"Get off me!" Struggling, Omah used her shoulder to push against him and crawled away. "Why…." She broke off whatever she was about to say when her sister raised the spear again. "Saa!" *No!*

Her sister, Kiaayo, slowly lowered the spear, her confused face darted back and forth between the two wolves that stood before her. "Why can that wolf talk, Omahkap'si? We don't understand. Is…is he like you?"

Omah shook her head slowly side to side. Adrenaline from the fight still coursed through her and she was edgy, ready to fight some more. She answered her sister in Blackfoot as she paced in front of the shocked Wolf and her tribe. "I don't know, Kiaayo! I just found out. Asaksiwa!" *Leave us!* "I need to settle this."

"Bring him to us when you know what to do." Returning the spear to the disgruntled brave, Kiaayo motioned for the others to follow her.

Once alone, Omah stared into the blue eyes of Wolf. He glared back, ignoring the blood again running down his leg. "We need to talk, Wolf."

"You think?"

Omah bared her teeth at him. "Sarcasm will get you nowhere. Follow me."

Wolf sank down on his haunches. "This is fine with me."

With a glance up at the sky, she snorted and turned away to leave. "Suit yourself, but it's going to rain any minute. Not that you couldn't use a good bath…."

On their arrival, the clear sky overhead had been a brilliant, clear blue. But, typical of the Midwest Plains, small clouds had come in, one by one, unobtrusive by themselves. Bumping together, joining into darker, threatening shapes, the sky now darkened. A steady wind had picked up, blowing ahead of it dust and leaves. She knew it would soon turn fierce, both wind and rain lashing at the thirsty ground. Just as she spoke, the first fork of lightning streaked across the sky. With a disgusted shake of his head, Wolf realized, again, that he had no choice but to follow his hostess.

Instead of taking him to her tent in camp, Omah knew they would have more privacy if they went back to her cave in the hillside. Protected on three sides, it became a haven from the storm outside. With the brightness of the sun obscured, her den was even darker than before.

Eyes now adjusted to the dark, Wolf went first to the item that caught his attention earlier. He put his paw on the picture of Peter and Cate peeking out behind Lance. "Where did you get this and how did it get here?"

Curled up comfortably on the floor, her tail protecting her feet, Omah was amused by his demanding tone. "The 'how' should be obvious by now even to you. I took that photo just after I found the two kids in the Mansion. I figured I'd need it again to find them. It's amazing how popular that boy is around the Park. I learned from the cast members how to find his father and the rest was easy."

Wolf could tell by her relaxed position that the fight was over… at least for now. He knew, however, not to trust her.

At his continued silence, Omah knew he was confused as well as intrigued. Even though it didn't show, excitement ran through her. Impatient to find out about his past, her mind filled with questions. *Why was he like me? Can he do what I do?* When she finally did speak, her tone was carefully neutral as if she didn't care whether he answered her or not. "So, tell me, Wolf, how do you come to be this way? I thought I was unique."

Hearing her question, his head jerked up from the picture of his two little friends. Yet he still remained silent as he thought. *What should I tell her? How much?* It was too fascinating to pass up.

Her impatience got the better of her. "litsi'poyi!"

His head tilted to the side, not understanding the word. The command in her voice was obvious enough but he kept silent.

"I said speak!"

"Arf."

The irritation in her eyes faded as she began to chuckle. Her mouth dropped open into a wolf's version of a grin. "I've used that one myself." She looked away and shook her head. The movement caused the different shades of red in her beautiful fur to blend and dance in the dim light. "All right. Let's call a truce and start over. I'd say 'shake on it,' but I don't want you flinging dust all over my den. How about at least sitting and quit glaring at me. You're safe...for the moment."

Wolf did sit, but it was near the opening of the cave. "You apparently forgot who was pinned on the bottom. It wasn't me."

His reminder elicited a growl. "I was just catching my breath."

"Uh huh."

"Be that as it may, we are at an intriguing impasse right now. We both want to know how the other came to be and neither of us wants to go first. Am I correct?"

Now it was Wolf's turn to laugh. "Yes, that about sums it up." A boom of distant thunder echoed through the cave. The storm was almost over. Would the battle begin again? "How long have you been this way? How long have you been able to travel?"

"All righty, I see that we'll start with my favorite subject: Me." She got up to stretch. The three fights had taken a toll on her, unused to them as she was. The movement caused Wolf to be instantly on the alert, ready for anything. "Oh, relax, Wolf. I think you put a kink in my neck. You're quite safe from vicious attack."

"I know I'm safe. I just don't want any surprises."

She gave a huff as a reply and padded over to her sleeping mat. Pushing aside some of the paper debris with her nose, she found what she wanted. A granola bar was shoved over to Wolf. "Aooyiwa."

He glared at the wrapped bar at his feet. "If you insist on talking Blackfoot, I'll switch to Lakota and we'll never get anywhere."

"I said 'eat'." She rolled her eyes as she crunched on her own treat. "Have you always been this sensitive?"

"Have you always been this messy?" The granola was shoved aside.

"Suit yourself. I'm hungry." As she snatched it back, she carried it over to her original place in the cave.

Wolf stomach grumbled as he watched her eat what probably was all he would get for dinner. "Are you quite finished? I think we have a lot to talk about."

She used a paw to brush away a sticky crumb off her whiskers. "Yes, we do. I believe I have the floor."

Wolf mumbled, "Messy floor," under his breath.

"I heard that." At his pointed silence, she felt the need to justify. "I've been busy with traveling back and forth. You know how difficult it can be."

His silence continued.

"Fine." She huffed a dramatic sigh. "I've been able to travel since I was about thirteen or fourteen. I found out quite by accident. It was a lovely spring day, actually. I was thinking about my mother who had died right after I was born. She had been attacked...."

"By a rogue wolf with blue eyes. He bit her." Wolf's voice was so low she could barely hear him. What she couldn't hear was the sudden pounding of his heart.

"Yes! How did you know?"

"Go on with your story."

He acted like he was having difficulty breathing. "All right," she answered slowly as she closely watched him. *How did he know? Why are his eyes the same color as mine?* "As I said, I was thinking about my mother, and, poof, I was suddenly there."

"What do you mean? You were where?"

Omah lifted a shoulder in a shrug. "I apparently had traveled back in time and saw my mother before she was married. She was learning to do beadwork in front of her tipi. She was quite lovely. So young. I just stood there staring at her." In her mind she could clearly see the young woman from the settlers from Lincoln, Nebraska, who would become her mother. Her red hair caught the glowing light and shimmered like a wave down her back.

"Wasn't she terrified to suddenly see a wolf in front of her?"

Irritated that the only memory she had of her mother was interrupted, the dreamy look in her eyes vanished. "Wolf? Who said anything about a wolf?"

"You turned into a wolf when you traveled back in time."

Omah shook her head, confused. "Who said I turned into a wolf? I never said that."

"But that's what happens to me when I travel back in time. Isn't that why you're a wolf now?" Getting frustrated and angry again, Wolf jumped to his feet to pace the littered floor.

"I am a wolf now because I wanted to be a wolf now. I did that to exert my power over you, to show you who was boss. Apparently my surprise wasn't as great as I thought."

"But you obviously were a woman when we were in Disneyland. Now I can only assume we went back in time and you are now obviously a wolf."

"Obviously."

Her dry comment got him to stop pacing. He abruptly sat again to glower at her, his mouth slightly open. "Do I understand that you choose how you want to appear? Is that what you said?"

"Can't you? What's wrong with you?"

"Call the storm and show me."

Confused, Omah stared back at him. "What do you mean? Call what storm?" She glanced out the entrance of the cave at the clearing sky. *Is that what he meant?*

"That's how I travel. I howl for the storm and it creates a portal for me to go through. It's accurate…more or less."

"How archaic. No wonder you're always so angry. That must be exhausting."

"I'm not angry!"

"Yes, you are. I can tell by the way you're yelling at me."

Wolf had to stop and take a deep breath. They were falling back into their previous aggressive relationship. *I need more answers. I'll have to be more….nice.* He let out a low growl that was instantly met with a mocking laugh. Ignoring her, he again began to pace as he thought back to earlier. "There wasn't any storm or even a whirlpool when we vanished at Disneyland." He had to stop here, baffled by the events. "Was that still today?"

Omah gave an unconcerned shrug. "No clue. Time moves differently here. It might have been months ago. It could be tomorrow. We won't know until we go back." She gave him a sly look. "That is, if I choose to take you back."

"Don't threaten me. I can still do it my way."

"Surprised you haven't ended up inside a wall or something." She shook her head and grinned. "I could teach you, I suppose."

"Teach me what?"

"How to do it right."

Wolf bit back the words he was about to throw at her. Could he learn something new, something different than what he knew? He glanced over to where she sat. Sure, she was mocking him and sarcasm dripped like water from her lips. Could they put aside their differences and work together? Did he want to work with her?

His silence grew as she watched him. Wolf was obviously trying to work something out in his mind. She knew he didn't trust her. He had no reason to. Did she want him to trust her?

Her own musings stopped when she came to a decision. She had to show him she knew something he did not. And, there was only one way to accomplish that.

Quietly she got to her feet and padded out the opening of the cave. The rain had stopped and there were small pools of water here and there that were being absorbed by the thirsty ground. The air was fresh and invigorating, far different than the closeness of her den with two damp wolves sharing the space.

Wolf stayed where he was as she walked out of sight around the boulders that formed one of the protecting walls. Not sure of what he was supposed to do, and regretting not eating the granola bar when he had the chance, he just waited.

Within moments, his wait ended. Omah returned to the cave. Only now she was a woman, dressed just as she was when they fell over the railing at the Motor Boat dock.

His mouth fell open in surprise. "Why are you dressed? Where did you have identical clothes stashed?"

"Excuse me? Why wouldn't I be dressed?"

Wolf stammered. He would have blushed if he had been a man. "Er, uhm, I come back…unclothed. Don't you?"

Omah started to laugh until tears ran down her face. "Oh, my dear Wolf! I have so much to teach you!"

Chapter 3

Disneyland

"I'm so glad your mom let you come today, Peter. I wasn't sure you'd be able to since I just saw you Tuesday night. What's your little friend's name again? I just can't seem to remember. How did you do on that math test yesterday? I don't think it's fair at all to give us a surprise test on Fridays." Lisa had kept up a steady stream of chatter since the moment she met up with Peter and Catie on the steps of the train station on Main Street. Now riding on the top level of the Omnibus, her eyes were on Peter, not the shops or the quaint architecture on the street below.

On Peter's other side, a hurt frown on her face, sat Catie. "My name's Catie. As I already told you three times…." Ignored again, she gave a longing glance at the Candy Palace as they putted by. They were making English Toffee. She and Peter usually liked to stop for a few minutes to watch the candy makers inside and sniff the enticing aroma wafting out of the hidden vents. She knew she would have to speak up or she would be a silent third wheel all day. "Hey, Lisa, I really like your necklace. Where'd you get it?"

A brief look of irritation transformed Lisa's pretty face before she managed to control it. With a deep, dramatic sigh she reluctantly turned away from Peter. "What did you say, Cathy?"

"Catie. Her name is Catie, Lisa!"

Grateful to Peter for standing up for her, Catie's lips turned up in a brief smile. She realized she'd have to fight her natural shyness to counter the confrontation Lisa seemed determined to provoke. "I…I just asked about your necklace. It's so pretty."

Lisa's hand automatically went to the pendant that hung from her neck. As she looked down at it, she seemed more confused than flattered by Catie's compliment. "I, uhm, can't remember exactly where it came from." She held up the golden bird so she could see it better. The small eyes were red like rubies and the body was a shimmering green gemstone. Moments passed as she stared at it as if mesmerized. The darker green deep within the stone appeared to swirl and move in front of her eyes. With a shake of her head to try and clear the confusion, she looked up to see the questioning looks coming from her two companions. "I think it's a raven, but I'm not sure. It must have been in the back of my jewelry box. I guess I just forgot it was there."

"It looks really pretty with your top. I've never seen a purple that deep." Catie was still trying to get on some friendly ground with this girl.

"Yes, doesn't it?" With a smug look of amusement at the plain tee shirt Catie was wearing, she flipped her hair off her shoulder and turned back to gush at Peter. "So, tell me, Peter, what's your favorite thing to do in Disneyland? You and I are going to have so much fun today!"

And so they were back to square one.

The Omnibus dropped them off between the entrances of Tomorrowland and Fantasyland. They were in the heart of the Park and could go in any direction from there.

Peter grinned at Catie and pointed over to the left at the Hub. "Let's go say hi to Walt and Mickey."

Catie immediately perked up. That was a tradition of theirs every time they came to Disneyland together. *At least he isn't forgetting me.*

"Say hi to who?"

They stopped dead in their tracks to stare at Lisa. Not sure if he had heard her correctly, Peter had to clarify. "Walt and Mickey." He gestured again at the bronze Partners Statue, its base surrounded by an intricate swirl of golden mums and purple anemones. "You don't know who Walt is? You're kidding, right?"

She gave an unconcerned shrug of her shoulder as she looked from one stunned face to the other. "Should I? Who is he?"

Not wanting to provoke Lisa any further, Catie dropped her eyes to hide the amusement within them. This day just got better.

Peter could never like someone who didn't even know who Walt Disney was.

"He's only the founder of the Disney Studios and the person who built Disneyland."

"Oh. I thought it was just a name like Orville Redenbacher or Colonel Sanders."

"They are real people, too." Hands on his hips, Peter couldn't believe she didn't know who Walt Disney was.

Lisa gave a light laugh. "Gosh, you look so offended. You sound like you know him or something."

At her dismissive statement, Peter had to bite his lip. There was no way he'd tell her that, yes, he had met Walt. His time-traveling friend Wolf had insisted that the facts about their trip had to be kept a secret. "Everyone should know who Walt is, that's all."

"And now I do. So, let's go over to Big Thunder and get Fastpasses so we don't have to wait long in line later." With another flip of her hair, she grabbed Peter's hand and led them through the wooden fort entrance of Frontierland.

As they walked past the flagpole just inside the gate, Peter had pointed out a Hidden Mickey in the rocks on its base. Always ready with Disney trivia, he had a tidbit to share. "Hey, Catie, did you know someone backed a truck into this flagpole back in 2005? It snapped right off and fell onto a popcorn cart!"

"Oh, wow, really? I'll bet they were pretty upset. It's been here since opening day."

"Yeah. It got fixed pretty quickly and put back into place."

Unseen by the others, Lisa rolled her eyes and hoped this wasn't what she could expect for the rest of the day. When they each had a Fastpass, she took control again. "How about the Haunted Mansion? We have an hour before we can use our passes." There was a look exchanged between Peter and Catie that she misunderstood. "Or is it too scary for you, Cath...I mean, Catie?"

"I'm not scared of the Mansion!" Catie found she had crumbled her Fastpass in her fist and stuffed it into her pocket, hoping they hadn't noticed. "Let's go."

Lisa and Peter had to hurry to catch up to the angry girl. She was already past the white entrance of the *Mark Twain* and *Columbia* dock.

With a reassuring hand on her shoulder, Peter leaned in to give her a quick whisper. "It's okay, Catie. I don't think she meant anything by it. She never acted this way at school. Maybe she's just having a bad day."

Her arms folded across her chest and rigid stance told Peter that Catie didn't quite believe him.

"Okay." Peter gave a silent sigh. *This is going to be a long day.* "Lisa, did you see those eight flags flying over the *Mark Twain* landing? Do you know what they mean?"

"That's there's a nice breeze and it won't get too hot?"

Since he really didn't know her all that well, he wasn't sure if that was sarcasm or not. "Uhm, yeah, I guess. But each one also represents an important time in America's history. Like that flag over there came over on the Mayflower and that one went up Bunker Hill and...."

"Didn't you do a report on that in Mr. Russell's history class?" *Please say yes.*

"Yeah, last year."

"Then I remember. Interesting. Ooh, look!" Eager for any excuse to stop the history lesson, Lisa pointed at the Frontierland River. "The canoes are running! Do you want to go on those?"

"Thought we were going to the Haunted Mansion."

Lisa threw an irritated look at Catie but turned it into a smile when Peter looked at her. "We are. I meant after." The threesome joined the queue going through the bricked entryway of the Mansion. As they shuffled past the graveyard, they took turns reading the quirky sayings on the tombstones. "I like this one under the pig: Rosie. She was a poor little pig, but she bought the farm. 1849."

"This is my favorite: Dear departed brother Dave. He chased a bear into a cave."

As they continued to share some laughs, the building tension began to ease. All three of them fit into one Doombuggy, which pleased Catie who figured she would have to ride alone. Peter kept the conversation light as they wound their way through Master Gracey's neglected house. As they passed through the Ballroom, he pointed out the three plates pushed together into another Hidden Mickey pattern. He kept his memory of meeting the real Master Gracey and Constance to himself.

As they exited the tomb with the haunting call of "Hurrrrry baaaack" in their ears, they turned left to head to the canoes. Lisa took his hand again as they walked past the drop of Splash Mountain, a log-full of riders screaming their way down into the briar patch below. "So, Peter, what do you like to do best at Disneyland? Do you always just ride the rides?"

With a side glance at Catie and a small grin, he gave a shrug. "No, not just the rides. I like to find things."

"You mean, like the Hidden Mickeys you've been pointing out?" *Like, everywhere.*

"No, not just that. I like finding lost things. Ouch!" He had to wince when Catie punched his arm. "Hey, I wasn't going to tell."

"Tell what? You've got a secret?" Lisa's eyes narrowed as she watched the silent interplay between Catie and Peter. *Finally! Now we can start getting something accomplished. I don't know how much more of this I can stand.* "You mean like that door you came out of on Main Street? I went up to it later and it was locked." Her free hand played with the raven pendant hanging from a thin golden chain as she intently stared at Peter.

"You…you saw that?" He looked from Lisa to Catie and saw her eyes were wide. "I guess it would be all right to tell her since she saw us."

Catie wasn't going to back down. "No, Peter! You know what Uncle Wolf said."

"You have an uncle named Wolf? That's funny." Lisa stopped walking before they got to the wooden railings that marked the entrance to the canoe dock. They could see from where they stood that there wasn't much of a line that early in the day. As she leaned against the fence that blocked off that portion of Splash Mountain, she narrowed in on Peter. It was obvious she wouldn't get any information out of the girl. "So, tell me what you find. I won't tell, if that's what you're afraid of, Catie."

"I'm not afraid of you."

Lisa gave her a small smile. "I didn't say you were afraid of me." *You should be, though.* "I was just talking." She turned her wide green eyes on Peter as she held her necklace between her fingers. "Tell me what it is you find. Tell me, Peter…." Her voice was low and inviting.

Peter gulped and ignored the persistent nagging in the back of his mind that told him not to say anything. He had stepped between the two girls as if to shield Catie, not knowing exactly why he felt he needed to protect her. "I find things that have been lost."

The intrigued look on Lisa's face faded. "You mean, like a wallet or sunglasses? Why?"

Peter wanted the look of interest to come back to her face. He was sorry, somehow, that he seemed to be disappointing her. "No, not like that. Interesting things that have been lost a long...."

"Peter!"

He motioned behind his back for her to keep quiet. "It's okay, Catie. We can trust her."

"Yes, you can trust me. What do these things look like?"

Peter pulled his fingers free from her grasp, not even aware she had been holding them. His hands went about a foot apart. "They're usually gray canisters about this long. The thickness depends on what's inside. There's usually a clue or riddle and a prize of some kind."

"A clue to what?" Lisa's heart began to pound.

"Where the next one is hidden."

"So, you can find anything that's been lost?"

"Hey, Lisa, I didn't say that. They were put in place a long time ago and I just happen to find where some of them are hidden. Catie and I are pretty good at figuring out the clues."

Behind her back, Lisa reached into the bushes that were planted at the base of the mountain. As she pulled her hand back, still unseen by the others, she was holding a gray canister. "So, they can be anywhere? Like here, for example?"

"Here?" Peter frowned and looked up at the towering mountain as if he wasn't sure where he was. "Here? Oh, no, not here. Splash Mountain wasn't built in Walt's time. They have to be from when Walt was in the Park."

Lisa tossed the container back into the bushes. "Oh, I see. That makes it more difficult." She had been thinking to herself and didn't realize she had said it out loud.

Peter, though, thought she finally understood. "Yes! That's right. It *is* hard. Everything has to have been, well, lost before 1966. And there are still lots and lots of places I haven't explored yet."

"If we're going to ride the canoes, we need to do it soon. It's almost time for our Fastpasses."

Catie's reminder broke through the swirling mist in Peter's brain that was overriding his better judgment. If he had been asked to describe it, he would have called it green. "Canoes? Oh, yeah, that's right. We're going to ride the canoes."

"Are you okay, Peter? You look funny."

Pulling his gaze from the canoe dock, he looked into her worried brown eyes, familiar eyes that he had known forever. "Yeah, Catie. I'm fine." He reached out to lightly touch her arm. The contact seemed to clear some of the conflicting emotions running through his mind. "I guess I'm just anxious to find another clue, that's all. You know how much fun we have with them."

"And now there are three of us to find them." Lisa stepped in between them to break their connection, and threw a smile at the girl. It would not have been described as a warm, caring smile.

Catie had had enough. She didn't want to spend the rest of the day in Lisa's company. With a fake cough, she leaned against the rail that Lisa had just left and put the back of her hand against her forehead. "Peter? I don't feel really good right now. I'm going to go see my mom."

"Really? You seemed fine a minute ago." *Girls, sheesh.* "Aunt Beth is working Pirates today, isn't she? You want me to go with you?"

"No, you go ahead and ride the canoes. I have my walkie-talkie if I, uhm, feel better later and want to find you." *Much, much later, when Lisa is gone.*

He wasn't sure what to do. Catie didn't look sick and Lisa wasn't acting at all like she did at school. His mind was telling him to let her go, but he knew that wasn't right. "I should go with you, shouldn't I?"

"I'll come, too. You look really, really bad."

Lisa's piping up was the last straw for Catie. "No, just stay and go on the canoes. You're already here. I'll be fine." With an angry shake of her head and tears in her eyes, she quickly turned and walked back the way they had come without a backward glance.

Not completely sure what had just happened, Peter watched until Catie was out of sight. His hand curled into a fist. Something wasn't right. Whirling around on Lisa, he had to stop himself from actually yelling at her. "That wasn't cool, Lisa! Catie's my best friend. She should be going with me on the canoes, not you!"

So, the boy does have some spirit. That's good. He might need it later. Lisa let her face fall and managed to look repentant. "I'm so sorry, Peter. She looked so sick I thought she really wanted to leave. Should we go after her?" She placed one hand on her pendant and lightly touched Peter's arm with the other. "It's up to you. Don't you want to stay with me?"

At the touch, Peter's eyes dropped down to his arm. He could feel the warmth of her fingertips and his worry and concern over Catie slowly melted away. "She'll be fine once she gets to Aunt Beth."

"I'd like to see that room over Main Street."

The warmth on his arm spread up to his shoulders. A big grin spread over his face. "Sure, that would be great. When do you want to go?"

Lisa returned the smile. "No rush now, Peter. No rush. Let's ride the canoes. But I don't feel like paddling."

"You don't have to. I'll do enough for both of us!"

As soon as she got past the entrance to the Haunted Mansion, Catie turned right and headed into the shaded grove of Magnolia Park in New Orleans Square. Just above her, the steam train *Ward Kimball* had just pulled into the station and let off a mighty blast of steam.

Unseeing, her eyes on her feet, Catie walked unerringly through the twisting streets filled with quaint shops, ornate wrought iron balconies, and meandering people. Next to the Blue Bayou restaurant was the exit of the ride, Pirates of the Caribbean, where she knew her mom was working. She felt rather than saw the bright sunlight fade as she went up the ramp into shadowy darkness. Her nose picked up the chlorine smell that was unique to the last ride that Walt Disney himself had worked on.

Going against the traffic of guests who had just ended their voyage through the world of pirates, Catie wound her way over the wooden bridge to the unloading station. Only then did she look up. Her mom Beth was nowhere to be seen.

"Anne, have you seen my mom?"

The lead in charge of the ride that day, dressed as a pirate, turned from the operator's desk at the edge of the dock. Even in the dusky light lit only by flickering lamps Anne could see Beth's little girl was very upset. "Hi, honey. Your mom's up in the control booth. You want help in getting over to the other dock?"

Grateful that she wasn't being asked for any explanation, Catie just nodded as Anne held up a hand for the loader on the other side. "Coming over, Laura. Give her a sec."

Catie waited for the last guest in the first row of the flat-bottomed boat to get out before she hopped down onto the seat and ran to the other side. She smiled her thanks to Laura as she mounted the steps that lead up to the control booth. Her mom faced a panel of screens that showed the entire ride. Alert to anyone who stood up in the boats or took pictures, Beth was also responsible for each boat as it headed out below her. Properly filled and spaced correctly, Beth's job was to make sure everyone was safe.

Aware it was time for her break, Beth thought the person who just entered was there to take over for her, so she didn't look away from the screens. She had been watching one particular boat as it wound through dark tunnel of the Treasure Cave. "I already told you once, you stubborn man." As she muttered to herself, she pushed a button on the console and leaned into the microphone. "Please remain seated at all times. And no flash photography," she added when a bright flash lit up the next screen over. "I tell you, Dawn, these people just don't listen."

"It's Catie."

At the sad voice, Beth's head jerked up. "Catie! I thought you were with Peter and…what's that girl's name? What's wrong, honey?" With a last, quick glance at the monitors, she rushed over to her daughter to give her a hug. "Did something happen?"

"Am I ugly?"

Oh, dear, what did that silly boy do now? "Okay, it's break time." Beth went to the entrance to the small room and glanced down the ladder. "Dawn? Could you come up, please? Thanks. I need to take my break. Can you take over a little early?"

"Sure thing, Beth." With a kind smile to the girl who looked both miserable and embarrassed, Dawn sat in the chair in front of the monitors.

"Come on, honey. Let's go to the break room in the back." Beth smiled to herself when her girl's eyes lit up. Whatever it was that upset Catie was probably not as world-shattering as Catie thought.

"We get to go through the bayou!?"

"You know the way. Lead on."

Known only to the cast members, there was a secret path that traveled along the border of the bayou. As the guests were slowly pushed along by an invisible current of water, they drifted past the dark houseboats, glowing lanterns, and fireflies flickering in the darkness. The sky above was in perpetual night; the Blue Bayou restaurant off to the right was bathed in romantic dusk and lit by individual candles. Bullfrogs croaked in the distance and moss hung from the trees completing the complete immersion of senses. However, beyond the edge of the houseboats was the unseen edge of the water. There was a gap between the channel and the background paintings of an endless, misty forest of moss-draped trees.

It was through this gap that Beth and Catie now walked. If anyone had been looking closely enough between the houseboats, they would have seen two heads as they bobbed along, briefly visible against the blue of the matte painting.

Behind the final houseboat from which the soft strands of banjo music could be heard was a door that led backstage and to the room in which Beth and Catie now sat.

"Thanks for the dinner, Peter. I still can't believe I didn't bring any money with me."

"That's okay, Lisa. It was only a corndog." Peter paused, his hand on the knob that led to the secret apartment. His anger at her treatment of his friend had faded as the day progressed. The girl had changed her attitude once Catie left and was more friendly and fun. All the warnings from Uncle Wolf and his parents had shrunk into irritating gnats that he had swept away. Still, Peter hesitated at the door. Something wasn't right. He just couldn't pinpoint exactly what it was that was off.

"Aren't we going in?" Lisa saw Peter's reluctance and placed her hand on his shoulder as she leaned in behind him. Her words tickled his ear. "Turn the knob, Peter. We're starting to attract attention by standing here."

Her words and the warmth of her touch seeped into his brain once more. Thoughts of Catie and Uncle Wolf winked out and were gone. "Yes, just a sec."

That's a good boy. Let's get this game going. I need to gain your trust so you can lead me to what's mine. "Ooh, it's so dark in there! You sure this is the right place?"

"We have to go up the ladder, and then you'll see. It's really cool!"

Lisa let herself be led around the small room as Peter excitedly explained the clue search that had brought him to this place. "Oh, you're so smart. That's really clever. I don't know how you do it." She kept up a mindless, steady stream of compliments as he talked, which encouraged him to reveal more and more.

Peter was about to explain the history behind Walt's bronzed hat when he had to excuse himself. "Sorry, too much soda."

When he went into the small bathroom in the back of the apartment, Lisa slumped against the nearest wall, totally spent. "Oh, by the Sacred Gemstones of Merlin, how do they do it? How do they stand all these hormones racing through their bodies? It's…it's exhausting! And I thought it was bad when Aurora was mooning over that wretched Prince Phillip! This boy has to know where my red diamond is. I can feel it close by…so close, I just know it. If those meddling fairies hadn't interfered and blocked it…. Oh, it would be so much easier if I could just entomb him in a tree until he tells me what I want. That worked with Merlin…."

With a disgusted shake of her head, she reminded herself to get back to work. Using the girl's eyes, she looked around the room she had already examined earlier in the week. This time, though, she needed to 'discover' a reasonable hiding place. *I think I have a sufficient clue trail in place to lull him into a false sense of security. If this works like I think it will, I'll trick him into revealing where my heart is. I didn't travel all this way to be denied what is mine.* The mental tirade stopped when she heard water running in the sink in the bathroom. Her time limited, she summoned all her remaining strength, eyes closed as she continued to stroke the pendant.

Peter came back into the room to see Lisa standing up from the floor. About to ask what she was doing, the words caught in his mouth when he saw what she was holding.

"Peter! Look what I found!"

"Where did you find that?"

"My, uhm, thing rolled under the couch and this was under there! Isn't it exciting?" Lisa held out the gray canister for Peter to take. She could see the excitement in his eyes. "What are the odds, huh?"

Eager to have another possible clue from Walt, Peter took the case a she held it out for him. He appeared to be speechless.

Having expected him to probably rip it open with his teeth in his excitement, Lisa was confused when he merely stood there and stared at it. "What's wrong? Aren't you going to open it?" *Don't tell me it isn't right. I did just what you described, you miserable…*

.

"No, no, it's fine. It's just…." He looked up at the sharp green eyes that were glaring at him. How could he tell her he wanted to open it with Catie, not her?

Forcing her gaze to relax into a kinder expression, Lisa put her hand on Peter's arm. It was the only way to get him to talk. "What's the matter, Peter? I thought you'd be pleased with me for finding it."

The smoky, green swirl slowly worked its way back into his mind. "Oh, I am. It's just that I usually do this with Catie."

Oh, is that all? Finally! Now I can leave and get some strength back. "That's all right, Peter. I know you and your little friend like to solve the clues. Just let me know what you find, okay?" Her hand dropped from his arm when she went over to the window. "It's really late. My mom should be here to pick me up any minute. I'll see you in school Monday."

"Do you want me to walk you to the pick-up lot out on Harbor?"

"No, I'm good. Mom's coming to the lot behind Rainforest Cafe. I'll just take the Monorail. If you went, you'd have to go through the security check-point again. Thanks for a fun day!"

"Yeah. Fun." Peter could only watch as she gave a light wave of her hand before she disappeared down the ladder. His emotions were mixed as his hands moved over the cold plastic of the canister. The further Lisa got away from him, the clearer his mind became. "Fun? I guess part of it was fun. I need to check on Catie. Gosh, it's late. Aunt Beth has probably taken her home by now." As Peter mumbled to himself, he lifted his backpack off the floor to retrieve his phone. As he scrolled to her number, guilt began to seep into his brain. His finger hesitated over the Connect button. "She's probably really mad at me. I don't blame her." Peter hit the Message button instead. "I'll send a text." As he began to type, he let out a disgusted snort. "When did I become such a *coward?*"

Catie, guess what? Found another canister in apartment!

When can we open it?
    Her answer was immediate. *Ask Lisa.*

CHAPTER 4

The Great Northern Plains

The longer Omah laughed, the angrier Wolf became. Had she still been a wolf, he would have tackled her again, pinning her to the ground until she realized he was still the boss. If he did that now, it would probably break her back. A low, warning growl came from deep within his throat.

Omah finally managed to get herself under control and wiped the tears from her cheeks. Every now and then she would break into a chuckle as the mental image of Wolf desperately trying to find his clothes somewhere in Disneyland came back to her mind. "Oh, that was rich! Sorry, it's just so funny…. Why do you still look like you want to go for my jugular?" Her eyes narrowed as she smirked at him, purposely walking closer to his position. "Do you still want to fight me, Wolf? That can be arranged, you know." Just as she reached out with her hand toward his unflinching face, she changed back into a wolf. A snarl was her only warning before she leaped at him.

Momentarily stunned by the instant transformation, Wolf wasn't prepared to be attacked again. The weight of her body slamming into him shoved him against the back wall. Lights exploded behind his eyelids.

"Is this more of what you want, Wolf? We really need to get beyond this, you know. Ouch!"

Quickly recovered, Wolf bit the closest thing he could find—her foreleg. As she recoiled, he maneuvered away, turned and jumped on her back, crushing her to the floor.

"I think you made your point." Her words came out muffled,

strained because he was lying on top of her with his full weight.

There was no move to get off of her. "And what point would that be, Omah?"

"Get. Off. Me."

"I'm sorry, what did you say? I couldn't hear you. You sound like you're out of breath or something. Perhaps you need more exercise."

Unable to reach any part of his body to snap, she realized she would have to concede to his superior weight and, sigh, apparently his superior fighting skills, too. "Do you want me to say Uncle, Uncle Wolf?"

He took a long moment as if he was thinking about it. "That's a good place to start."

"And yet you're still not moving. Get off me or I'll change back and grab the knife out of my shoe!"

Wolf's answering chuckle irritated her even further. That little knife of hers never had intimidated him. He remained in position for a few more minutes just because he could. "So, are you ready to discuss this like a rational adult?"

"Coming from the man who outweighs me by fifty pounds and is currently crushing the life out of me."

"Is that a yes?" He could feel her body shaking with rage.

Her pride had taken enough of a beating. It took a lot out of her to finally answer, "Yes."

"Sorry. What was that? I still can't hear you very well."

"YES!"

With extremely slow movements, Wolf got up to release her from the hard ground. He sat back to wipe the dust from his face with a paw, his mouth open in a lopsided smile.

Omah threw him a disgusted look as she tried to get to her feet with some semblance of dignity. Turning her back on him, she stretched each leg to make sure they all still worked. "Quit smirking. It's not becoming." With a mighty shake of her body, all the dirt was cleared from her red fur. She was secretly pleased when most of it drifted over Wolf. "At least you didn't break anything. You might consider going on a diet."

"If granola bars are all you have to eat, I might be forced to."

"I usually eat with my family." She glanced out the entrance of the cave at the placement of the sun. "They should be sitting down to dinner about now. Shall we join them?"

Wolf wasn't too interested in going back to the camp. His first encounter had been less than friendly and he didn't want to be goaded into another fight.

"At your silence, I assume that's a no. If you're afraid, you needn't worry. They won't hurt you now."

She was trying to attack Wolf's dignity—and he knew it. Amused, he slowly shook his head as he answered her. "Unless you want to end up crushed to the earth again, quit trying to start another fight. I am not afraid now nor was I then. Is that clear?"

Omah could tell by the look in his eyes that she had best not press him further. With her back still sore, she didn't think she could take another beating. The offensive posture she had assumed was dropped. "I will give you that," she admitted grudgingly. "You are known for your bravery. I suggest we call a truce—a real one this time—to see what we can work out. You do have a lot to learn, and I want to figure out how we both came to be as we are."

Wolf looked at the paw she held out to him. He thought she was being sincere. At least he hoped so. All the fighting was making his body ache, not that he would let her know. His paw touched hers. "Deal. Now, to start, how come you and that woman who speared me have red hair? It's not a trait of the Blackfoot."

Knowing the fighting was over for now, Omah relaxed as she sat back on her sleeping mat. "Her name is Kiaayo. She is my sister—my older sister. Our mother wasn't Blackfoot, just Dad." She fondly thought back on the oft-told tale about her family. "One day Father was at a trading post in the Idaho Territory and saw this beautiful redhead. Her family and other settlers had just arrived in a wagon train from Nebraska. He was instantly drawn to her. Her name was Sadie Temple, and the feeling was reciprocated." Omah paused as she tried to put the rest of the story into non-judgmental words. "Let's just say her family wasn't too thrilled to learn about her infatuation. So, to make a long story short, she ran away to join the tribe. Just packed her bag one day and walked out of town in broad daylight. Even then, the Blackfoot were more, how would you say, progressive in their thinking. She was quite welcome. Especially by Father."

"And her family?"

Omah lifted one shoulder in a shrug. "The usual. Mother tried to go back to visit after Kiaayo was born, but, well, that just wasn't done then. She never saw them again."

Wolf just nodded. His tribe faced the same prejudices.

"Kiaayo was about two or three when Mother was expecting me. They were quite happy until...."

When Omah broke off and didn't continue the story, Wolf felt he knew why. It was the same ending that his parents had suffered. "Until the gray wolf came and ended their happiness."

Her sharp sapphire blue eyes swung to face him. "Yeah, but why? Why were both of our families hit like that? Why do you have the same color eyes I do? My mother's eyes were green; my father's a deep brown. How can we both travel like we do? And why a wolf?"

"Why, indeed." Wolf got up to pace the small cave. These were the same unanswered questions he had asked for centuries. "Was it the same wolf that tried to kill both of our pregnant mothers? It sounds like it, but how do we know? And how would that even be possible? My tribe lives nowhere near here—from what I can tell of the landscape. Then there is the fact that, after I was born and my mother died, my father tracked down the wolf and killed it. He wears the skin to this day. Your mother would have to have been attacked before then." Wolf broke off pacing and suddenly gave her a grin. "You know, that makes you older than me."

"Oh, shut up."

"Gosh, you could even be *decades* older than I am."

"It doesn't matter! I am thirty-five and I'm sticking to that."

"I usually say thirty-two."

"Hmmp. You would." She shook her head in disgust. "Men. Tell me, what do you mean that your father *still* wears the wolf skin? You meant in your youth, didn't you?"

Irritated at his slip, Wolf didn't want to tell her his family was represented by the Friendly Village situated on the Rivers of America back in Disneyland. Experience taught him that anything done at Disneyland in the current day affected the past. Since he didn't know what she would do with that knowledge, he didn't want her messing with his loved ones. She had a long way to go to earn that much trust. "Yeah, sure, when I was a kid. I still go back to visit when I can."

Her eyes narrowed. Positive he wasn't telling her the whole story, she decided to let it pass. There would be plenty of time later to discover what he wasn't explaining. "And you are always a wolf when you go back in time?"

"Yes, I am and don't look so amused. Obviously you know how to do it differently. *That* I am eager to learn from you."

With no desire to end up flat on the ground again, she held back the sarcastic remark on the tip of her tongue. "Why don't you show me how you travel, and then I'll teach you how to do it right."

"It isn't wrong. It's just different."

"Archaic."

Seeing they were headed for another argument, Wolf stalked out of the mouth of the cave. The breeze carried the tempting aroma of roasting meat from the Blackfoot camp. Nose to the air, his empty stomach began to rumble.

Omah followed and stood off to the side. "Why do you hesitate? It'll be dark soon and I'm hungry."

"I hesitate because I don't know where I am." He hated to admit he was completely lost, but there was no way around it. More facts were needed and she was the only one who could provide them. "I usually know the portal I am going to use and where it comes out. More or less...."

"Antiquated."

"Don't start with me! I'm sure I would eventually find my way home. Now tell me, where are we?"

With a procrastinating look around the clearing, Omah now had to admit something she didn't want to. Since her tribe traveled so often, she wasn't completely sure. "Let's just say somewhere in Montana." She hesitated and then mumbled, "Or Canada."

The confession caused Wolf to pause. He had never used a portal to travel that far north. There would be no way of knowing where a random portal would dump him. "This is going to be interesting."

"And you will travel forward in time, right? To our own time, if I understood you correctly. And you won't have any clothes." She just had to add that.

Wolf growled. "Yes. Hopefully it will dump me either at Disneyland or my own place. But, the closest thing in Disneyland that resembles Montana is...."

"Absolutely nothing. The Grand Canyon Diorama is sort of applicable. Or somewhere on the River in Frontierland. It's a Small World?"

Imagining boatloads of children running into him, Wolf gave a groan. "Let's hope for the River. I have clothes stashed all around there."

"Why?"

He shot her a look. "Never mind for now. You ready?"

"Almost." She padded back into her den and emerged with a blanket in her mouth. She dropped it at his feet. "This might help if we don't end up where you think."

Wolf was surprised at her thoughtfulness. "Thank you."

As she tried to help drape it over his body with her teeth, she gave a snort. "Don't let it go to your head. There. I think that will hold, depending on what you have in store for us."

Once they were ready, Wolf tilted back his head and let out a long, lingering howl. It traveled through the waving treetops to bounce back in a subdued echo. The effect was immediate as the gentle breeze left over from the passing storm began to intensify. Soon it was a twisting fury of leaves and dust, swirling into a funnel that reached into the dark storm clouds that once again appeared overhead. Lightning shot out from the black clouds, angry, jagged forks that twisted over the ground, leaving pink flashes of light behind wherever they touched.

Intimidated, Omah took an involuntary step back as one bolt crashed merely feet in front of them. "Pink? Your color is pink?" However, the laugh that accompanied the taunt was weak and wavering. Fear of the violence made her shake.

Wolf ignored her as he kept his eye on the approaching storm, looking for the center, that one moment when they would leap. "Hold on to my tail with your teeth. Do not let go. Get ready. It's almost time." He winced when Omah, happy to oblige, clamped down. That would be dealt with that later. "Ready…. Now, run with me and jump."

He took off at a run, almost falling when she didn't keep up and his tail pulled him back. The pain lessened when she caught up. "Jump!"

She leaped at the same time as Wolf, his tail crushed in her jaws. *How can he do this time after time? We're falling, twisting. Don't let go! Everything hurts….*

Disoriented, not knowing what to expect, they were both stunned when they landed in water. The force of the storm had been greater than the depth of the water in which they found themselves. As they collided with each other, they hit the bottom.

Eyes open, they quickly located the wavering light above them. With the hope that it was open air, they headed for the light. Gasping in big gulps, they tried to get their bearings.

Omah pressed the palm of her hand against her forehead as she floundered in the water. "How do you do this over and over? Oh, my head is pounding! This is barbaric."

Wolf made a grab for the blanket before it was carried away by the current. More concerned about their location than her headache, he wiped the water out of his eyes so he could look around. A smile broke out on his face. "It worked. I'm home."

"Home? You live in a river? That would explain a few things…"

Wolf ignored her sarcasm. "We're back in Disneyland. If we go around that bend we'll be at the Mark Twain dock."

"I know where the Mark Twain dock is." Turning back she noticed the white patch of hair on his chest that was in the same place as the white patch of fur when he was a wolf. With a tilt of her chin, she indicated his bare chest. "The more important thing is: Where are you nearest clothes?"

Before he could answer, they both heard the shrill whistle of a train. "What in the world was that? Did they change the Mark Twain's sound?"

"No." Wolf's head shot around as he looked more closely at the banks of the river opposite Tom Sawyer Island. Eyes wide, he grabbed for her head. "Hold your breath." Without giving her time to respond, he shoved her back under the water and followed. When she immediately struggled against his rude treatment, he hugged her to his body to still her.

Unable to get out of his grasp, Omah had had enough. In the blink of an eye, they were back in her den, dripping wet, his arms still wrapped around her body.

As soon as he perceived the change, he pushed through the shock and moved away from her. Grabbing the soggy blanket that had somehow made the trip back, he wrapped it around his waist.

Furious, Omah pushed limp tendrils of hair out of her face.

"What's the matter with you? Were you trying to drown me?"

"Didn't you see it?"

"See what?"

"The Mine Train was coming through Twin Sisters Falls."

"The Mine Train…." She broke off, her anger draining away like the water running down her legs. "How could it have been the Mine Train? That closed down in 1979."

"I don't know. We traveled to the future, but apparently not far enough."

"How is that possible? What did you do wrong?" Before he could defend himself, Omah turned to disappear into the recesses of her cave. Wolf could hear her rummaging through something inside. When she came out, there was a pair of deerskin trousers in her hands. "Put these on. I want to dry out my blanket."

"How come you have a pair of men's pants in your cave?"

"Don't we have more important things to discuss?" Turning away, she draped the blanket over the rocks near the entrance. It immediately started to steam from the warmth of the sun. Somehow it was now midday, not evening as it was when they left. At his pointed silence, she gave a sigh. "I was married. Can we get back to the Mine Train now?"

Wolf could tell it was a subject she did not want to pursue. "So, where is he? Did he get fed up with your sarcasm and leave?"

Head tilted to the side, she stared back at him, her face pulled into an emotionless mask. "He died in a buffalo stampede. Anything else you want to know?"

Not expecting that, immediately sorry for her, Wolf reached out a hand, only to let it fall back to his side. "I'm sorry. That must have been horrible for you."

"It was." With an effort, she shook off the memory and the melancholy that threatened to overwhelm her at the thoughts of her long-lost husband. "It was a long time ago. Even now, back here," with a wave of her hand to indicate the present time, "it was a long time ago."

"I never even considered marrying." The admission sprung involuntarily from Wolf's mouth and heart. He'd never told that to anyone and immediately wished he could take it back.

Intrigued that the closed-off Wolf would ever share anything that personal, she had to dig deeper. "Never? Why not? Haven't you ever met anyone?"

He bit back a sigh. *She will never let it go.* "I thought you'd understand. Since we don't seem to age, how could I watch someone I love grow old and die in front of me? You went through that—for a different reason—so I thought you'd get it."

Walking up to him, she put a sympathetic hand on his bare shoulder. "You've missed out on a lot."

"But you saw someone you love die."

Stepping back, she folded her arms over her chest as she looked into his face. It was a strong face, a handsome one she had to admit to herself. When she spoke, her words were soft. "People die all the time, Wolf. My husband went too soon. And we both lost Walt. Your family all died in their time, right? Mine did. But, I can push away the reality that I'm alone by coming back here to visit them. Is it the same with you?"

Wolf just silently nodded as she went on.

"We are alone, you and I, Wolf, but I don't think it has to be that way. I chose not to look for someone new. But, the choice is also mine to accept someone if I do find him. I think it's worth the eventual heartache. I…I loved my husband and I miss him very much. Tell me, Wolf, have you ever let someone special get away just because you worried about the eventuality?"

Wolf saw no way of getting out of this conversation. She seemed to be sincere, but he figured a sarcastic remark might not be too far away. That *would* bring things back to normal between them. "I don't know. There've been a few women that've caught my eye, but I never pursued it." He gave a shrug. "And they moved on."

Omah knew it was time to change the subject. She had already revealed more about herself than she would have liked, and figured it was the same for Wolf. "Speaking of moving on, should we talk about the Mine Train and why you didn't hit your real time?"

As she intended, irritation snapped back into his eyes. "I told you it wasn't an accurate science. Since I don't know exactly when or where I am, and I didn't come here on my own power, thanks to you, I'm not too surprised it didn't work quite right." He looked down at his blanket-clad torso. "And why am I still a man? When I jump to the past I always turn into a wolf."

Omah shrugged her shoulders. "Perhaps it's because *I*

brought us back here. If I had let you control it, who knows where we would have ended up."

"Like I said earlier, I usually use portals I know. This was a blind jump."

"Well, at least you went back to the place you wanted to go, correct?"

Wolf had actually wanted to go to his apartment, but declined to admit that little fact. "Close."

"Hmmm, right. Well, I'm exhausted by that little stunt of yours. I'm going to sleep and, in the morning…or later today—whenever the heck it is—we'll start doing it right."

Without another word or waiting for his answer, she walked into her cave to throw a pile of clothes into a heap on the floor. Pulling another blanket around her, she used the lumpy pile as a mattress and promptly went to sleep.

Watching from the door, Wolf just shook his head in amazement. *If she was as good at traveling as she said she was, why didn't she bring a real bed and a couple of pillows?* He tested the blanket draped over the rocks to find it was already warm and dry from the sun. Putting it around his bare shoulders, he went to the other side of the cave, away from the bright light filtering in through the entry. As he leaned back against the far wall, he picked up the picture of Peter and Catie. While he was wondering how much time had passed since he last saw them, he, too, fell asleep.

Chapter 5

Fullerton

"Peter! Hey, wait up!"

Peter heard Lisa call his name but didn't stop as he quickly headed for his locker. His aim was to get his books put away and get to the bus before she could corner him. Successfully avoiding her all day, he didn't think he'd make it this time.

"Gosh, you're hard to catch! Didn't you hear me?" Pushing her bangs out of her face, Lisa was breathless when she ran up beside him. The other kids, glad school was out for the day, passed them by without a second glance. "Anyone would think you've been avoiding me!" Her words came out in a light, flirty manner, but the look on her face indicated that she hoped she was wrong.

Cornered, with the realization he would have to say something, Peter slammed the door to his locker with more force than was necessary. He didn't want to hurt anyone's feelings, but now she was forcing him to talk. "Yeah, well, I didn't have anything to say." Eyes on his backpack, his fingers needlessly fumbled with the zippers.

Her cute face fell. She hadn't been wrong after all. "Oh. I thought we had a fun time together at Disneyland."

Peter's head jerked up, his green eyes flashed with anger. "Fun?" Now, two days later, Peter's head was finally clear and he had had plenty of time to go over all the events. "You were so rude to my friend Catie that she had to leave and hasn't spoken to me since!"

Lisa stood there slightly stunned. To her, the events of that day were still somewhat fuzzy, confusing. All she could clearly remember was going on the rides with Peter. Then there was something about a room somewhere on Main Street, but those details seemed to be all jumbled. "I was? I...I don't remember that. I know Catie left early, but I'm not sure why."

"You don't remember.　Oh, that's convenient." Frustrated, Peter ran a hand through his hair.　Mentally, he tried to count to ten before he continued, but only got to four.　"She tried to give you a compliment on that silly necklace you had on and you turned it into an insult."

The girl's fingers unconsciously went up to her bare neck. "Necklace?"　She looked down at her hand as if wondering why it was empty.　"Wasn't it shaped like a bird or something?"

Peter rolled his eyes.　"It's your necklace.　You should know what it looks like."

A blush crept up Lisa's face.　She seemed more confused than anything else.　Thinking back over the day she had spent with Peter, she looked out toward the buses with unseeing eyes.　"Yeah, I should know, but I can't find it anywhere.　I even asked my mom to help me look, but she didn't remember anything about it.　Maybe I dropped it at Disneyland or somewhere."

"Well, all I know is that you were wearing it when you left."

"I was?"　She gave a small shrug with her shoulders.　"I don't remember.　It's just gone.　It's like I never had it at all."

"Well, necklace or no, you were rude to Catie and I really don't want to talk to you right now.　I have to catch my bus or I have a long walk home."

As he stalked off, Lisa looked after him, her face miserable. "I'm sorry.　I just...I don't remember."　Her whisper was spoken to an empty corridor.

Kimberly looked up when she heard the front door slam. Since the younger boys, Michael and Andrew, were already home from their schools, it had to be Peter.　When the windows quit rattling, she headed for the hallway.　Something had to be wrong.　That wasn't like Peter.

Muttering to himself as he jerked off his backpack, he was stomping up the stairs when she reached him.

"Afternoon, Sunshine."

"Yeah."

Okay, an attitude, too.　Great.　"Peter Percy Brentwood."

If the tone in her voice hadn't stopped him, the added treat of hearing his full name would have done the trick. He immediately came to a halt on the second floor landing. What he didn't manage to stop was the dramatic sigh as he turned around. "Hi, Mom."

"Don't 'hi, Mom' me. Come down here and tell me what's wrong."

"What makes you think something's wrong?"

Kimberly didn't answer him. With a tilt of her head, she just put her hands on her hips.

Peter had to smile in spite of himself. "You look like you're thinking the word 'duh'," as he came down the stairs.

"I am." She took him in her arms for a quick hug before he even had a chance to protest. "Now, come on in the kitchen. I think your dad left some fruit untouched. And we can talk."

"No cookies?"

"After you tell me what happened at school."

Peter first opened the back door to let in Dug, their Golden Retriever, which resulted in several minutes of a joyous reunion. Kimberly watched as the boy played with their dog. She could see some of the tension ease out of him as he fended off drooling kisses and a whipping tail that could probably decapitate someone. Now seated at the big island in the middle of the kitchen, it was duly noted that most of Peter's apple was being stealthily dropped into a waiting mouth below. That, too, was allowed to pass.

When two pairs of expectant eyes looked to her for the next, more savory, treat, she could only grin as she passed over the plate of chocolate chip cookies. "You still haven't told me anything. And don't give Dug any chocolate. It's not good for her."

"I know I'm not supposed to feed the dog from the table."

Wow, a look of wide-eyed innocence! How does he manage the same trick as his dad? Kimberly held up the apple core as she pointed at the excited Dug who obviously expected more.

When it didn't work, Peter dropped the look on his face and stuffed another cookie into his mouth. Seeing the movement, the dog's head eagerly swung back to him. Dug had to settle for licking his sticky fingers. Disappointed, she turned away to head for her enormous pillow in the far corner of the kitchen. With three full turns and a loud sigh, all eighty pounds of delicate golden fluff settled down and promptly went to sleep.

"Well, now that you've allowed Dug to distract us for ten minutes, let's get back to the original question. What happened at school?"

Peter made a face behind the napkin he had been handed to wipe the chocolate from around his mouth. Somehow, someway, his mom never seemed to forget her original question—no matter how long he stalled. He gave a longing glance at the kitchen door.

"Your brothers are upstairs doing their homework and won't interrupt. Or save you, as the case might be."

"I do have math and history...."

That earned a grin. "Glad to hear it, Pete! You usually tell me you finished it on the bus."

Rats. "Okay." There was no use trying to stall any longer. He figured he might as well get it over with. "You remember that girl from school, Lisa?"

"She's the one who went to Disneyland with you and Catie Saturday, right?" Kimberly grabbed the last cookie and slowly nibbled on it. "You didn't seem to have a very good time with her. All you said was that she was mean to Catie and Catie left early. Did something happen today? Was she still acting the same way?" Catie and Peter had been friends forever and she knew Peter was protective of her. She just hoped whatever happened today wouldn't escalate into a problem she and Lance would have to step in to handle. Peter was usually pretty forgiving after he had been wronged. He might pout for a while, but he usually got over it.

"Well, I avoided her all day—not easy since we're in some of the same classes." He momentarily perked up and looked rather proud of himself. "I showed up late to class and then got out right away. Oh, that reminds me.... You'll have to sign a couple of tardy notes from my teachers."

"Peter!" Kimberly had to stop and bite back her ready lecture on being late to class. There was more here that she needed to know. *I couldn't have had a nice, peaceful, obedient little girl. No, I had to have three boys. Well, four, counting Lance...* "Okay, so you never talked to her. Then why are you so angry?"

Peter fingered the notes from his teachers that he dug out of his backpack. He would rather work it out for himself and try to get Catie to talk to him again. There was also a gray capsule hidden under his bed that he was dying to open—and he wanted Catie to be part of it when he did. "She finally caught me at my locker before I could get to my bus."

"And she made fun of Catie again?"

"No! She tried to apologize, I think. I don't know. I made a run for it." He broke off, suddenly realizing what he said.

"Oh, no! She apologized! How awful."

Peter didn't bother to hide rolling his eyes when he saw the small grin on his mom's face. "You're making fun of me." The notes were crumpled into his fist. "Catie won't talk to me. I've tried texting her and she doesn't answer. It's all Lisa's fault. And then she says she can't remember anything that happened! She acted all confused and stuff. Like she couldn't even remember that ugly necklace she was playing with all day. Hmph." He tossed the paper onto the countertop so he could fold his arms across his chest. "And then, after Catie left, we found another capsule from Walt in the apartment and I can't even open it 'cause Catie won't talk to me!"

Kimberly held up a restraining hand. "Wait, wait a minute. There're two things that bother me here. One, you took Lisa into the secret apartment. And, two, you never mentioned another capsule. Pete, you know what we find from Walt is not for general knowledge. We have a special duty as Guardians to keep Walt and his plans for the future of Disneyland safe. If he leaves us something special like an unknown room above Main Street, it is for our use only. I thought we made that clear."

"But, Mom, she said she saw us coming out of the door! How could I say there wasn't anything there when she saw the door open and close?"

Looking out the window over the sink, Kimberly thought back to that exciting Saturday night. She could not remember seeing anyone nearby who even gave them a second look. That girl Lisa hadn't approached Peter until later when they were almost at the Opera House. She turned back to her son. "Did she say anything about the apartment today?"

The boy just shook his head. "No, she was more interested in talking about the necklace she apparently lost. She didn't even mention the capsule or want to know what was in it."

Kimberly leaned back against the kitchen counter. "What *is* in it?" As she asked, she was picturing the holographic map of Disneyland in the War Room on the third floor of their house. Kimberly knew the map hadn't shown any undiscovered capsule in that vicinity. The house itself had been built by Walt Disney for the first Guardian, her late father. That special room, though, was a technological wonder, and was the central hub for the Guardians of Walt. Kimberly, Lance, Wolf, and now Junior Guardian Peter, all took turns making sure the Park ran smoothly—just as Walt had wanted.

"I don't know yet. I haven't opened it."

This wasn't like Peter. He was usually so excited when he discovered one of the canisters that he would attack it with anything at hand to get it open. "Really? Why not, honey?"

He paused before he answered, stalling by trying to press the crumbed notes from school smooth again. Embarrassed by the admission he knew to be true, he didn't want to say it out loud. His shoulders raised in a sigh of defeat. Kimberly would just keep asking. "I wanted Catie to be there."

Mumbled in a low voice, she barely heard his words, but caught 'Catie' and knew what he meant. His body language was clear enough. She didn't want him to get any more self-conscious by making him repeat it. With a kind hand on his shoulder, she let him off the hook. "Well, you'll figure it out. If you need any help, you know you can come to me or your dad. Now, about those late notes...."

Peter's head shot up when he realized the interrogation was over. With a big grin on his face, he sprinted for the door with an energized Dug barking at his heels. "Won't happen again. Thanks, Mom!"

Yorba Linda

Catie looked at the blinking light on her phone again. It was another text from Peter. About to hit the delete button, curiosity got the better of her. "This'd better be good, Peter."

I'm sorry. Didn't talk to Lisa all day. I want you to open the capsule with me not her.

Catie's face lit up with a big smile. He didn't want Lisa. He wanted her.

The hurt and anger that had lingered over the past two days

was slowly melting away. Peter had acted so strangely at Disney-land that he had seemed like a different person. He never acted like that toward her. Maybe her mom had been right: Let him sweat for a couple of days. He'll come around. Worked on your dad!

Still, she waited another hour before she replied to his message.

I guess. I'll see if we can come over next Friday. It's a school holiday.

Fullerton

"**D**ad! Can we go to Walt Disney World?"

Seated in the living room with their guests, Adam and Beth, Lance heard Peter's yell as three pairs of feet thundered down the stairs and headed toward their location. Always ready for anything, he gave the Michaels a grin. "So, you guys busy tomorrow? Want to go to Florida?"

Andrew and Michael, playing with the steering wheel of the Mr. Toad's Wild Ride vehicle over by the fireplace, became all ears. Initially irritated at getting booted out of Peter's room while he, Catie, and her twin brother Alex, worked on some clue, they immediately perked up. "I want to go to Florida!"

Andrew's confirmation was right behind his brother's. "I wanna go to Florida! Me, too!"

"Quit copying everything I say, Andrew!"

"I didn't copy you! Quit copying everything I say, Michael."

"Boys! Your dad's just kidding." Kimberly glanced over at Lance, a 'you-are-joking-right?' look on her face.   "At least, I think he is…."

Adam glanced at his watch. "Well, we could catch the red-eye."

"What's a red-eye?"

Beth lightly punched him in the arm as she pulled Andrew into her lap. "You're not helping."

A loud jumble of voices all discussing the likeliness, the impossibility, the fun, the choices of rides, and the dining experiences of Walt Disney World greeted Peter, Catie, and Alex when they reached the living room. Coming to a halt in the doorway, they could only look from face to face as four adults and two boys all chimed in with their own reasons for going or not.

Peter glanced over at his two companions. "Wow. I think I started something."

Enjoying the fray, Alex leaned against the entryway and folded his arms over his chest as he got a grasp on what was being said. "From what I can tell, my dad and your dad are for it. Our moms keep talking about school. Michael is planning out the day in the Magic Kingdom and Andrew wants to go to Animal Kingdom."

"But we need to go to Epcot."

Peter, still enthralled at the chaos in front of them, grinned at Catie. "I think Michael is getting to that park now, Catie! Gosh, I thought we'd have to talk them into it."

"Uh oh, your mom spotted us, Peter. She doesn't look like she wants to go."

The loud clanging of a brass bell that had come off the Chicken of the Sea Pirate Ship stopped everyone mid-sentence. When Adam and Lance resumed their talk about air flights, Kimberly rang it again.

"Okay, okay, honey! What? Wow, I didn't remember that bell being so loud."

Beth, seated closest to the bell, seemed to be checking the hearing in her right ear. "That's because it used to be in the middle of Fantasyland, not an enclosed room. Am I yelling? I can't tell if I'm yelling."

Adam patted her knee. "Yeah, you're yelling. You'd better not talk anymore."

She shot him a dubious look and then glanced at her hostess for confirmation. Kimberly gave a short shake of her head. Before Beth could get back at Adam, Kimberly motioned the troublemakers into the room. "You three, come on in here. What's this about Walt Disney World? I thought you were opening that capsule and working on a clue."

Not sure if they were in trouble, their walk into the room was a slow one. Peter found himself in the lead as the twins stood behind him, somewhat out of sight.

"Umm, yeah, we were working on the clue, Mom." He pulled a yellowed piece of paper out of his pocket and glanced at it.

The four adults felt their hearts beat a little faster. They were all experienced clue-solvers, having all been on joint and separate clue hunts in the past. While Adam and Beth had come across an actual treasure chest deep under the Pirates of the Caribbean ride, Lance had probed further by himself. Then later, with Kimberly's help, they had discovered their own secret room on Main Street and an eerily beautiful treasure no one else knew about. They each had private mementoes from Walt Disney, not the least of which were pieces of paper—like that one in Peter's hands—that contained clues written by Walt himself. And now Peter had just pulled another one out of his pocket and they became as excited as the kids.

Lance spoke first, having to hold himself back from grabbing the ancient paper out of his son's hand. The adults had agreed the first time Peter found a clue to let the kids have their own adventures and see where it took them. Usually Wolf was with them, but he hadn't been seen for a month since he ran down Main Street after Omah. "So, why do we need to go to Walt Disney World? The clues never included Florida because Walt didn't actually work on that park. His brother Roy got it built after we lost Walt."

Kimberly looked puzzled for a moment. "Didn't you say Wals went to Florida for one clue? Something about the Carousel of Progress?"

"Yeah, but that was just because the ride got moved from Disneyland to Florida. It was the only way for him to find out where the trail led."

"What other rides moved to Florida? There's the Country Bear Jamboree, but that was built after Walt's time. What else?"

"Don't they still have the PeopleMover?"

"Yes, but that was their own model, not our ride transplanted."

Alex edged closer to Peter so he could whisper in his ear. "I think we can back out of here and not be noticed. They're in their Ancient History mode now."

Lance's ears were sharper than Alex thought. His head swiveled in their direction just as the three kids started to edge backwards. "Hold on, guys. We're getting off track, aren't we, Alex?"

Alex got a sappy grin on his face when he realized he had just been caught. He gave Peter a light shove in the back. "Peter has the note."

"Traitor," Peter hissed at Alex. When he saw that all eyes were on him, Peter held up the yellowed paper. "From what we can tell,

I think we need to go to Morocco."

"First Walt Disney World and now Morocco? What's next? Transylvania?"

Adam sat back with a smile. "Sounds like an even more exciting trip than ours was. We just got to go to Marceline, Missouri, and Tobago."

"Don't forget San Francisco. That was fun."

"Right, Lance. Rappelling into a Disney warehouse in the middle of the night was fun. I remember the look on your face when the sirens started wailing."

"You guys got caught? You didn't tell me that part!"

The two men turned at the sound of Peter's intrigued voice. "We didn't get caught," was said at the same time by both of them.

"Jinx."

"Funny, Lance. What are you? Thirteen?"

"Hey!   I'm standing right here."

"No offense, Pete."

"We're getting nowhere fast." Kimberly rang the ship's bell again while Beth and the younger boys held their hands over their ears.

When order was again restored, Kimberly asked Peter to read his clue out loud so they could all try to make sense out of it.

"You want adventure? I'll give you adventure. But, we need to make a deal before you accept my challenge. If I give you the treasure you seek, will you give me my heart's desire? The first clue to <u>my</u> heart's desire is this: A red as deep as blood.

"If you accept, you must climb to new heights. The pink Moroccan face is carved, its two windows barred.

"Don't break your neck."

There was complete silence when Peter quit reading. He looked up expectantly as if the adults should now see his wisdom and agree they needed to go to Florida. What he saw instead were four confused looks.

"That doesn't sound like Walt." All eyes turned to Beth, but she didn't notice. She was still contemplating the odd wording. When she did look around, she could only shake her head. "He sounds so…so, I don't know. What? Angry? Demanding? It's so different than what we all got."

"Can I see it, Pete?" Lance held out his hand and read it over himself. Peter hadn't added to or left anything out. That was what it said. "What do you make of the handwriting, Beth? You're the expert."

"Hey, I'm the one who collects Walt's autographs," Adam reminded him.

Lance covered the word 'Fake' with a cough.

Adam heard him and let it pass. He had paid a couple thousand dollars for a signed picture that Beth immediately knew was a forgery. It had been fourteen years since the discovery and Lance still wasn't about to let it go.

Beth let the guys banter while she examined the writing, her fingers testing the feel of the paper. It certainly looked authentic, but, somehow, slightly off. She felt *something* was not quite right about it, but she couldn't figure out exactly what it was. She passed the note along to Adam, mainly out of courtesy. "It kind of looks right. Maybe Walt was having a bad day or not feeling well. If this was written closer to 1966 when he died, perhaps his style changed. Who else would it be from?"

Peter, anxious for any sign that he could keep going with the hunt, jumped on her last words. "It has to be from Walt. We found it in my apartment on Main Street. No one else would know it was there, right?" They could hear the hope in his voice.

"Wish Uncle Wolf was here. He would know all about this."

"Still haven't heard from him?" Surprised by Peter's words, Adam turned to Lance for confirmation.

Since Adam, Beth, and their children didn't know anything about the Guardians of Walt, or even the secret room upstairs, the Brentwoods had to be speak carefully. Kimberly tried to keep it light when she answered Adam. "I'm sure he's just making sure Omah knows she can't come back and threaten the kids ever again. Once that's done, I'm sure we'll hear from him. Or maybe he just went to visit his family." She repressed a slight shiver knowing how Wolf usually took care of problems. And a trip back to his family— through a terrifying time portal—was the usual way.

"So, are we going to Walt Disney World or not?" Tired of the chatter, Peter wanted to know for sure that he could get to work on the clue's actual location. He was sure 'Moroccan face' meant the Morocco Pavilion in Epcot's World Showcase. He'd just have to figure out the where part once they got there.

"Not. Walt didn't have anything to do with the actual building in Florida, as we told you earlier. You know that, Pete." Lance looked at the clue still in Adam's hands. "It has to be somewhere in Disneyland. You just need to figure out where."

"Awww." The chorus of five young voices made the adults smile behind their hands. A trip to Florida would be nice and they would probably plan one for next summer, now that they thought about it. Not that they would tell the kids yet, of course. They would never hear the end of it until they actually boarded the airplane nine or ten months from then.

"But, Dad, we looked online and some of the buildings in the Morocco Pavilion are pink. Not sure why," Peter added in a mumble. "That has to be the answer."

Lance thought he knew the correct location, but would let the kids find it themselves. "You'll figure it out."

As Peter and Catie filed out, Alex chose to stay with the adults. Once he learned he wouldn't be going to Walt Disney World and ride Expedition Everest and Test Track, he lost interest in the clue search. "Can I play a game of pool, Uncle Lance?"

"Sure, that's a good idea. Let's give this a rest while those two work it out." Glad for the distraction, Lance stood from the sofa and motioned for the abandoned younger kids. "Come on, Michael, Andrew. You can help me mess up Uncle Adam's shots!"

As the men left for the billiards room, Kimberly and Beth looked at each other.

"Rats. Florida sounded like fun."

"I know!"

Chapter 6

The Great Northern Plains

Alone with his still-sleeping adversary, Wolf stood in the entry of the messy cave. The low position of the sun told him it was early morning. Exhausted, they both must have slept through the previous afternoon and all night.

After the uncomfortable dampness of Omah's cave, the warmth in the air was welcome. Eyes closed, he lifted his face to the source of the heat, allowing the blanket to fall from his bare shoulders. Motionless, moments passed as the heat soaked into his abused body.

An unwelcomed snicker interrupted his tranquility. "Working on your tan? I would've thought you'd be working on your sadly lacking travel skills."

Wolf's eyes remained shut as the fiery red light from the sun circled and danced behind his eyelids. "I'm surprised you're awake. It isn't noon yet."

"You know, if someone attacked you right now, you'd be as good as blind after staring into the sun like that."

Wolf still didn't move. The last thing he needed was advice on his survival skills. "You could always protect me with that cute little knife in your shoe."

She wasn't going to take the bait. "Perhaps it would be me attacking. Then what would you do?"

One eye cracked open to look at her. He would never admit that she was a cloudy, wavering mass of red. "Do you require another demonstration of what I can do? I'd be happy to oblige."

Omah didn't answer as she took a bite of the deer jerky in her hand. Still stiff from getting pinned to the ground those two times, she could hardly move. "Let's just save that for later. Are you hungry?"

"Steak and eggs would be good. You cook?"

"Don't sound so surprised. I've been known to." *When no one else was around and it was the only option to keep me from starving to death.* "I was going to offer you some jerky."

Wolf, his eyes back to normal, looked at the black *thing* she held out to him. "What is that? A burnt offering?"

"Hey, it's not that bad. It's teriyaki."

Wolf raised an eyebrow. "Really?"

"No."

His chest rumbled with a laugh. "Thought that sounded too good to be true." Wolf held out a reluctant hand for the meat. After taking a bite, he winced. "Tell you what, you show me how to travel correctly and I'll have the Cooking Woman from my tribe show you how to cook correctly."

"At least you're admitting that you don't travel the right way. That's a start."

Unable to swallow what was in his mouth, Wolf walked to the edge of the clearing and spat the wad as far as he could. "I have a feeling that'll still be lying there when the next Ice Age comes."

"Are you always this charming when you're hungry?"

"It's been ten minutes and you still haven't taken another bite. Point made."

Omah shrugged her shoulders as she stared at the jerky in her hand. "I hate it when you're right." With a mighty hurl, the meat was thrown in the same direction as Wolf's. "It was my first attempt at jerky."

"How long ago?" Knowing how difficult it was for a tribe to find fresh meat, Wolf couldn't believe someone would desecrate it like that.

Five years. Taking a moment to dig some dirt from under her fingernails, Omah didn't answer. "Why don't we get back to something important rather than my cooking skills?"

"Skills?"

Having had enough buttons pushed, her anger, never too far away, finally resurfaced. Eyes flashing, she whirled at him and snapped, "Enough, Wolf! You have things you do well. I have things I do well. We can bicker all day or we can try to teach you something."

Wolf held up a placating hand that irritated her more than it calmed. He, too, didn't want another fight. Even though he had somehow come back to her past as a man, he figured she could transform him into a wolf again if she so desired. Plus, he had a firm conviction that members of her Blackfoot tribe were always watching, hidden within the shadowy depths of the forest. That was what his Lakota tribe would do and he had no reason to doubt hers would do the same. He didn't fear them, but knew they would rush to her defense if it appeared he would hurt her. Absentmindedly rubbing the fresh spear prick in his side, he didn't need any more of those. He was tired of fighting.

During his silence, her sharp eyes went from his upraised hand to the one placed over the angry, red welt. As her eyes moved over his muscular torso, there were more scars to be seen. Her anger faded. A normal man would never have marks like that on his body. Until she had learned how to control whether or not she appeared as a wolf, she, too, had been hunted and hurt. They had both been through a lot in their lives. And now it was time to help him. Perhaps he wouldn't have to be hurt again.

Wolf saw when the anger drained away from her, wondering what prompted the change. As her eyes slowly moved over his bare chest, he understood and tensed, waiting for the pity or shock his friends usually displayed when they saw the unexplainable battle scars. But, that didn't happen this time with Omah. What he saw instead was understanding. "You, too?"

At first she didn't comprehend what he asked. Her eyes rose to his impassive, waiting face as he stared back at her. It took a moment, but, then she gave him a brief nod. "You'll excuse me if I don't remove my shirt to show you my back. But, yes, I have similar marks." She slowly walked up to Wolf to put a tentative hand on his shoulder. When he didn't shove it away as she half expected, she gave a light squeeze. "Let's fix it so that doesn't happen anymore."

His large hand covered hers. "That sounds good to me. What do we need to do? What's first?"

Surprised by his touch, Omah stepped back out of reach. When his hand fell back to his side, she felt deprived of its warmth.

"Well, to be honest, I've never had to teach anyone before." Arms folded over her chest, she quickly turned away to hide whatever conflicting emotions her face might betray. She'd have to analyze her reaction to his touch later. A slight movement in the forest caught her eye, distracting her from her confusing thoughts. With a slight flutter of her hand, Omah signaled her hidden sister that all was well. In all that had been going on, she had forgotten her tribe was always close by.

"In case you wondered, I saw her, too."

"Just now?" Omah gave a little laugh. "Kiaayo is usually more discreet than that."

"Maybe she can get me something to eat...."

The warm, odd feelings of a moment ago were forgotten as Omah shot a less-than-friendly glare at him. When she saw the smile on Wolf's face, she relaxed, realizing he was joking. "And they say you don't have a sense of humor."

"Who says that?"

"Everyone you work with at Disneyland."

That stopped him. He had to think back. "I keep forgetting you worked at Disneyland. Nothing about you screams the happiest place on earth."

She let that slide. "I knew about you when I was a mermaid in the Submarine Lagoon." A womanly grin played over her face. "*All* the girls knew about you. You were quite the man of mystery."

"Still am."

"I suppose that'd be true. Walt sure was fond of you."

A brief look of sadness passed over Wolf. "It was mutual." When he realized what she had just said, he frowned. "You talked to Walt about me?"

Omah gave another shrug. "I knew you were more than just a security guard. It was obvious to me, more so than anyone else, because I was more than just a mermaid. I didn't know about your traveling abilities, of course. Just that there was something *different* about you. For me, the job was a means to an end."

Wolf let that sink in. He had known Walt had used other people in various capacities. Wolf worked with Kimberly's father to get the clue searches in place and helped see that Walt's visions of the future came true. As Guardians of Walt, as they came to call themselves, it was their job and their privilege to protect their boss.

"What was your other work?"

Omah had hoped that her past failure wouldn't come up again. The fiasco had sent her from Walt's good graces to Florida where she had to wait out the building of Walt Disney World to get her position back. Then, when Walt suddenly died in 1966, her hopes of finally proving her worth to him came to an end. It had snapped her power of reason and she became fanatical in her attempt to bring that clue search to the end Walt had wanted. She had to relive all of those bitter memories after she found Peter and Catie in the Haunted Mansion with the object she had spent decades trying to find. And Wolf had been witness to her breakdown while he relentlessly pursued her as she used Peter to track down the mermaid. When she finally spoke, she looked embarrassed. "You know about my search for the mermaid all those years." Without waiting for his reply, she just forged ahead. "I had been assigned to help Walt set up a clue hunt. Whoever found the hidden clues would be rewarded at the end if they could figure out the riddles he put in place. It was a pretty easy hunt and Margaret, Catie's grandmother...."

"I know who Margaret is."

Her train of thought broken, Omah momentarily looked confused. "Of course you do. Anyway, it got all messed up and I could never find the mermaid once the Submarine captains started hiding her. It never got back on track and I...I failed Walt. He sent me to Florida."

Wolf was stunned as the implications of what she just said and what she had said to Peter slowly became apparent. Back in 1965 there had been a search Walt set up without him. It had bothered him that Walt used someone else, but, that was Walt. He always had more than one iron in the fire. Questions began to pour into Wolf's mind: *Did Walt originally plan on having her work with him and the Blond-Haired Man? What would have happened if her quest had been fulfilled? Had Walt been setting her up to become another Guardian?*

"Why do you look like that? You look like I just stepped on your puppy."

Her voice snapped him out of his daze. Her question ignored, he asked instead, "Did Walt ever say what the end result would be?"

"I already told you. The person who followed the quest to the end would get some sort of prize. Knowing Walt, probably some piece of animation."

Wolf licked his dry lips. "No. I meant what *your* end result would be?"

"Oh." Omah had to shrug. "I figured he'd use me again for different things over the years. Different positions of trust. He never really said. Then, when he died, well, that kinda ended everything for me." Her eyes narrowed as she looked at Wolf. There seemed to be so much that he wasn't saying. It was written all over his usually expressionless face. "Did you know about those treasure hunts? I always had the feeling that mine wasn't the first. Did he use you, too?"

How much do I tell her? A Guardian is effective because of the anonymity. Walt had said nothing to me or to Kimberly's father about Omah. "Yes. I had set up a Hidden Mickey hunt or two myself."

"And?"

"And what?"

"Why did Walt do it? Did he use you later for other things?"

Wolf just nodded. "Yes. We had a close relationship. I would help him do whatever he needed."

"And I missed out on that because I failed with the mermaid." Not realizing he hadn't really answered her, bitterness over the past slipped back into Omah's voice. "Everything would have been so different." About to continue her rant, a confused look slowly began to overshadow her anger. Mouth clamped shut, she walked to the edge of the clearing to stare out over the trees.

Becoming used to her mercurial changes of mood, Wolf just waited. "What's wrong?"

Slowly turning back, Omah's face was still a puzzle. "I just had another thought. Now there's another thing we have in common: the wolf attacking our pregnant mothers, the ability to travel through time, and that we both worked with Walt on secret plans." She turned away again. "Don't you think that's odd?"

"I never thought about that. But, you're right."

A smile briefly crossed her lips. "I'll add that to my ever-growing list of things I'm right about." The smile was gone as quickly as it came and the seriousness returned. "Do you think it's all related?"

"That our mothers were both attacked by the same wolf and we ended up working for Walt? Sounds more like a coincidence.

An odd coincidence, but a coincidence just the same. Look at how many employees have worked for Disney over the decades. There has to be a lot of shared traits in there somewhere."

Running a hand through her messy red hair, Omah began to pace in front of her cave, the plans to help Wolf shoved aside. "Possibly. Possibly. But...." She broke off as another idea suddenly surfaced.

"But what? What are you thinking?"

"But, what if we were attacked *because* we worked for Disney?" Her eyes were wide as she spoke this aloud. "Is that too weird? We can't possibly be the only ones who can travel through time. What if we were targeted?"

Wolf was silent again as he thought about her supposition. There had been a lot of strange things that happened in his travels. He had met Merlin a couple of times throughout the centuries. And, then there had been that battle with.... His mouth fell open as his past ordeal with helping Aurora came back to mind. Way before Aurora's lifetime, his opponent had been known as Merlin's apprentice Nimue. She had lost a valuable piece of jewelry Merlin had given her. Once she knew where it was and who had it, she wanted it back. And that had meant many centuries of trouble and many name changes as she traveled. In Aurora's time, she went by another name, one that struck terror into those who whispered it. Wolf and his friend Wals had taken Aurora home and ended up in a battle with the evil fairy. She had enchanted all her followers—including Wolf—and turned them into a snarling pack of wolves, herself being the largest, most powerful. "But I defeated her. She was too weak to do any more. Merriweather told me it would be a long time before she recovered. But it's only been seven years."

"Who are you talking about? Who did you defeat?"

Wolf snapped back to the present, not realizing he had spoken out loud. He wanted to think about this and analyze it in private. If *she* was somehow involved, the effects could be far-reaching—and devastating. Aware Omah's eyes were on him, intently staring as she waited for his explanation, he knew she would have to wait. There wouldn't be one just yet. "Sorry. I hadn't expected your reasoning."

In spite of the seriousness of what they were discussing, Omah gave a slight grin. "What? That I can reason or that I might have a point?"

"Both." Wolf rubbed a hand over his face. "I need time to think this through. Can we get back to what we originally planned to do? We can discuss this again later."

"Oh, we will. You can depend on that."

"So, how do you travel? What do you do to get where you want to be?" In an effort to change the subject, Wolf waved a vague hand around the clearing. "You obviously don't use portals."

"I just think of a happy thought."

"And then you can fly?"

They both laughed and some of the tension drained away.

Omah shoved all the unanswered questions to the back of her mind. Yes, she and Wolf would have another long discussion. But, obviously, not now. She allowed Wolf to distract her. "To me, now, it's just about that easy. At first, I did use portals like that. Terrifying things...."

More relaxed now and keenly interested in what she might show him, Wolf was all ears. "How did you realize there was a different way to travel? How did you figure it out?"

Omah gave a small laugh as she thought back. "I came out of a portal—much like what you just put me through at Disneyland—only I was dumped on top of that mountain," she pointed to the far north at a tall, snow-covered peak, "not here with my family. In case you're wondering, that range has snow all year. And, yes, it was freezing."

Wolf shrugged, not seeing the connection. "I've made mistakes, too. I wanted to visit Walt and ended up back in Marceline when he was nine years old. Scared his little sister Ruth so badly that you can probably guess where the song '*Who's Afraid of the Big, Bad Wolf*' came from."

"Well, this mistake almost killed me. I wasn't prepared for the cold and there was no way down without starting an avalanche."

"What did you do?"

"Got mad."

Wolf chuckled. "You? Really?"

"Yeah, hard to believe, right? Anyway, I started fuming, which, by the way, helped keep me warm.... Anyway, I started yelling that I didn't want to be there and I wanted to be with my family. And, suddenly, I was."

Wolf thought he must have missed something. "Wait, back up. What?"

She shook her head slowly side to side as the wonderment of it came to her again. "That's all it took. I was so focused on where I wanted to be—and with whom—that I was instantly transported there."

"As a wolf or as a woman?"

"That's a good question. At first, since I was traveling from our current time, I was a woman and I arrived in the snow as a woman. But, when I came off the mountain, I was a wolf. I couldn't figure that out for the longest time."

"What did you figure out?"

Her blue eyes filled with amusement. "Apparently in my ranting, as I thought back on what I had said, I had said something about wolf fur would have been welcome for once. I must have mentioned that right before I said I wanted to go to my family. So, apparently my wish was granted—or whatever prompted it—and I was a wolf when I arrived."

Wolf found his heart was beating faster in his chest. If what she said was true, if this is what it took to travel like she did…. This could make his life so much easier, so much more enjoyable when he traveled. His father…. Wolf recalled when Merriweather had allowed him to travel one time as a man to see the Shaman. It had been the first time since he was a young boy that his father had seen his face. He had never seen his father cry before. "I want to do this."

"Of course you do. That's what this is all about."

"No, I mean right now. I just think where I want to go? Is that all?"

"All?" Omah didn't know whether to be insulted or amused. "There's no 'all' to it. There's more to it than that. Haven't you been listening? And don't growl at me. It's not becoming."

Wolf had to take a deep breath to keep from becoming irritated at her again. She was quite capable of refusing to help if he kept pushing her. "Sorry."

"Oh, that sounded sincere."

"Listen…." Wolf bit back the rest of his words and lowered the hand that pointed at her. "Sorry. I'm just intrigued and anxious to try it. Can't you understand that?"

"Yes, I can. Once I first learned how to do it right I traveled all over the place! But, it can still go wrong if…."

"So it won't go wrong." Wolf interrupted her to keep from having to listen to a lecture. "I want to try it now."

"I'd rather take you somewhere myself the first time so I can talk you through it and you can see my process."

"I don't need that. You've already shown me the results a few times."

Omah kept her mocking thoughts to herself. If he wanted to do it himself alone, fine. She'd be here waiting when he came back. And then she'd show him the right way. "Since I can't seem to stop you, go ahead. Think of where you want to be, and with whom. Let the power do the rest."

Wolf had to stop and think. Where did he want to go first? Who did he want to see? "Since I don't know how long we've been gone, I should probably check in with Lance and Kimberly. If it's been too long, they might be worried."

Omah gave an indifferent shrug. "Then you have what you need."

Wolf closed his eyes and concentrated on his friends and fellow Guardians.

Fullerton — Current Day

A shrill scream suddenly pierced the air. Startled, Lance dropped his full coffee mug and bounded up the stairs two at a time to the master bedroom. Heart racing, he started yelling for his wife. "Kimberly? Where are you? Are you all right? Honey?" He could hear the water was running in the bath and then the shower door slammed.

Wrapped in a towel hastily thrown around her body, an embarrassed, angry Kimberly rushed out of the steamy bathroom. "Where is he? Where's…."

Lance threw his arms around her to keep her from rushing out of the bedroom. "What happened? Why did you scream?"

Once she realized Lance was holding her, Kimberly relaxed her rigid posture. As she pushed a dripping strand of hair out of her face, her eyes darted around the empty bedroom. "It was Wolf! Wolf got in the shower with me! Where is he? I want to…."

Lance held her at arm's length so he could look into her face. "What? How could Wolf be in your shower? We haven't seen him in weeks. He certainly isn't here. Look around. I would have seen him, wouldn't I?"

"Well, he certainly saw me!" Kimberly jerked the towel tighter around her body, her face a bright red. "You don't believe me! I know what I saw, Lance."

"I'm not saying you didn't. But, there wasn't any lightning or wind, was there? That's what we usually see when he…travels, shifts, whatever it is he does. How could he just show up like that?"

"I don't know. It was like he just appeared next to me and then he was gone."

Lance was trying very hard not to break out laughing. He didn't figure it would help right now. "Did he say anything? Was he a wolf?"

"No, he wasn't a wolf. He...he was a man." The red began to creep up her neck again. "And, no, he didn't say anything. To be honest, he looked about as surprised as I was."

Lance had to bite the inside of his cheek to keep from smiling. "I'm sure he was. Maybe something happened while he's been gone." Another thought came to mind that put a damper on his mirth. "I wonder if Omah was involved in any way. The last time you saw him he was with her."

The mention of the woman who attacked her son made Kimberly forget her humiliation. "Omah? Wolf hated her. He wouldn't work with her. Would he? You've known him longer than I have."

Lance could only shrug as he took her in his arms for another hug. "I don't know, sweetheart. He's been gone a long time. Things change over time. Maybe there's more to it than we know. Plus, you're dripping all over the carpet."

Glancing down at the floor, Kimberly saw the large water stain beneath her. With a loud 'hmmph,' she stormed back into the bathroom to finish her shower, mumbling all the way. "Just wait until I see him again. I'm going to give him a piece of my mind."

Lance waited until the shower door had slammed shut once more. It was only then that he started laughing, his face safely—and wisely—muffled in one of the pillows from the bed.

CHAPTER 7

Flashback — Disneyland 1962

"I can never stand still. I must explore and experiment. I'm never satisfied with my work. I resent the limitations of my own imagination." It was early in the morning, hours before Disneyland opened for the day. Walt could see a thin layer of coastal mist swirling around the flagpole in the Town Square as a sweeper hurried through the same area to make sure everything was clean and ready for the day. Turning from the window of his apartment, he looked over the men who stood waiting for the daily walk-through of the Park. They were a good group of men, ones who had been with him for years and had shown themselves capable of taking his ideas and dreams and turning them into reality. "You all know how involved the company's been with the New York World's Fair coming up in two years. Well, that's all well and good, but Disneyland can't suffer while our minds are elsewhere."

As one they nodded in agreement. "Walt, you still planning on bringing the rides you're building for the Fair back to Disneyland?"

Their boss turned to shuffle through some drawings on the table before he answered. "Yeah, they'll fit in nicely. The Lincoln show will be talked about for years to come—once we get all the bugs worked out. Ah, here it is." A rendering of New Orleans Square was pulled out of the pile. He pointed to the back of the quaint streets and plant-hung balconies. "How's the work going on putting the train station in Frontierland on the other side of the track and moving the route away from the Rivers of America?"

"Good, Walt. There'll be plenty of room for your Haunted House. The footbridge that separates Frontierland from New Orleans Square will be removed. The water will be have to be piped and the area paved over."

"Great." Walt let the drawing drop back to the table and rubbed his hands together. He always looked forward to this part of the day. "Let's go do the walkthrough. I want to see the progress in Adventureland, too."

The men again nodded as they made sure their notepads and pens were ready at hand. If Walt made any comment or observation along the way, it was a cue for them to get busy and fix/repair/enhance/move/replace whatever it was that had just been subtly pointed out to them. Usually he would just say, "Well, let's go a little farther with this," or "Let's change it to something like this." Sometimes the cue would just be a slow shake of his head as he stood and glared at something.

Their route took them by the turn-of-the-century restaurant Red Wagon Inn on Main Street, There was a beautiful pepper tree that had been planted next to the building. The day before, as they walked by that same tree, Walt had made a passing comment that it seemed a little too close to the curb. Today Walt just smiled to himself as they went by. During the night, the ten-ton tree had been moved back a few feet.

The group rounded the corner and paused at the Tahitian Terrace. Made to look like it just came from the South Seas, it was a marvel in thatch and bamboo. The hardwood floors led inside to a large African coral tree under which the guests would enjoy watching the fire walkers and hula girls while they ate their dinners.

Walt led the way inside, arms folded over his chest as he surveyed the progress. "I'm glad we changed out the tree."

"Well, Walt, you said the real one we had brought in wasn't big enough."

"If it was going to hold all the sound and lighting equipment, it wasn't. Glad you got it cut in half and raised to the proper height. And, this tree," as he patted the trunk, "will always be in bloom!" Hands on his hips, Walt then walked over to the right side of the restaurant, nodding hello to the workers who made room for him. Satisfied for the moment, he went back to his group. "That's a good view into the Jungle Cruise. It'll give the guests something to watch when the shows aren't on."

Glad to hear his work on the imitation coral tree passed inspection, Bill patted his stomach. "I'm looking forward to trying those teriyaki steaks and the raisin ice cream."

Walt looked over his shoulder at the landscaper and grinned. "Now you've made me hungry! Let's go back to the Red Wagon Inn for a bite. I'm buying!"

Disneyland — Current Day

As Peter and Catie walked down Main Street, enjoying an extra day off from school, Catie paused to look into the window of the Crystal Arts shop. There was a faceted crystal horse with its flying mane in the center of the display. Surrounded by colored gemstones, all lit by hidden spotlights, it sparkled and gleamed, sending out a myriad of rainbows. Catie was quite taken by the piece and stared at it every time she passed the window. "Isn't it beautiful, Peter? I just love horses."

Peter, however, wasn't paying attention to where they were or what she was seeing. "Horse?" He looked around for the horse pulling the streetcar. "What horse? Oh, that. Yeah, pretty."

Catie gave a slight "hmmph" and turned back to the crystal. "You didn't even look at it. What's wrong? You've been looking over your shoulder ever since we got here." A feeling of dread pricked at her stomach. "Are you looking for someone in particular?" She sincerely hoped Lisa didn't plan on joining them again. After the disaster the first time—even though Peter assured her the girl hadn't meant it—Catie wasn't keen on repeating the experience.

Distracted, Peter ran a hand over the back of his neck as he frowned. "No, I'm not looking for anyone exactly. It...it just feels like we're being watched or something. Like if I turned around, someone would be right behind me."

"Peter, it's a Friday. There are thousands of people in the Park. There's *always* someone behind you."

Not wanting to worry her, Peter just smiled and agreed. He felt somehow responsible for her bad treatment a week ago and wanted her to enjoy the new treasure hunt. Perhaps he was just being paranoid. Yet, before, their movements had been followed by Omah. That had been a real experience and something he didn't want to go through again. With one last glance, he turned his attention to the window. The huge spun glass Sleeping Beauty Castle with golden turrets in the back was what caught his eye. "Wanna get a corndog?"

"Peter, it's only nine in the morning."

"I'm hungry."

"You're always hungry!"

With one last mutter of 'starve to death,' they headed for Central Plaza to say hello to the Partner's Statue of Walt and Mickey.

"I think starving to death will be the least of your worries, boy. If you take any longer to get started on this fool's errand I've set up, you'll have to deal with my goons. Given the right incentive, they can be quite, how shall we say, creative." The woman broke off into an eerie, cracking laugh. Mindless of the parents who pulled their children away from her, she majestically strode down Main Street as she kept Peter and Catie always in view.

Sitting in the shade of a jacaranda tree in the Hub, a small bronze statue of Chip and Dale kept watch over Peter and Catie. Heads close together, they examined the Park map they had grabbed at the entry ticket booth. Even though they both knew Disneyland inside and out, it was still helpful to have something printed in their hands.

"I still think we should've gone to Disney World." Peter was doggedly determined that his idea of going to the World Showcase in Florida was correct. Not wanting to admit he might be wrong, he felt today was a waste of time—clue-wise, of course. He would never turn down an opportunity to go to Disneyland.

"That does sound like fun." She looked up from the map to give him a sly grin. "Guess what I heard? Mom and Dad were talking when they thought Alex and I couldn't hear. All of us might be going next summer!"

Peter's head shot up at the news. "To Walt Disney World? Really? Oh, wow! That'll be great. But, what if I'm right and we don't find the answer to the clue here in Disneyland? That's a long time to wait." Already planning ahead, he figured he might be able to convince them to go during the winter break in three months.

Catie was glad to see his expression change. He hadn't been his usual cheerful self. "Well, all our parents seemed to think we needed to come here. You know that's why they let us come again today. Mom says that if we need to stay overnight, she'll come and stay with us in the apartment. She kinda sounded excited about it for some reason." Catie turned back to the map and then remembered something else. "Oh, and don't let on that you know we're going to Florida. It's supposed to be a surprise."

Peter gave a private laugh. Oh, he'd let them know, all right—not that he would tell Catie at this point. "Then I won't say anything to Michael. He can't keep a secret. What are you pointing at?"

Her finger rested on the upper part of the map, indicating a very familiar-looking white structure. News delivered, she wanted to get back to the clue. "The only thing I can think of that sounds like Morocco is inside It's a Small World."

As expected, Peter let out a loud groan and dropped his head on the top of the bench. "No! We rode it like a million times last time. I don't want to ride it again. It has to be somewhere else."

"Last time we rode it we had to look for mermaids. This time we have to look for something with a carved face that's pink. I think it's in there."

Arms crossed over his chest, Peter had to challenge her. "Okay, then, which room?"

"Either the Africa section or the Mexico one. The buildings in there were really different from all the others."

His face fell at her ready answer. "Oh. You've thought this one out."

Now it was her turn. "Haven't you? Where do *you* think we need to go?"

"Umm." Peter hadn't really figured it out at all. He just hoped to wander around the Park, ride a few rides, and hope they might stumble across something that looked right. And when that didn't happen, as he knew it wouldn't, he would let them all know that his brilliant idea about Florida had been correct. While stalling, his glance fell on nearby Tomorrowland. More exactly, it fell on the walls near the Star Tours and the Buzz Lightyear buildings. "Well, what about those?"

"Those what? What are you pointing at?"

"Come on." Springing up from the bench, Peter dodged through the families taking pictures of the statue. They had to wait for the Omnibus to park before rushing across the street to the entrance to Tomorrowland.

A crush of guests was coming and going around the Astro Orbitor situated in the middle of the entry. Rising high like a cosmic kinetic sculpture, the rocket jets were being loaded for a whirling adventure high above the heads of the onlookers.

Off to the side, Peter paused in the shade of the PeopleMover track near the busy entrance to Star Tours. The building used to hold the Adventure Thru Inner Space where guests were 'shrunk' as they explored the wonders of water and molecules. Even though the multi-tiered fountain outside had been removed years ago, the silver, curved outer wall with its futuristic design still remained. "What about that?"

Catie looked at the two small trees in front of them and the manicured hedges that formed geometrical patterns. "What about what? The trees?"

"No! The wall. There's another one just like it over by Buzz. It looks all carved and stuff."

The look he received was one of 'have you lost your mind?' "You're kidding, right?"

In an attempt to redeem himself for his impetuous suggestion, Peter waved an arm at the wall. "It could be right. It has designs all over it and I could easily break my neck if I fell from it!"

The dubious look on her face didn't alter. "First, this is supposed to be the future. Not Morocco. That's the idea of Tomorrowland. Second, it's obviously not pink." She stopped to walk further back under the PeopleMover track, toward the restrooms hidden between Star Tours and the neighboring Plaza Inn restaurant. When she came back, she had one more to add to her list. "And, third, it's just a thin wall. There can't be anything up on top."

"It could be pink if those lights hidden in the trees were pink."

Catie just tilted her head to the side as she silently stared at him.

"Fine." Peter let out a huge sigh. "It's not this wall. Let's go ride It's a Small World." The name of the ride seemed to stick in his throat.

Catie looked dejected. "I really thought those walls were pink. They didn't look right at all."

After his stupid suggestion earlier, Peter held back from the 'I told you so' on the tip of his tongue. "Well, it was a good try, Catie.

We'll just have to come up with something else. Want to ride the bobsleds?"

"What does that have to do with the clue?"

"Ummmm....."

As they walked past the Storybook Land Canal Boats, Catie gave him a exasperated sigh. "I'm beginning to think you don't have any real answer to the riddle. Or, that you even want to be here." She left out the 'with me' part.'

Depending on his answer, he knew she would be quite capable of calling her mom to come pick them up to go home. Not wanting the day to end badly again, he rushed to assure her—even if it meant admitting she was partially right. "Well, um, I don't exactly know the answer. I still think it's in Florida, so I didn't plan out today very well."

"Very well?"

"Okay, fine, at all. But that doesn't mean I don't want to be here. In the small chance I'm wrong, we still might come across the real answer."

Catie had to smile at his self-assuredness. For years she had heard her mom and dad talk about Peter's father, Lance, and his almost cocky knowledge that he was usually, irritatingly, right. Sometimes you just had to put up with stuff like that from best friends.

"Excuse me." A tall woman dress in deep purple pushed through them. "Sorry, didn't see you. Come along, my dear, let's go to Adventureland. I hear there are some interesting buildings there."

Peter and Catie looked at each other and shrugged. There had been plenty of room to go around them. As they wondered who the rude woman had been talking to, they resumed their interrupted conversation.

Catie, pacified that their day would continue, pulled out the map again. "What about Adventureland? I never really looked at the outside of the shops across from the Jungle Cruise."

"Wasn't there an Indiana Jones stunt show or something in that area a few years ago? I remember seeing him come out on the roofs and crack his whip."

"I never got to see that. Sounds like fun. Want to check it out?"

In the shade near the Tea Cups, the woman rolled her eyes as the two kids walked past her position. "By the Sacred Gemstones of Merlin, this is taking forever. Maybe I misjudged the boy's intelligence. At least the girl took the hint." She let out an exasperated huff of air. "I was just about to take his hand and walk him over there myself. Maybe if I stand in front of the building and point at it." Still muttering to herself, her fingers circled the green gemstone at her neck. She fell into step behind Peter and Catie just as they headed through the archway of the Castle. "Should have turned him into a rat. But, then, he couldn't willingly hand me my treasure. Meddling fairies. Should have turned them into toads when I had the chance."

She glanced at the Castle rising above her head. "Pink. How disgusting. Why are so many things in here pink? Hmmph. This would make a fine pile of rubble." Green light snaked out from her pendant and the walls around her shuddered. With a sneering laugh, she dropped her hand and the grating noise stopped as the walls settled back into place. "Later," she promised.

"Want to ride the Jungle Cruise?"

"No."

"How about a chicken kabob at the Bengal Barbecue?"

"Peter!"

"Fine. We'll look at the buildings. If you're right, at least there are some stairs to use."

"What are you talking about?"

Peter gave one last, longing look at the menu of the Bengal Barbecue. There was a tantalizing spicy aroma coming from the small outdoor restaurant. He pointed back at the buildings they had unseeingly walked by as they argued. "Right after that big arch on the Bazaar, there's a little arch. Then, these stairs. That must've been what Indiana Jones used for the show."

"They do sell Indy stuff in the Outpost...." Catie broke off as her eyes scanned the pink tower next to the Indiana Jones Adventure Outpost. Peter yelped when she suddenly hit him in the arm. "Are we stupid or what?"

Not sure if or how he was supposed to answer that, he turned away from examining the dark posts that went up the side of one of the buildings. They sort of looked like a loosely-formed ladder.

"What was that punch that for?"

"What did the clue say about windows?"

"It said that two windows would be barred. Hey! Look up there! Just like those!"

Catie grinned when she saw he knew where she was headed. "And the front of the building looks just like a carved pink face to me!"

Now energized, Peter again looked up at the side wall as he thought. "I could probably get up that ladder…. It goes all the way to the top."

Not yet sure they were correct, Catie put a hand on his arm to keep him from heading back to the stairs. "Don't you think we should find out what's inside first? It might just be empty space over the store, or storage of some kind. You might not have to go up from the outside." Catie didn't think the posts sticking out of the wall looked too safe. There were only four that she could see and they had a rope tied near the outer edges for support. Since she had never seen the Indy show, she didn't know if that part of the building had been used or not.

With a shrug at her suggestion, Peter headed inside the store, glancing longingly at the Indy hats piled near the door. Looking at the different cast members at work, he picked one who had been to the Security Guard and Princess party at their house earlier that summer. They waited until she was done with a customer.

"Oh, hi, Peter! How are your mom and dad?" Patty gave him a warm smile and turned to the girl. "Who's this?"

"This is Catie Michaels."

"Michaels? Beth's girl? I remember you from the party. Your mom working today?"

"No, she has the long weekend off."

Peter wanted to get down to business. Since both his and Catie's parents were so well known around the Park, the chitchat could go on and on. "Patty, I have a question for you. That pink building right next door? What's in it?"

The cast member looked slightly confused and answered him in an overly kind, slow voice. "It's just part of the shop, Peter. You can see it right through there," as she pointed to her left.

Peter grew a little red around the ears. "No, I don't mean that. I mean what's up above the store, behind those two windows?"

"I'll be right with you, ma'am. I have to get back to work, Peter. That part of the building just hides the vents from the kitchens. Say hi to your folks for me!" With that information, she returned to the cash register and didn't give the kids a second thought.

Back outside, Peter and Catie looked up at the wall again. "Vents. Why did it have to be vents?"

"What did you say, Peter?"

He gave her a grin. "Nothing. Just kidding around. Well, if the inside is off limits, then I'll have to go up on the outside. That's probably why it says not to break my neck." Peter didn't seem at all dismayed by the dire warning. In fact, he looked quite eager to get started.

Catie, though, still didn't look convinced. "I don't think our moms are going to be too happy about this. Maybe my dad can help. He did say that he and Uncle Lance had to go up the side of a building in San Francisco to follow one of their clues."

"But they didn't have a handy ladder built into the side of the wall."

"That doesn't look very safe. I think we need to tell them what we found. If something happened to you, well…." She let the rest of her sentence drop off. Even Peter had to admit that didn't look like the best way to get up to the roof. "Is it all right if I call Mom and Dad? I don't want to get into trouble later for not asking."

Peter had already gone back to check out the stairs leading to the area behind the façade of the Bazaar. That area, from what he could tell, looked pretty flat and accessible. And it led right to the place he needed to go. Which, unfortunately, wasn't flat and accessible. "Yeah, I guess. My dad's gone for the day with Michael and Andrew. All Mom said was 'Spa Day.' Maybe Alex will want to come and help."

Catie had her own opinion of her twin's willingness to help with a clue, but kept silent. If it meant Alex could get on some of the rides, he might come along. "We'll see."

"**W**ell, there's no way we can get up there in broad daylight." Adam and Alex, much like the way Peter had done, had looked at the access to the roof from every angle available to them. Excited about the prospect of finding another clue hidden on the roof, Adam had to remind himself that this was Peter's and Catie's clue search.

Turning to his wife, he could see skepticism on her face. "What do you think, Beth?"

"Are you sure there isn't a way to get up there from inside?"

Peter was quick to again tell them what Patty had said. "I think the only way up there is that ladder."

"Your mom is going to kill us." Meant to be private, Beth didn't realize her mutter had been heard by all.

"I wasn't planning on telling her."

Beth looked over at the eager boy—and her equally eager husband. "You really think that it's safe, Adam?"

"Only one way to tell. We'll have to wait for dark and go up there to check it out."

Peter shook his head. 'When Fantasmic! is over, they funnel everyone through here. There are always people around."

Adam looked at Beth with a silent question. At her slight nod, he tried to hide how much he really wanted this. "Well, I guess we'll just have to spend the night in the apartment you found. I haven't gotten to see it yet. Would that be all right with you guys?"

"Yes, yes, yes!"

"Well, if you're sure...." Adam let them jump around him for a moment more. "All right, I'll give Lance a call and give him the head's up. Beth and I, um, took the precaution of bringing along a few things we might need in the apartment. They're in my backpack. You know, toothbrushes and the like."

Peter, Catie, and Alex didn't care if he brought homework or an anvil in his backpack. They were going to spend the night in Disneyland hidden away in a secret apartment! Then they would have to keep out of sight of the cleaning and maintenance crews who worked at night. It could be their ultimate game of cat and mouse.

While the kids were busy planning their daring adventure, Adam and Beth continued with the boring pre-plans. "We might wait until the fireworks start to get inside the door of the apartment. Kimberly told me that's what she and Lance did and it worked really well."

"That's a good idea. Oh, do you have the key to get inside, Peter."

"What? Oh, yeah, I always have it with me. Uhm, don't tell Mom...."

Adam rubbed his hands together. "Okay, then. We're set until tonight. You guys want to go home, grab some dinner, and come back right before the Park closes?"

That broke them out of their planning mode.

"Home? I don't want to go home!"

"What if we get stuck in traffic? We might not make it back in time!"

"I thought we were going to ride something."

Smiling, Adam held up a hand to stop the protests. "Just kidding! We'll stay."

That earned a chorus of "Yea!"

"But," as he watched their faces fall with the dreaded word, "Beth and I missed lunch when we hurried over here. You guys hungry?"

"Peter's always hungry."

"I could eat a horse."

"I could eat a buffalo."

"Water buffalo?"

"Eww."

Adam threw Beth a look. Maybe teasing them wasn't such a good idea. "Okay, I get it. You're all hungry. Where do you want to eat?"

"Blue Bayou."

"Pizza Port."

"Big Thunder Ranch Barbecue."

"Rancho del Zocalo."

"Club 33."

Amused, Adam glanced over at his wife at her submission. "Nice try, Beth. I think we'd need advance reservations for the Club. And, Peter, you voted twice."

"Worth a shot." Beth gave a good natured shrug. There would be another time.

With a desire to keep it democratic and fend off possible arguments, Adam had a question. "Okay, who got to choose where we ate last time? That's person's suggestion will be taken away."

"You did, Dad."

"Oh, that's right. Rats. I was going to suggest the Blue Bayou."

Catie raised her hand. "That was my choice."

"You all agreed with Catie? Blue Bayou it is."

"Hey." The boys felt they weren't given a real say in the matter, but, since they loved eating on the water and watching the Pirate's boats going by, they didn't raise any more of a fuss.

As the group headed over the bridge that curved above the line for Pirates of the Caribbean and into New Orleans Square, there was a long, disgusted sigh. "Oh, my stars! How many people does it take to find a clue? Apparently five. Maybe I should have just plunked the next clue down in front of them and said it fell off the roof. Maybe I should just poison their food and get it over with. I'll find what I want another way. There's always that girl Lisa. No, that wouldn't work. She doesn't have any idea about my treasure. These humans are infuriating. How do any of them ever survive?" Knowing where Peter and Catie were now headed and when they would be back, the woman raised her arms to make a dramatic exit. Suddenly remembering she was surrounded by more of those sniveling humans, she glanced around. There was a flight of stairs leading up into a tree. "Oh, whatever. If it was good enough for Merlin, it's good enough for me." As soon as she stormed up the steps, there was a blinding flash of green near the overhead exten-sion bridge.

And she was gone.

CHAPTER 8

The Great Northern Plains

"**W**hy are you all wet?"

Embarrassed and angry, the silent Wolf strode past her into the cave. Grabbing the first dry thing he could find, he began to wipe the water off his body.

"Hey! That's my best dress! It's not your personal towel!"

Wolf held the garment away from his face to look at it for the first time. "Sorry." The soggy dress was tossed back onto the heap and he snatched up something else.

"Well, I never really liked that blouse, but it is silk."

"Then find me a towel!" as the ruined blouse was hurled to the floor.

"My, you have such a temper. Here, use this. It's all I can find." Omah waited a few minutes as Wolf fumed and paced, giving him time to calm down. Her intuition told her not to prod or question him, to allow him to tell her in his own time when he was ready. "So, what happened? Did you end up in the River again? I thought you wanted to see Lance." *So much for intuition….*

As he looked up at the ceiling, teeth grinding together, he knew he was going to have to explain that he made a big mistake. And, to add probable insult to injury, he would also have to ask her for more help. Anticipating the laughter and sarcasm that was sure to come, he didn't relish relating what had happened. With a mental count to twelve, he took a deep breath in an attempt to rein in his temper. *How can I face Kimberly again? That was awful! She's the wife of my best friend and the daughter of a man I truly cared for. And now I have to grovel for help. Wonderful.*

"Are you going to tell me what happened, Wolf, or would you like me to guess?"

His head jerked in her direction. "I thought I just did."

"You haven't said anything since you got here." A half-smile crossed her lips as she walked back out into the clearing. "Come sit in the sun. You'll feel better."

Wolf detected no sarcasm or ridicule in her voice. *But*, he forewarned himself, *that didn't mean there wouldn't be any*. After he ran his fingers through his dripping hair, he reluctantly joined her on a rocky seat and raised his face to the sun.

"Better?" Omah could tell he was slowly calming down. Aware that now was not the time to push any more of his many buttons, she kept her hands folded in her lap as she quietly sat beside him.

"Yes." The warmth seeped into his body. She was right—it did feel good to sit in the sun. He shook his head and gave a small, humorless laugh. "That wasn't what I had intended."

"Ending up in the River?"

He cracked an eye to look into her face. Again there was no trace of mockery, only interest. It was a welcome change and it helped him to open up. "No, I didn't end up in the Frontierland River. I ended up in a shower."

"Rain? It's raining back home?"

"Nope. Not that kind of shower." He cleared his throat before he continued, a tint of red staining his cheeks. "I ended up in a bathroom. In the shower. With Kimberly."

There was a burst of muffled sound from her lips. Knowing it would not go over well, she tried to cover the laugh with a cough. "Oh? That must've been a surprise for both of you."

"Go ahead and laugh. You look like you're about to explode. Then you can tell me you were right."

Omah managed to get herself under control and swallowed the laughter. An argument with the embarrassed Wolf was the last thing she wanted after the progress they seemed to be making. Still a surprise to her, she found she would rather have him on her side than opposing her. "I'm sure she'll forgive you. Eventually…. Were you able to talk to her and Lance and tell them where you've been?"

"Geez, Omah! It wasn't exactly the right time for a long chat. I didn't even see Lance—thank goodness. I'd have to bore my eyes out…. As soon as I realized where I was I came back here."

"See? Something good did come out of it."

Wolf looked at her as if she had lost her mind—an expression she saw way too often. "Care to explain that?"

"You just said it yourself, Wolf: You came back here. See? It did work...after a fashion."

His mind churning, he glanced around the clearing as if seeing it for the first time. "You're right. How'd I do that?"

Omah patted his knee in encouragement. "You tell me. How did you do it? What happened?"

"I've got to think. It all happened so fast." Excited now, he sprang to his feet to pace. He just had to be moving. If he had been a wolf, he would have broken out in a run. "I thought about Kimberly and ended up...and went to her. When I saw what I did, I got upset and embarrassed, of course, and then I...and then I thought of you. And I was here."

"With me. Just like you wanted to be."

He stopped his furious pacing to stare at the beautiful red-head. *Why did she word it that way? She just meant that I wanted to return to where I started, right? That is what I wanted, just to come back to learn how to do it correctly. Right? I could have stayed where I was and worked it out with Kimberly. Eventually I'd be able to teach myself. But I came back. To Omah.*

"Why are you staring at me? Did you remember something else?" She couldn't read the expression on Wolf's face and squirmed under the intensity of his gaze. Suddenly self-conscious, she glanced down to make sure she was wearing everything she was supposed to.

Like a kid caught with his hand in the cookie jar, Wolf swung away from her. "No, that was everything." He cleared his throat again and ran his hand through his now-dry hair. "What do we do now?"

"Turn into wolves and have a good fight?"

He turned back to face her, his face puzzled. "What?"

Omah gave him a broad smile. "Just kidding. Your mind seemed to be...somewhere else. I think we need to try to travel again. This time with me along."

Glad to have his thinking back on safe ground, he nodded. "Where do you want to go?"

"Take me to meet your family." The words sprang from her

mouth before she had time to stop them. "I mean, um, you've met mine and you talked so much about your father...." She broke off before she started to ramble, not sure how to take it back.

"All right." One shoulder raised in a slow shrug. "I guess that's as good a place as any. I did want to try to go back to my past." Wolf gave her a pointed smile. "Perhaps you'll get the same warm welcome as I got when I arrived here."

Now it was her time to blush. "Sorry about that. They were just protecting me. Well, you did keep attacking me, you know."

Wolf let out of breath of disbelief. "I attacked you? Care to think back on that?"

She waved an airy hand in his direction. "I attacked you. You attacked me. What difference does it make? We're in a different place now."

Not wanting another showdown, Wolf let it slide. They were in a different place now—one that he liked considerably better. He just didn't want to dwell on *why* he liked it better. "Fine. We'll go see my father. I'd rather be a man than a wolf. How do I make sure of that? And, how do you come along? Do you just follow me?"

Happy to see she was getting her way, she stood from the rocky bench. "Remember how you got to Kimberly?" At his nod, she continued with more instruction. "You have to be more specific in your thoughts. You have to picture it in your mind exactly as you want it to be. If you want to see your father as a young man, you picture him that way. If you want to see him as he is now, you imagine him as he looked the last time you were there. Do you want it to be in the camp or somewhere else? See what I mean?"

"And, apparently, I have to picture myself as I am now and not a wolf."

"Yes! Oh, and don't let your mind wander at the last moment." She shuddered as she thought of the blizzard in which she had landed.

"There's a lot more to it than I imagined."

Omah put a soft hand on Wolf's arm. "It takes a strong mind and determination. You have both. You can do it."

"And how do you come with me? You haven't answered that yet."

She looked down at her hand. "Just like this. Just like when I traveled with you before. Remember? I held onto your tail. We were touching. That's the best way."

Taking her hand, Wolf tucked it through his arm, his hand staying over hers. "This should do it. Now, do you think you can keep quiet long enough for me to think?"

That earned a chuckle. "If it's that difficult for you to accomplish the Herculean feat of thinking, we're doomed."

The Island

The Shaman gestured to the five braves as they sat in front of him, arranged in a semicircle under the stony outcropping. The story he told was how the flute came to their people. His oldest son, Mato, did his best not to fidget. A grown man of his own, he had heard the story regularly while growing up. Now he could repeat it word for word, as his mind was now doing, one word ahead of his father. Out of respect for the leader of the tribe, he remained as he was. This would be his position someday, his responsibility and privilege. It was expected of him as the eldest son.

As Mato forced his eyes to remain in focus and aimed at his father, the Shaman suddenly toppled forward as if pushed from behind. The braves scrambled to rescue their leader from the man who had somehow appeared right behind him, a woman clinging to his side.

In the pandemonium that ensued, Mato, after seeing his father was all right, drew his blade at the intruders. The man tried to push the woman behind him, but she sprang away and pulled a knife out of her boot.

"Ayúštaŋ po!" *Stop!* "Mato, drop that knife! Omah, this is my family. Knock it off!"

"But he's attacking...."

"That's my brother, Mato."

When Wolf's words sunk in, Mato's arm slowly dropped as a look of shock replaced the anger on his face. The danger over, now recognizing Wolf, the braves began to press in on every side to greet their friend.

"Sumanitu Tanka? Is that you? Wolf!" Mato let out a happy shout and embraced his brother, slapping him on the back.

"Do you mind if I say hello?"

At the droll voice of their father, Mato gave Wolf one final pound and released him. "Sorry. I'm just so surprised to see him."

"As are all of us."

All the men stepped back to give the Shaman room to approach his son.

"Atewaye ki." *My father.* Wolf dipped his head in respect. "It's good to see you again."

Smiling, the Shaman ran a hand over the face of his youngest son. It was rare to see him as a man. "You're still the handsome one of the family."

"Hey! I'm standing right here." Mato pretended to be insulted. His father said the same thing to him.

"So, what can I say? You're the smart one."

"Hey!" Now it was Wolf's turn to play indignant. At least he hoped his father was joking.

"Come sit by the fire. It's cold today. My bones are acting up again." Turning to their other guest, the Shaman took the silent Omah's arm in his and led her over by the fire. Since Wolf had spoken to her in English, he tried to do the same. It was laborious, halting, since he had been learning from Mato only a short time. More and more traders from Rainbow Ridge regularly approached the camp and he realized he needed to know more of their strange tongue. "We haven't met yet. We don't get to meet many of Wolf's...friends."

Omah noticed the odd way he said 'friends,' and wondered what the older man thought was going on. With the changes in hers and Wolf's relationship lately, she wasn't sure how she would answer if asked. "I'm Omah." What the heck, she might was well go all the way. "Omahkap'si."

"Ah, you're Blackfoot. Welcome to our camp, Wolf Woman."

She was pleased and relieved when he kindly patted her hand as he guided her to a seat. "Thanks for the kind welcome. I wasn't sure what to expect."

The Shaman looked surprised. "Why would it be any other way?"

A blush crept up her neck, blending in with her fiery hair. "My people took Wolf captive." At the alarmed look on the old man's face, she rushed to explain, her hands gesturing wildly. "Well, they didn't know him and he was fighting me. Beat me rather soundly, I hate to admit." She could immediately see that she hadn't chosen her words well. Before the Shaman could storm over to his son, she put a restraining hand on his arm. "I said that wrong. You see, we were both wolves and had been fighting…. Oh, rats. Let Wolf tell you."

"Oh, he will." The Shaman covered her hand with his own as he examined her face. *This one is a beauty.* "Are you still fighting?"

"No, that's all over now." *At least, I hope it is….* "I've been trying to teach him how to travel correctly."

His dark eyes stared into her blue ones. They were the same blue as his son's. The scrutiny continued as she held herself rigid and didn't squirm. "I see we have a lot to talk about. Go, have something to eat. I want to speak to my son." A glance over at Wolf put a fond smile on his weathered face. "That is, if I can pull him away from his nephews. I see word's gotten out he's back." He was curious about this woman and wanted to determine if she might also be a traveler like his son, not like his friend Wals who just came along for the ride. "Usually an intense and sudden storm announces his arrival." When Omah nodded her understanding instead of looking confused, he knew he had his answer.

"I learned how to do it a different way. One less violent and chancy."

"Change can be a good thing." With a mild grunt of pain, he rose from his place on the log. "Go eat something. You're too skinny."

That made her laugh. "Okay, Dad."

The Shaman gave her a wink as he walked away.

Sitting on the bank of the River, deep in thought, Omah watched the reflected moonlight waver and ripple on the ever-moving surface. The sounds from camp, so familiar to her, were muted into the background as she listened to the noises from the surrounding forest. Every now and then she would look over her shoulder at the camp, puzzled. It looked so familiar to her, as if she had seen it before. "But I've never been here. Why do I feel like I've seen it a hundred times? Even Wolf's father seemed like someone I know."

"Talking to yourself? That's never a good thing." Wolf had just come from the rocky outcrop where he and his family had been in deep discussion. "What were you saying? You were mumbling."

"I never mumble. I just talk to myself…in a low voice, indistinguishable to anyone else."

"You're right. How could I mistake that for mumbling?"

She looked back at the camp one more time as Wolf sat beside her. A fish jumped in the river, breaking the silence between them. "I was just wondering why this camp looks so familiar to me. That's all." She pointed off to the right. "Is that a little cabin on the other side of the River? It's too dark to see it clearly."

Wolf still wasn't ready to tell her that this camp was represented at Disneyland as the Friendly Village on the Frontierland River. It was too close to him. Things were changing between them, but he wasn't at that level of trust just yet. He gave a non-committal shrug. "Perhaps it reminds you of your home."

"This looks nothing like my camp and you know it. I'll figure it out eventually. So, have you worked it all out with your family?"

Wolf gave a grunt. "I should push you in the River. From what you told him, my father thought I literally beat you with my fists. I had a lot of talking to do to explain everything."

"Sorry about that. I could tell by the look on his face—what little I could see under that wolf skin—that he took it badly." She turned to look at Wolf's face, lit by the full moon as it was. The silver tips of his black hair glimmered in the nocturnal light. "Tell me something. Is that the skin of the wolf that attacked your, and possibly my, mother?"

"Yeah. He's been wearing it ever since the day he hunted it down and killed it."

"What if…."

Her voice had been so soft only his wolf-like hearing could have heard her. When she stopped, he turned to her. "What if what?"

It took her so long to answer that he thought she wasn't going to. She seemed to be staring at the bend of the River, when, in fact, she wasn't seeing anything. "What if we could go back and save them? You got us here just as you wanted, so I think you'd be able to go back to the right time. What if we could save our mothers?"

Now it was Wolf's turn to be silent. It was something he had thought about over the years, the decades, the centuries. Now he had been given the tool to possibly make it come true. But, what would be the consequence? What would happen if they were able to succeed? "I've thought about that before. I never could come to a decision."

Omah shook her head. "Me, either."

"What would it mean if the wolf never bit them and they were to live? What would it mean for us?"

"We probably wouldn't have blue eyes, that's for sure."

Wolf gave a low chuckle. "That's probably the least of our worries. What would happen to the future us? If we weren't who we are, we would have lived out our lives with our families in our camps."

"And we would have been dead for almost two centuries."

"Yeah, there's that. But we have lives in the future. We know people and they know us. We have jobs. Well, at least *I* do...."

She hadn't seen the small grin on his face. "Don't start, Wolf."

He bumped his shoulder into her. "I was kidding. Just thinking out loud. Would we just disappear in the future? Would we be like the Haunted Mansion?"

Her head turned to stare at him. "What? What in the world are you talking about? What does Disneyland have to do with this?"

"Oh. I forgot you wouldn't know about that." Wolf settled back on his elbows as he prepared to tell her the story. "I was going back to see my family, and Peter, rebel that he is, followed me through the vortex. He ended up staying with the Gracey's, and we somehow changed their story. When we got back to our time, the Haunted Mansion was no longer in New Orleans Square. The Chicken Plantation was back in place, as well as the Circle Dances. What made it even odder was that no one we talked to had ever heard of the Haunted Mansion. It had been wiped out of everyone's memories."

"Well, I followed Peter and Catie into the Mansion. It's there now."

"Yeah, I know. We had to go back and figure out what went wrong and fix it. When we returned to Disneyland the second time, everything was back to normal."

Omah was quiet again for a long time. "Is that what would happen to us? Would our memory be erased from everyone's minds?" She felt, rather than saw, Wolf's shrug.

"I can only guess that the answer would be yes. No one would know we ever existed."

"Are you willing to risk that?"

Wolf didn't answer. He didn't yet know. "Think of what it would mean to our families, our fathers. We'd be able to get to know our mothers. They'd have a chance to live the life that was cut short."

"And we'd never get the chance to know who did this to us or why."

"I doubt the gray wolf would explain it before we killed him."

"Your father said the wolf spoke before he died. 'I'll see you again,' isn't that right? I wonder if that came true."

An idea began to form in Wolf's brain. What if that gray wolf had just been a puppet? If someone had been behind the scenes controlling him, the gray wolf dying would have had no effect on the one in control. But, it always goes back to: Why them? Their only connection was Walt Disney. Wolf is a Guardian and Omah…well, she might have been a Guardian if things had worked out. Is that the answer? There were only two people he had encountered over the centuries with enough power to go after them: Nimue and Merlin.

Wolf suddenly gasped as the idea he was formulating started to take more shape. He then recalled that Merlin had him give something to Walt in the jungle of Columbia in 1940. It had been a strange pendant with even stranger powers. At the time, he hadn't known it had once belonged to Nimue. And she had been chasing after it ever since. The connection to Wolf seemed obvious. But, why Omah? Ah, maybe…maybe Nimue didn't know Omah failed…. And, if the Guardians were gone, Walt would be on his own to fight Nimue.

"But why attack in the first place? If we just lived a normal life and then died, we wouldn't have been in her way."

"What are you talking about, Wolf? What attack? On our mothers?"

Wolf suddenly realized part of what he had thought had been said out loud. "I…I might have a theory, but there's some unanswered questions."

"Some? That's putting it mildly. Tell me what you think."

Since Omah wouldn't know about the pendant, Wolf left out some of the particulars that she didn't need to know. After he was done, he studied her face. "What do you think?"

She shook her head slowly side to side. "I don't know. What you said is intriguing, to say the least. But, your final question of why still remains."

"If our mothers weren't attacked...."

Wolf finished her sentence. "We wouldn't be here discussing it."

"Right. So there has to be another reason for us to be given our abilities. Why would someone who desperately wanted something back give us the ability to protect it?"

Omah turned to look at him, the moonlight shimmering in her eyes. Under different circumstances, he would have found the effect intriguing. "But, Wolf, what if we weren't meant to protect whatever it is. What if we were supposed to work *with* this Nimue person, not against her? Do you really think she has the ability to do that to someone?"

His skin suddenly crawling, Wolf recalled his trip into the evil fairy's castle. He had been put under a spell and did whatever she told him to do—even to the point of attacking his brother and his best friend. His voice was a mere whisper. "Yes, she has the ability."

Flashback – England – 1289

Nose in the air, Wolf had sensed the approach of the pack. He knew they were wolves and that they were coming fast. And... he knew they were coming for him. With a parting warning yell to Wals, "Get in the house!," he turned and plunged into the thickest part of the trees.

When the following pack easily picked up his trail, Wolf tried to lose them with a twisting, erratic path. He leaped to the tops of huge boulders in an attempt to end his scent. From there he would jump onto a large tree branch and crash into the nearby river, swimming to the opposite side. But, whatever he did, they followed—unceasingly, unerringly. She seemed to anticipate his next move and follow his every step. Even when Wolf did a sweeping turn and doubled back on his own trail, she followed.

For hours the chase continued. Wolf was beginning to feel the effects of the long run and the strain. But, he knew she and her followers would never tire.

He was thinking about opening a portal, any portal that might be near, and escaping that way. He could always come back. But, that would leave Wals and Rose to face her anger alone. They didn't know where he had hidden the pendant. He knew Nimue would not accept that answer. No, he couldn't leave them.

In his contemplation, he got careless and missed the turn he should have made. Caught in a narrow ravine, the surrounding boulders were too tall for his leaps and the sides were too steep for his claws to get to the top. Hearing the sounds already behind him, Wolf slowly turned, head down to face the onslaught of fangs and claws that would be on him in an instant.

Only he didn't face a pack of wolves. Nimue stood behind four of her strongest men as they hurled a weighted net over the snarling Wolf. With nowhere to escape, he crouched down to lessen the impact as the heavy ropes and stone anchors landed on top of him. It was so heavy he couldn't even lift his head to snap at the hands that slid long poles through the mesh. The men grunted at his sheer weight as the poles were placed on their shoulders and the wolf hung swaying in defeat between them.

In silence they trod back to the Dark Castle, their triumphant leader, the Evil Fairy, ahead of them all.

Flanked by a row of sharp spear points, the net was removed from the exhausted Wolf. He had not been allowed to sleep or eat for two days. Knowing his defenses would be at their lowest, Nimue had finally called him into her presence.

"Welcome to my humble castle," she smiled broadly, throwing her hands out. "I am so glad you could join us, wolf. May I offer you some water?" She clapped her hands and a terrified lad of about fourteen scurried out of the darkness with a bucket.

Wolf saw the look of fright on the boy's face and refrained from snapping at him. He could tell the boy was here about as willingly as he himself. Turning his head away from the much-needed water, the wolf stared defiantly back at the woman as the boy vanished back into the depths of the shadows that lurked everywhere in the castle.

Nimue appeared shocked. "What? You aren't thirsty?" Her eyes narrowed and she spat at him, "Then perhaps this is more to your liking!"

The green orb glowed and the water in the bucket was changed into a bubbling, spitting acid. With a derisive snort, Wolf kicked it away with his hind leg. The acid spilled out of the bucket and ran toward his guards who screamed and backed away from the red, hissing flow.

At first surprised by Wolf's insolence, she soon began to chuckle. That chuckle quickly turned into full laughter. Her men looked at each other, unsure of what they should do. A couple of them gave a nervous laugh at their mates who were still dancing away from the spilled acid.

"Oh, wolf." Once her emotions were under control, she let out a deep sigh. "I can see that we would get along famously if you would just let us. You see," she added confidentially, leaning away from her throne, "I know you are more than just an ordinary wolf. I also know you can talk. You have been too stubborn, or perhaps afraid, to do so. So, I give you permission to speak freely." A regal hand was waved in his direction.

Wolf sat on his haunches and tilted his head at her, his blue eyes steady. *No chance, lady.*

"Come now, it's all right. We all know it's true, wolf." She waited for his mouth to open, intently watching the muscles play around his face. When she saw his black lips part, her smile was triumphant.

Wolf just let his tongue loll out of his mouth. Rather undignified, but that was all she was going to get.

He could see her gray eyes change in anger. "Very well. If that's the way you want to play it." Her index finger stroked the waiting orb as her eyes closed.

Seeing the gesture, the swords around him wavered as the guards fell back a few steps. They would have fled the room, but they didn't dare.

Coming warily to his feet, Wolf's eyes narrowed as he waited. A streak of green light curled upward from the throne and slowly snaked its way over to him. Around his body it swirled. Tensed, waiting, Wolf felt nothing. He slowly relaxed his stance. Thinking quickly about his options, he decided it would be better if he let her think the spell actually worked. He figured correctly that the next attempted spell might be a lot worse. He closed his eyes so she wouldn't see them rolling upwards in derision.

"What is it you'd like me to say, madam?"

The deep voice coming from the beast shocked the guards surrounding him. The spears were quickly lowered into place as their eyes widened in fear. They apparently had no memory of their own transformation just days before.

Nimue, on the other hand, was delighted. "I made an animal talk! Oh, imagine the possibilities. I should have tried this years ago with my poor Diablo." She glanced out the glassless window at the stone raven that used to be her pet. Stuck forever on the turret, it was frozen as if in mid-flight, its mouth open for a warning that never came. That malicious Blue Fairy had done that.

Whatever you want to think, witch. He'd like to be around when she tried it again, over and over, only to fail each time! But, then again, perhaps it'd be better if he wasn't.

She turned back at his amused chuckle. "Something you'd like to share with the group, wolf?"

"No, not particularly. But, thanks for asking."

Her eyes narrowed. "Do not push the limits of my good temper, wolf! I can just as easily turn you back into a common brute."

"My apologies." *When pigs fly.*

"I think you know why I brought you here, wolf. I want what's mine. It has been out of my possession far too long. You know that of which I speak?"

"Yes, Nimue."

"Ah, you do know who I am. Interesting. And you will take me to it?"

"No, I shall not."

There was a grunt of "ooh" that went through the surrounding men at his reply. Again they held themselves back from leaving their posts. *At least her anger won't be directed at me this time.*

Nimue calmly stood from her throne and descended the four steps. Her men unconsciously leaned away from her as she paced back and forth in front of the waiting wolf. "Well, I see we are at an impasse. I want my pendant back and you do not wish to give it to me." She stopped directly in front of Wolf and looked down at him, grudgingly respecting the fact that he didn't cower. "Is that how you see it as well?"

"Yes, madam. That's a succinct summary."

She snorted. "You sound more and more like that blasted owl, Archimedes. But, yes, that is where we stand. Unless..." She stopped to tap a finger on her black lower lip. "Unless you decide to join my happy little group here." A waving hand indicated the men-at-arms, each of whom winced as her fingers flew past his position. "Think of what fun we could have together! The pendant would be shared equally with all."

Wolf bowed his head briefly. "Again, I must decline the honor."

She spun on him before he had time to react. Her specter pointed at him, its tip glowing with prickling heat. The black lips formed soundless words as Wolf was bombarded with unseen forces. Too much for him, not even knowing how to resist, the evil penetrated his body and his mind. Scenes of darkness and pain played through his brain, overshadowing his memories of friendship and love and family. Try as he might, already exhausted, he couldn't fight off the intrusion. He couldn't regain his own self. Flung to the cold stone floor, spent, he lay panting from the exertion.

When a film darkened his blue eyes, Nimue smiled smugly. "Now, let's talk about my pendant." With a swirl of her robes, she retook her throne and settled into its depths.

Wolf staggered into Wals' small room at the back of the tavern. "There you are," Wals smiled. "I wondered what happened to you after that pack ran you off. You've been gone for days." He broke off at the lowered head and narrowed eyes. "You okay, Wolf? You look a little beat up."

Fighting every new instinct deep within him, Wolf could only snap out a few words. "Come with me. Quickly, Wals."

"You don't sound very good, Wolf. What's wrong?"

A growl forced itself out of his mouth and he had to snap his mouth shut. "Can't explain it. Just come."

The wolf blended into the darkness of the forest and followed the path to the sea. Wals looked around. "Hey, this is where I met Rose. We haven't been back here since we were attacked."

"Quit talking!" Wolf yelled at him.

At the surprised, hurt look on Wals' face, Wolf shook his head. "I'm sorry. I can't help it. I...I'm supposed to kill you now, Wals. That's what I've been sent to do."

Wals gave him a big grin. "Who sent you? King Stefan? I

know Rose's father wasn't too happy with her sneaking out that night like she did."

Wolf picked up a piece of driftwood in his mouth and easily snapped it in his jaws. "This is supposed to be your neck. No, it isn't the King. It's Nimue."

"What?" Wals was shocked. "That...that was centuries ago! How did she get here?"

"She is known here by another name. She follows the pendant. She will always follow the pendant until she gets it back."

Wals held up his empty hands. "But I don't have it. You know that. You saw that burly guy take it from Rose. I tried everything I knew to stop him." He broke off, shrugging his shoulders, angry at his failure to protect Rose.

"Wals, Nimue forced me to join her side. I...she put me under some kind of spell. It's taking everything I have to keep from leaping at you as I've been commanded."

"You're serious." Wals' eyes got big as the truth of the situation began to sink in. Wolf was acting far too differently for him not to believe. "What do you want? Why did you bring me here? You can't kill me! I'm your friend."

Wolf snarled and snapped at the darkness, obviously fighting a powerful force attacking him from the inside. "I know you are, Wals." The film covering his eyes wavered for a moment as Wolf tried to do the decent thing, the right thing. "That's why I brought you here. You have to go back."

"Back to the castle or my room?" Wals was confused. He didn't know what Wolf meant or what he was capable of doing.

"No. Back to the twenty-first century. You have to bring back help. I...I can't fight this off by myself. I need help."

"Who? Who can help with this?"

"Mato." Wolf winced as the evil in him surged against the thoughts of family and friends.

"Your brother? How can I get to him? He's back on Tom Sawyer's Island in 1817!"

"There's a way."

"How? The portals only open with your howl. That much I do know."

"In my locker. In the back there's a recorder. Get Lance to help you. Use that recorder, or I'm as good as dead," he panted, hopeless.

"Wolf, I can't leave you here like this. There must be something I can do."

"If you stay, I won't be able to fight this spell any longer and… I…will…kill…you."

Wals quickly looked about. Unarmed, there was only the broken driftwood near at hand. He had no delusion that the wolf was joking. He knew Wolf was totally serious. Trying to reach out to touch his friend, he quickly jerked his hand back when he saw Wolf starting to snap at him, the dark film coming back to cover his blue eyes. "Call the portal. Now, Wolf! You were always there for me and I'll do everything I can to come through for you. Remember this: I will be back." Wals made his promise, torn by the knowledge that he wanted to help his anguished friend, but, to do so, he had to leave him behind in this condition.

Head back, Wolf let out an angry, anguished howl. It was different than any Wals had ever heard before. Stepping back from the divided animal, he could see the ocean start to change. The fog came very quickly this time, as if sensing the urgency, the desperation of the summons. Falling over themselves, the waves became a swirling whirlpool as lightning split the sky above them.

The electricity in the air somehow sparked the new evil deep within the wolf. In a sudden frenzy, he snarled and bit at the waves crashing onto the sandy shore. Just as the whirlpool neared the beach, Wolf began to turn on Wals, setting himself to jump at his throat. Seeing the legs bunch, Wals took the initiative and threw himself into the gaping darkness.

Wolf sailed through empty air where the man stood only moments before. Turning quickly he bit at the edges of the water. Once Wals had fallen through, the terrifying pit closed and sparkled out, its job was done.

Seeing he was alone and his prey had vanished, the wolf dropped into the placid, lapping water, his energy totally spent. "Hurry, Wals," he gasped, his sides heaving. "I don't know how long I can hold out."

The Island

Omah's words broke into Wolf's tormented memory. "Then

that must be it. We weren't supposed to work for Walt. We were supposed to work for her. I wonder what happened."

Trying to pick up the thread of their conversation, Wolf suddenly put his hands on her shoulders, forcing her to look at him. "Have you ever…have you ever had an uncontrollable anger when you came out of a vortex? Have you ever turned on someone you loved?"

"Well, back when I traveled that barbaric way, yes, now that you mention it." She placed her hands over his. "I tried to attack Kiaayo a couple of times. The more I traveled that way, the worse the aftereffects became." She paused, her fingertips mindlessly rubbing his. "Do you think that was the start for us to turn bad?"

"I can only guess yes. I only came out of the rage because of Mato and his persistence. He kept telling me he was my brother and he loved me. Not that he would admit that now."

Omah chuckled. "I never had a brother. Only Kiaayo. It was the same with me. Maybe we were able to fight off the tendency enough that it, I don't know, went away?"

Wolf only shook his head. When he realized his hands were still on her shoulders, he slowly eased them away.

"What do you think we should do, Wolf?"

"I think I need to talk to my father again. See what he thinks. It was his wife, my mother. He never remarried. What about you?"

Her eyes suddenly filled with tears. "I missed so much without a mother. Kiaayo would talk about her to help me feel connected, but it wasn't the same. I never knew her. Oh, I'd go back in time to see her, but it wasn't the same. She wasn't Mom then. And I was just some stranger with red hair." She swiped at the tears that ran freely down her cheeks.

Wolf put an arm around her shoulder and pulled her into his side. As she sniffled, he could only hug her. "I think we need to talk to Walt, too."

"Walt? Why? I already did that. He told me my quest never mattered."

He gave her a companionable squeeze. "Maybe he didn't mean it the way you heard it. It wouldn't hurt to try again. I'll go with you this time."

Omah didn't answer as she snuggled deeper into his side. It felt good to be hugged and comforted. She didn't want to talk to

Walt again. That hadn't ended so well the last time. There was something else in her heart that she felt she needed to do. And, if it was successful, then this would be the last time she would feel Wolf's arms around her. The thought saddened her, but her resolve kicked in. Perhaps they were wrong about the outcome. Perhaps….

"Wolf, you go talk to your father. Thanks for understanding."

Wolf had an uneasy feeling when she moved away from him. As he reluctantly rose, she smiled up at him, but the smile didn't reach her eyes. Her eyes were filled with sadness and, also, a determination he hadn't seen before. For what he didn't know. "Are you all right?"

"Yes. I'm fine. Go see your father."

Her words were spoken too brightly. He frowned, but had nothing else to go by. "Okay. I'll see you a little later. If you get tired, there's a sleeping pallet for you in the family tent."

"Yes. That sounds wonderful. Thanks."

Wolf slowly turned away and went in search of the Shaman. Halfway across the quiet compound, he had to stop. The uneasy feeling still pushed at his mind.   Unable to shake it off, he looked back toward the River.

Omah was gone.

CHAPTER 9

Disneyland

Like a general leading his troops, Peter stood in front of his friends, feet wide apart, hands clasped behind his back. Adam, Beth, Catie, and Alex formed a loose semi-circle as they received their instructions for the night. As impressive as Peter looked, his stance belied his actual feelings. Nerves, combined with excitement, threatened to make his hands shake and knees wobble. By holding his hands out of sight, he could hide the shivers that went up and down his arms. Now was the chance to do something he had always wanted to do—spend the night in the empty Park. However, he knew it was never completely empty. Once the guests were gone, the crews got to work cleaning and repairing. There was a nightly ritual that was going on below them and he would have to lead his small band of adventurers through and around it so they didn't get caught. Aunt Beth might have her cast member I.D. with her, but there would still be the questions of why they were all there and where they had been hiding. No, it would not help Aunt Beth's career if they were caught.

"Okay, then." Peter had to stop for a moment when he heard his voice crack. Alex snickered at him, but the rest pretended not to hear. "Okay. I think we've agreed that Uncle Adam will go with me to the roof. Just to make sure I don't fall, right?" He shot a glance at Uncle Adam to make it clear that he, Peter, would be the one going up the intriguing ladder built into the side of the wall. Uncle Adam looked way too fascinated by this clue search, so Peter wanted to be sure they were on the same page.

Amused at the intense, meaningful stare Peter was giving him,

Adam just nodded solemnly. *Lance would love seeing this.* "Yes, that's right. Just for backup in case you need it."

The stare continued a minute longer as Peter tried to determine if he meant it or not. Uncle Adam had the oddest gleam in his eyes. "Okay, um, thanks." Peter turned to his other minions for the night. "Aunt Beth, you and Alex will cover the area around the Tiki Room and Jungle Cruise to make sure no one comes from that direction. Catie, you'll be up in the Treehouse to watch the entry from New Orleans Square and Frontierland." He put a hand up to shade his eyes when the beam from Alex's flashlight hit him square in the face. "Right, Alex, you and Aunt Beth have flashlights to signal Catie if someone comes and she will use our walkie-talkie to alert Uncle Adam."

"Honey, put that out. We know it works." Using the diversion to hide her smile as she turned to her son, Beth wondered if Peter was going to make them drop and give him ten push-ups before they set out. *Kimberly would love seeing this.* "I think that sounds like a great plan, Peter. I know I can't talk you out of going up that ladder, but, please be careful!"

The room seemed overly dark when Alex's flashlight clicked off. All he could see of Aunt Beth was a dancing white dot. "I will. It's already 2 a.m. Do you think we've waited long enough?"

As the only cast member present, Beth mentally went over the maintenance schedule she had seen posted backstage. The only major work being done that month was in ToonTown, the opposite side of the Park from where they were. Only general cleaning and touch-up painting had been scheduled for that night. She shook her head. "The Park didn't close until midnight. It usually takes at least an hour to herd the stragglers to the exit and close the shops. I don't think there's been quite enough time. Catie dear, peek out the window and see if Main Street is clear. Alex, put out that flashlight. We might need it later."

As excited as the rest of the group, Catie eagerly pushed aside the lacy curtains just enough to see. "Oh, wow! Look at the size of those hoses! No wonder the street is always so clean."

"I want to see!" Alex nudged in beside her as they watched the nightly ritual of cleaning Main Street take place.

Adam joined them at the window and grunted as he watched. "Hmm, we're going to leave behind footprints with all that water.

We'll have to wait until it dries."

Beth knew what she was about to say wasn't going to go over very well, but, as a mom, she had to try. "How about if we all take a nap until, say 4:30 or 5. It might do us some good to have some rest." *It would sure do me a world of good. Haven't done an all-nighter since Adam and I hid out under Pirates.*

"Nap!?" The three kids sounded insulted.

"Fine. Never mind. We'll just wait." She gave a small shrug when Adam flashed her a 'nice try' look.

"**O**kay, I think it's time. I haven't seen anyone go down Main Street in quite a while. You all ready?" Peter tried his best to sound calm, but excitement oozed from every pore. If he could have run around the room whooping without looking like a complete idiot, he would have.

Adam led the way down the ladder of the apartment and opened the door onto Main Street. Going to the edge of the entry-way, he slowly eased his head out so he could look in both direc-tions. The work lights had been turned off in their area. There was a glow that could be seen behind the Castle that was probably the workers in ToonTown. Whispering, he told the others to come on out.

"What's that noise?" Alex walked away from the dark edge of the buildings and looked toward the Castle.

"Get back here!" Beth pulled her son back into the deeper shadows. "That's the Wishing Well. It's always playing. When we came in early to practice for the canoe races, we could hear *I'm Wishing* everywhere in the Park!"

They were all dressed in the dark hats and jackets Adam and Beth had brought in his backpack. For Adam, it had brought back the memory of the time he had jumped from the steam train in the tunnel, curled into a ball on the ground, and hoped no one looked back. Dressed in black back then, he had blended perfectly into the darkness. Now he hoped the dark colors would help just in case someone came along.

Peter took the front position and led them to the edge of the Photo Shop. Now they had to cross Main Street to get to the Re-freshment Corner. "I don't see or hear anything. Let's go."

As one black mass, they quickly moved across the street and

headed for the bridge into Adventureland. Just past the Tiki Room, by the Dole Whip stand, they paused once more. Peter hugged the wall of tiki masks until he could see into the side entrance to Frontierland as well as the exit of the Jungle Cruise. At his wave, the rest joined him.

"Okay, Aunt Beth, you and Alex stay around here. We'll go through the shops instead of out on the street. See you later."

He was surprised when Beth pulled him into a hug. "You be careful now."

"I will." Embarrassed, yet reassured by her gesture, Peter motioned for Catie and Adam to follow him. Unnecessarily crouched low like a ninja, he wove a zigzag pattern through the silent shops as Adam and Catie walked along behind him, matching grins on their faces.

Once they reached the black metal gate that lead to the roof of the Bazaar, Adam did one last sweeping glance before taking Catie to the steps of Tarzan's Treehouse. A trash can had been pulled in front of the stairs to indicate the attraction was closed. After he pulled the can away to give her just enough room, he asked her one last time, "You sure you're okay all by yourself, honey? I could get Mom to sit with you up there." Even in the darkness he could see her brown eyes were wide. He needed to make sure it wasn't from fear.

Catie went in for a hug. "I'm okay, Dad. This is exciting! I'm a little scared, but I have the safest spot. I'll call you on the walkie-talkie if I need you."

"I have to get back. I think I heard the metal gate squeak." Restraining his fierce desire to protect his little girl, Adam watched her mount the steps until she was out of sight. *Seems like just yesterday we brought the twins home from the hospital.* The trash can was then pushed back into place. When he returned to the stairs next to the Bengal Barbecue, just as he thought, Peter had already opened the metal gate and was busy exploring the rooftop. "Hey, you were supposed to wait for me. Oh, wow, look at all the details in the walls up here. Did you see this tribute window to Harper?"

Peter wasn't paying any attention to the walls. He had found a doorway behind the Adventure Outpost sign that had probably been used by the actors in the stunt show. "Wonder where this goes?"

Still feeling the need to whisper, Adam ran a hand over the carved door as he spoke. "Well, probably to a dressing room like the ones near the Golden Horseshoe. There are probably stairs behind these buildings that go down to the break area that the Jungle Cruise skippers use. Beth told me," he added when Peter turned to question his knowledge of what was behind the scenes—or backstage as it was called by staff. "I'll point out the windows of the Frontierland dressing rooms next time we're over there. The entry is that huge stockade gate next to the Stage Door Café."

Peter turned from the door to put a hand on the first rung stuck into the side of the pink tower. There were seven posts in all. He didn't think he would have any trouble since they weren't spaced too far apart. Intent on what he needed to do, he jumped when Adam spoke again.

"You ready? Sorry." Adam was glad to see that Peter was a little nervous. That hopefully meant he might be more careful. "Before you start, let me check over the top of the sign to make sure no one's around." The main walkway through Adventureland was dark and quiet. A quick glance toward the Treehouse showed him how far away he was from his daughter. It was further than he had thought. He wouldn't be able to see any movement and would have to rely on the walkie-talkie. Looking across at the Jungle Cruise, he saw a movement in the shadows and hoped it was Alex. "All clear, Peter."

Peter put a hand on the second rung and began his slow, careful climb.

Catie had crouched down on the suspension bridge that led from the entry stairway to the main part of the Treehouse. As if her head was on a swivel, she kept in constant motion trying to watch all directions at the same time. The two-way radio ready at hand, she had already watched a security guard go through the queue area of the Pirates attraction. Then, when he turned away to go deeper into New Orleans Square, she let out a sigh of relief. Intent on watching for a flashlight warning coming from the Jungle Cruise, she was startled to hear the scrape of the trashcan that blocked the entrance to her hiding place. Her dad wasn't supposed to come back until Peter had gotten the next clue. It was way too soon for that.

A flashlight beam suddenly lit the inside of the tree trunk staircase and began to swing back and forth as someone came toward her position. It couldn't be Alex; he was supposed to be with their mom at the other end of Adventureland.

Heart pounding, Catie sprung from her spot to sprint to the first level of the treehouse. Usually she took her time in this hut to look over the figure of Jane as she sketched the nearby Tarzan. On the other side of the walkway was a ship's wheel inside a dark-paned window and various nautical knickknacks that supposedly had come from the shipwreck that stranded the baby Tarzan.

Throwing herself against the wall, Catie ignored all the fascinating items and peered back at the wooden walkway. The flashlight beam was making a lazy side-to-side sweep as the guard got closer to her position. Trying not to make any noise, the scared girl hurried up the next flight of stairs.

The next building was a hut that used to hold the master bedroom for the Swiss Family Robinson, the former occupants of the treehouse. Now the mother gorilla tenderly held the baby Tarzan as they watched scenes from his life play over a screen in the back. Catie realized she needed to hurry across the next exposed observation platform. From there was a wonderful view into Frontierland, all the way to the dock that held the *Mark Twain*. As she rounded the bamboo-covered windows that shielded the touching scene from the guests, ready to run up to the next level where the leopard Sabor screamed at the guests, she suddenly remembered something Uncle Lance had told them. He and Kimberly had to hide out in the Treehouse a long time ago and he had mentioned a hidden latch that opened the window. With one last, desperate look to see how close the security guard was, Catie reached inside the bamboo poles to frantically try and find that latch.

To Catie, the releasing *click* of the latch seemed to be super loud, but she couldn't think about anything except to get that window to swing upward. Through the loose slats below her, she could see the beam of light coming up the next flight of stairs toward her location. Scrambling through the now-open window, she had to jump to reach the panel to close it as quietly as possible. Pressed as closely as possible to the outer wall, curled into a dark ball, she tried to hold her breath as the footsteps of the guard could now be clearly heard. Try as she might, she couldn't keep her eyes closed.

She had to look at the slowly swinging light as it got closer and closer.

All of a sudden the mother gorilla behind her was brightly lit and the grinning baby could be easily seen. The light beam then swung over the other artifacts in the room as the guard, apparently a fan of the movie, chuckled in appreciation.

Taking his time, the guard finally moved higher into the tree-house, enjoying the tableaus as well as the star-filled sky over quiet Frontierland. Afraid to move or breathe, Catie waited where she was, feeling a little safer from detection but still anxious. What if her mom had signaled that someone was coming? What if her walkie-talkie went off right then and alerted the guard? What if the guard went into Adventureland and saw Peter climbing the wall? Peter had to have gotten to the top by now and was probably trying to get back down.

All these thoughts rushed through the poor girl's mind as she kept trying to determine the location of the security guard. Why couldn't it have been Uncle Wolf? He would have helped her and not made her so afraid. Where was Uncle Wolf anyway? He had been gone a long time. No one had seen him since he leaped out of the apartment window.

Catie jumped when the leopard high above her head screamed out into the night. That could only mean one thing: The guard was now down in the laboratory section on the ground floor. The leopard only screamed when someone pulled on the rope down there. When she heard the clanging of pots and pans, she knew her guess was right. The guard was playing with the kitchen items that had been set up for kids to make music just like the gorillas did in the movie. With a sigh of relief, she stood from her cramped position to stretch out her legs. Easily finding the release, she opened the window and climbed back out onto the wooden walkway. Leaving the security of the small hut, she peered over the edge and tried to see through the dense foliage. It was too thick. Easing onto the observation platform, she slunk down to peer over the edge. She could see the guard as he left Adventureland and took the sloping path down toward Frontierland. His whistling tune was easily heard in the silence of the night. Soon he was out of sight around the River Belle Terrace. On shaky legs, she made her way back down to her original position.

Peter carefully placed his feet on rung after rung. It felt odd not to have some kind of safety bar next to him as he climbed up hand over hand. A quick glance down at Uncle Adam showed him hovering as if to catch him when he fell. *I won't fall. I'm Indy!* With a quivering laugh that probably amused Uncle Adam, he reached the top of the wall.

With one hand firmly grasped on the ragged stucco edging, he felt a surge of security and safety. "I made it!" Both feet now on the last rung, he peered over the edge. All he could see was a flat, square roof. Not a gray capsule anywhere to be seen. "I guess he's not going to make it easy for me." To pull himself over, Peter put his arm over the edge to get a better grip. It was then that his hand felt cool, familiar plastic. "I found it!" He clamped his free hand over his mouth. He hadn't meant to say it out loud. The answering "Shhh," from below showed it was louder than even he thought. "Sorry."

"Get down here then!" Adam was getting anxious as Peter stood on the topmost rung of the posts sticking out from the wall. None of the posts had even quivered when Peter put his weight on them, but the contractor in him didn't trust anything he hadn't built himself. "Toss it down."

Peter then remembered he had to actually pick it up. Expecting it to be at least nailed into place, the huge, unnecessary jerk he applied almost toppled him off his precarious perch. "It wasn't even fastened down." Looking down through his feet, he could see Uncle Adam still hovering, so he dropped the capsule in his general direction. Easing his foot to the rung below, Peter slowly made it back to the deck over the Outpost.

Relieved, Adam pulled him into a bear hug. "You did it! I'm so proud of you. You all right?" He could see that Peter had an odd look on his face and became worried.

The boy broke into a wide grin. "That was so awesome! I could see over some of the roofs in Frontierland. There's some kind of scaffolding and ladders back there. You want to go see?" The nerves and adrenaline were making Peter almost giddy.

Adam put a hand on the boy's arm to calm him. "I'll take your word for it. Let's go get Catie and the others. We need to get out of sight."

Catie, having seen them move along the edges of the Bengal Barbecue, was now waiting at the bottom of the treehouse stairs. Adam was caught by surprise when she flew into his arms to hug him like she'd never let go. He could feel her heart pounding against his chest. "You okay, honey? We're all right. Peter did great."

Still too shaken by her close call, she gave him a quivering smile and just nodded. Her adventure would have to wait for the telling. This was Peter's time. "Let's go get Mom."

Safely back in the hidden apartment on Main Street, the five of them jumped around and released all their pent-up nerves. Peter waved the grey capsule in the air like a victory flag and gave a hushed war whoop. Disneyland would open in just a couple of hours and they all knew the leads, the cast members who were in charge of their departments, would soon be making their early rounds. Once the Park was open and enough people had streamed down Main Street, Peter and his crew could make their getaway.

Peter proceeded to tell Alex and Catie how dangerous his climb had been. They all attributed Catie's pale face to his exaggerated story and being overly tired.

After Peter was finished, Alex asked what everyone else wondered. "So, are you going to open it or what? Or do we have to wait until we get home?"

"Oh." Peter had only been thinking of finding the capsule, not what would come after. "That's a good idea. Do you want to open this one, Alex?"

Even though he only had a minor role in the activities, Alex jumped at the opportunity to open it. But, try as he might, the sealed cap on the end would not budge. He handed it to his dad. "It seems like it's glued on or something. You try it. You keep telling us you're all muscles."

Adam, after getting the go-ahead from Peter, took hold of the container. Even with all his muscles, he couldn't get it open either. "Wow, this one is really tight. None of the others were this bad." He handed it back to Peter. "I guess we'll have to wait after all. I might have to use a vise and slip joint pliers to get it open at home."

Disappointed, Peter just gave a slight nod. Fiddling with the cap to see what they had meant, he was surprised when it easily came off into his hands. "Thought you said it was tight. Look, I got it open."

"Adam must have loosened it up. You know, like a pickle jar." Beth gave her husband a knowing grin to help ease any damage to his ego this might have caused.

"Nope. It wouldn't budge for me. Peter must be really strong." Adam let the look Peter gave him slide over. It was odd that he couldn't do it, but, as long as it was open, that was all that mattered.

"What's in it?" Alex didn't care who had muscles or not. He was just hoping the next clue would give him more time in the Park to actually go on some rides. He hadn't been on the roller coaster in Disney California Adventure in a while.

As Peter upended the capsule, Adam turned to Beth. "I should call Lance and let him know everything went well."

"Adam, it's only five in the morning."

He gave her a wide, impish grin. "I know. I owe him. Apparently you haven't had an itinerary duct taped to your bare chest."

As he punched in Lance's cellphone number, Beth just shook her head. "Boys."

When the ringing phone went straight to voicemail, Adam hung up and called again. He grinned when Lance finally picked up, his voice heavy with sleep.

"This had better be good."

Adam let his voice go frantic. "Lance! Oh, no! You…you'd better get over here! It's Peter!"

"That is so cruel, Adam." Beth glared at him, arms folded across her chest.

Lance practically shouted into the phone, "What happened to Peter? Where are you? I'm getting…. Ouch!"

"Lance?" Kimberly's sleepy voice could be heard in the background. "What are you doing on the floor? What about Peter?"

"I tripped…. Never mind! Adam, what happened?"

"You sound all out of breath, buddy."

"Skip that. What happened?" Lance seemed to be getting confused. Adam could hear the bed squeak as he sat back down. "Talk to me, Adam!"

"I wanted to tell you Peter found the capsule."

There was dead silence on the other end. Adam knew Lance was staring at the phone. "And…..?"

"Wow, you can sure put a lot of sarcasm into one word."

"And the hysterical tone in your voice is now suspiciously missing. You woke me up on a Saturday morning at 5 a.m. to tell me Peter found the capsule? He's all right?"

"Of course he's all right. I'm here with him."

Lance rubbed a hand over his face. "Grrr. So, what was in the capsule, now that I'm awake."

"No clue. We'll call you later. Bye."

"Adam....."

With a satisfied smirk on his face, Adam slipped his phone back in his pocket and ignored the vibration when it immediately rang again.

Beth stared at him. "That was mean."

"I'll give him an hour to fall asleep again, then I'll call him back and apologize."

"No, you won't!"

"Oh, you don't want me to apologize?" Adam mimicked Beth's arm-folded stance as he bantered back at her.

Not amused, she ran a hand over her face. "I'm too tired for this. Peter, what did you find?"

Peter's face was a mixture of disappointment and intrigue. "It's just another clue. There's nothing else in here. No little treasure or anything."

Beth slumped wearily on the sofa. If the kids weren't there, she would have dropped down and gone to sleep. "Well, there doesn't always have to be a gift inside. Sometimes the end result is the treasure."

"I guess." Not wanting to appear greedy after all he had received so far, Peter turned his attention back to the paper in his hand. "Do you want me to read it?"

"You did well. You found the container. But, do you remember our deal? You must still bring me my heart's desire. The second clue to my treasure is: A heart of greater value than life itself.

"Now you must go in search of the next container to get to your treasure. It is behind the sign of the Admiral.

"Don't break your neck."

"I tell you, these clues are getting odder and odder. Can I see the paper, Peter?" Beth took the yellowed slip and felt it between her fingers, shaking her head as she did. "It feels right, sort of. The handwriting still looks a little off, though. I just can't put my finger on what's wrong, though." Puzzled, she looked over at Adam. "Where's there an Admiral in Disneyland?"

He gave a shrug. "Isn't there a boat in ToonTown with Donald Duck? Is he an Admiral?"

"But, Uncle Adam, ToonTown wasn't there in Walt's time. Doesn't it have to be earlier than that?"

"Yeah, you're right, Peter. Wow, I'm too tired to think." Adam ran a hand through his messy blond hair. "Should we go home, get some rest, and then you guys can do your research?"

Just as before, there was a steady chorus of "No!"

"I did bring my tablet." Beth yawned from the sofa. She was sinking deeper and deeper into the cushions and didn't seem to mind.

"Wasn't there an Admiral's Bar in the original Tomorrowland?"

"No, that was the Yacht Bar, honey. No, you need to plug it into the wall, Alex. There isn't enough battery power left."

Adam joined Beth on the sofa as the kids hovered over the tablet. She leaned into his chest and closed her eyes. Before the kids could ask "Who's Admiral Fowler?" she was asleep.

Adam looked down at his wife, jealous of the rest she was getting. When the overly-tired kids began to argue over the pieces of history and trivia they were uncovering, he knew they had had enough. "Guys, I know you aren't going to like this, but we all need to go home and get some sleep in our own beds."

As expected, the response was less-than-favorable.

"I know you don't want to, but that's the way it is." Adam knew he had to stand firm or they would be all over him at the least sign of wavering. "Once the Park opens, we'll make our way to the car. If Peter or Catie finds the right answer to the clue, we can always come back." At the sullen looks he was receiving, he gave a silent sigh. *I must be getting old. I'd usually be able to handle an all-nighter. Hope Lance doesn't find out about this. I'd never hear the end of it.* "Gather up your stuff. Quietly! Let's let Beth sleep as long as she can."

CHAPTER 10

Flashback — Disneyland — 1958

A satisfied expression on his face, Walt looked over the array of artifacts he had brought back from Europe. It had been an extensive, productive trip. On the same table, slightly apart from the relics pulled from sunken ships, was a lovely item he had gotten as a surprise for Lillian.

His eyes lost their sharp focus as he thought back on the trip. It hadn't been easy to buy the strand of pearls without her knowledge, but he managed to pull it off. When she had wandered to a far corner of that little antique shop in Zermatt, Switzerland, Walt quickly paid the clerk for the pearls he had spotted when they first walked into the shop. Safely hidden in the deep, overflowing pocket of his jacket, he had smiled broadly when she came back to join him.

"What are you so happy about, Walt? Find something interesting?" Lillian fully expected to see a suit of armor or an antique piano with his name and California address on it. However, there didn't appear to be anything in particular that had been set aside.

"Oh, nothing, really. Just happy to be here with you!" He took her by the arm, waved a cheery good-bye to the shop owner, and together they had strolled out into the bright summer day.

Fingers lightly resting on the pearls, cool to his touch, his memory of their driving tour through Europe was interrupted by the *ring ring* of the entry bell to his apartment. Knowing whom he had sent for, he called out, "Come on in, Blaine."

"Hi, Boss. You have everything you wanted to show me?" Blaine had been deep into his work of sculpting the mermaids for the new Submarine Voyage set to open next year. His responsibilities also included over 14,000 beads, jewels, and treasures that would soon be placed all over the seabed floor in the sunken ruins and shipwreck section of the ride. Aware of his deadline, Blaine really didn't want to be interrupted. But, knowing his boss as well as he did, he figured Walt probably had something new for him to do.

"How's everything going?"

It seemed like a normal question a boss would ask an employee, but this was Walt Disney. He knew every facet of the work being done and its exact progress. Not only was work being done on the Submarine Voyage, but also the Matterhorn Mountain was being built, and the Alweg Monorail system was scheduled to open at the same time. This was going to be a tremendous expansion for Disneyland. Blaine gave Walt a half smile. "We're all on point. Everyone's on overtime, as expected."

Walt's eyes strayed back to the brass items spread out over the table as a big grin came over his face. "Did you see those two postcards I sent from Switzerland to the Model Department?"

Blaine had to laugh. "Yeah, everyone did. When the first one came, we weren't sure if you were serious or not. When the second one arrived, we knew to get busy."

"Well, we had an ugly Skyway tower on Holiday Hill to cover up and we all wanted a thrill ride anyway, so I thought it was the perfect solution. I was already in Zermatt to check on the progress of *Third Man on the Mountain*, and there it was."

"It" had turned out to be the Matterhorn Mountain. Enraptured by the majestic peak, Walt found two postcards of the Matterhorn and mailed them to California. On the back were just two words: "Build this!"

"You like the design of the Monorail?"

When Walt changed the subject, Blaine realized he wouldn't be getting back to work any time soon. He leaned his hip against the table and folded his arms over his chest. "Yeah, I like the wraparound windshield and the bubble for the driver to sit in. Sure a lot better than the way Bob described the first monorail he saw when you sent him to Germany."

At the reminder, Walt started to laugh. "That was priceless! 'An ugly loaf of bread with a slot in the bottom sitting on a stick.' Glad he had background in car design."

"Yeah, that and being a fan of Buck Rogers. The Mark 1 might have looked really different if he hadn't." After a subtle glance at his watch, Blaine pointed to the things on the littered table next to him. "Did you want me to work these things into the Submarine Voyage?"

Walt had seen his glance and hid his smile. He knew Blaine would stand there all day if he was asked to, but decided to let him off easily. "Yeah, I love these brass portholes and ship's bells. I found an anchor, too, but the museum just wouldn't sell it to me." The expression on his face showed Walt was still annoyed at being told no. "I know everything you're doing is made out of Duraflex, but I think it would be nice to have a few real artifacts on the seabed floor mixed in with your sculptures. Even if they tarnish, it will just make it all look more authentic. These old silverware pieces and plates could have come from the Captain's Quarters." His eyes got that dreamy, far-away look. As the finished product came into sharp focus in his mind, he was already working on how to improve it.

The ringing of his phone interrupted his thoughts. After finding out who was on the line, Walt halted the call and put his hand over the mouthpiece. With a nod of his chin toward the table, he dismissed the artist. "Take everything with you, Blaine. I'll check on your progress in a couple of days. I've got to take this call."

Blaine hesitated as his eyes landed on a beautiful strand of pearls. There would be pearls on the mermaids, of course, but these…these looked real. "Everything, boss?"

Walt had turned his back to resume his conversation. Slightly irritated at the interruption, he gave a slight glance over his shoulder. "Yeah, I said everything. You'll have to see yourself out."

With a shrug, Blaine gathered up all the items, leaving the table cleared. The door to the apartment shut with a low *click* behind him.

As soon as the call was finished, an upset Walt grabbed his hat, jammed it on his head, and rushed out the door. It would be over a month before he was able to return to his little hide-away over the Fire Station.

The Great Northern Plains

Using his newly-acquired skill, a worried Wolf soundlessly appeared in the disorganized den of Omah. He had pictured her just the way she looked when the sun hit her brilliant red hair, the golden highlights gleaming in the light. His memory had been so sharp he felt he could have reached out and touched the silky strands.

The cave was empty. Shocked that his new method of travel didn't work, Wolf wandered into the dark interior. The mess was still there, but there was an air of neglect. It felt as though she hadn't been back in a long, long time.

Unable to figure out why Omah wasn't there, Wolf eventually picked up a pile of pictures from the floor. As he thumbed through mementoes of her past, an uncommon feeling of loss swept over him. Not wanting to face the implications of what it might mean, he pushed the emotion to the back of his mind as one photo in particular caught his attention.

"That must be why I came here." It was a picture of Omah in an open meadow, standing in the sun, her face turned up to the warmth. After another long look, he slipped the picture into a pocket in his deerskin pants, the only garment he was wearing. "Now what do I do? If this didn't work, how do I find her?"

With a groan, Wolf knew he would have to talk to her tribe if he was going to find out what happened to Omah. Most of the tribe had only seen him as a huge black wolf. Her sister, though, had seen him as a man when she watched the cave. He would have to try and talk to Kiaayo. He just hoped she wasn't armed with her spear this time.

As he approached the encampment, he was greeted by a chorus of barking dogs. Alerted that there was a stranger in the camp, he was quickly surrounded by both the snarling dogs and the braves. "Kiaayo." He made his voice commanding and sure, as the son of the Shaman should.

The men could see the stranger was unarmed and unafraid. With a gesture, they led him to a large tent near the edge of the camp. When the redhead emerged to see what the commotion was all about, her eyes widened when she recognized Wolf. "Sumanitu Tanka." When he acknowledged his name with a nod, she gestured for him to sit. With the sign language common to the Plains Tribes, she asked why he was back.

"I am looking for Omahkap'si."

"Why?"

It took Wolf a moment to figure out her question. Then it took him longer to figure out the answer. "She suddenly left me and I was worried about her."

Kiaayo looked down to hide a small smile. When she spoke, it was from the experience of growing up with a headstrong sister. "If Omahkap'si doesn't want to be found, she will not be found."

"I wondered if she came back here to say goodbye."

That confused the woman. "Why would she say goodbye? She leaves and she comes back. Probably the same as you do."

Why would she say goodbye? Even if she does what I think she's going to do, she would still be a sister to Kiaayo. That wouldn't change. How do I explain this? Wolf ran a hand through his hair and shook his head in frustration. "When did you see Omah last?"

Now it was Kiaayo's turn to look distressed. "It's been a long time. She usually visits more often. I'm afraid something might have happened to her." She turned away from Wolf. "If you don't know where she is, I don't think I can help you."

Wolf glanced around to see who might be close enough to know what they were saying. Once the newness of Wolf's appearance wore off, the members of the tribe had drifted back to what they had been doing. They were alone by the entrance to her tent. "Can you tell me anything about where she lives when she is not here? Has Omah ever mentioned another house or...." He broke off. He wasn't sure how the word apartment would translate.

Kiaayo knew what he meant but shook her head. "No, she never talked about that part of her life. No one here would be interested. We live now."

At that point, Wolf realized there was nothing more to learn. As he stood to leave, he turned back to the curious redhead. "If you see your sister, would you tell her I'm looking for her?"

"I can do that. And if you find her, let her know I miss her."

Rather than create a spectacle by disappearing in front of the tribe, Wolf decided to walk back to the cave. Touching nothing, he just stared into the darkness. His mind whirled as he thought about his last conversation with Omah and what it might mean. He hadn't yet decided what he would do. And there was no way to know what Omah was going to do. Or what she might have already done, he reminded himself.

After one last look around, Wolf decided to go ahead with something he had planned to do with Omah. Even if he couldn't find her, he could still make that part right.

His glance happened to fall on what he was wearing. A droll smile on his face, he knew he'd have to make another stop first. While it would be amusing to appear dressed only in deerskin trousers, he wasn't sure enough of his new-found ability to be certain of his exact landing spot. It would be better to be dressed more appropriately. Not as funny, but more proper.

Disneyland — 1966

"**W**alt, you have a minute? Wow, what happened in here? The maid quit?"

Distracted, Walt looked up at Wolf. The apartment looked like a tornado had hit it. "I didn't hear the bell. Come on in, Wolf. Oh, I guess you're already in…."

Wolf didn't know if he should be worried or amused. Usually unflappable, Walt seemed distracted and was visibly upset. The security guard picked his way around the cushions that had been thrown from the couch. "Redecorating?"

Walt stood after thrusting his arm down the back of the sofa. One hand on his hip, the other slowly scratched the top of his head. "I just can't find them. I've been searching everywhere." He waved one arm around in a circle. "This is just my big, last-ditch effort before I forget it forever."

"What'd you lose? Anything important?" From the look of the apartment, it must have been something Walt *really* wanted to find.

"You remember that trip Lillian and I took to Europe?"

Wolf smiled. "Which one?"

"What?" The question seemed to stump the already-distracted Walt.

"Which trip to Europe? There's been a few."

The irritation at not being understood faded from Walt's face. "Oh. Right. The driving trip we took in 1958." At Wolf's nod, he threw another exasperated look around the room. "I had bought something for Lilian, something special as a gift." He glanced over at Wolf and gave a small smile. "You know, for putting up with me for so long!" As expected, Wolf didn't comment on that. "Anyway,

I had brought it here to hide until the right time to give it to her… and I still can't find it."

As soon as he arrived Wolf had glanced at a newspaper sitting on one of the tapestry chairs and had seen the current year. "It's been eight years, Walt. That's a long time for something to be lost. How come you never mentioned it before? I might have been able to help back then. What was it, anyway?"

"I know it's been eight years!" Irritated at himself, Walt let out a sigh as he bent over to pick up one of the cushions. After tossing it back into place, he sat down on the couch and shrugged. "I don't know. I always expected it to just turn up. You know, behind the sofa, or in the back of one of the drawers. A closet." Walt paused before he continued, his brow creased in concern. "I'd hate to think someone broke in here and stole from me. Things happened before, but I can't think of anyone who would do that again."

"You still haven't told me what it is that's missing."

Walt turned from staring out the window over Main Street to look at Wolf. Before he could answer, a confused expression came over his face as he looked his friend over from head to toe. "What are you dressed in? That's not the uniform the security guards are wearing now."

Wolf glanced down at his outfit. In his hurry to change out of the deerskin pants and get going, he had overlooked that little point. "Uhm…."

His problem forgotten for the moment, a big smile spread over Walt's face. "Ah, I get it. You aren't really here. I mean…you're here on a visit from the future, aren't you?" Fascinated, he got up to scrutinize the uniform. "I like it. Very neat and official looking. Should I make notes?" The smile faded a little. "Wait a minute. The other times you…uhm, visited…you were a wolf. Scared the dickens out of the dogs at home. This is the first time you've come back as a man. Isn't it? Unless I missed something another time."

He always was too sharp. Should have thought about the uniform before I just jumped here. "Yeah, you're right. I…I've learned a new way to travel. If I keep doing it correctly, there shouldn't be any more storms and lightning."

Walt was intrigued. He knew about Wolf's special abilities, but now there was something new. "How did you learn? Did someone teach you or did you figure it out?"

Oh, great. "Someone showed me."

"Who?" It was said more like a demand than a casual question.

"Omah."

"The mermaid Omah? She was just here. Well, a couple of days ago."

Wolf had to stop and think for a moment. Walt didn't look at all surprised by the identity of his teacher. He wondered how much his boss actually knew. "So, you know about her...."

"Her ability to travel like you do? Yeah, I've known about it for a while." Walt went over to retrieve the other cushion. "I thought she might possibly work with you. I was going to get you two together after her test, but...." He let the sentence trail off. That clue search ended badly and she had been sent away. Any future hopes for Omah had been cut short. It hadn't helped when she came back with the mermaid, frantic and wild-eyed.

Wolf's mind was quickly going through the timeline he knew about. If Walt had already sent her to Florida, then she possibly could have already returned to him after confronting Peter. "You said she was just here. Which time?"

Walt gave a smile. "Only you would know to ask a question like that. She suddenly appeared here, like you just did, with the lost mermaid in her hands. She seemed to think it would make a difference."

"But it didn't."

"Well, it was already over. Your young friend already finished the quest, thanks to you. There wasn't anything else to be done."

Wolf removed his hat and ran a hand through his thick hair. "Walt, did you plan on her being a Guardian?"

"Getting a little territorial, are you?"

"No, I need to know. There are...things...going on in my time where it would be good to know."

Walt gave a half smile. "From our dealings in the past...using the term literally...I know I shouldn't ask you when that would be." He was amused by the wary look that came over Wolf's face and he held up a hand to divert what he knew would come. "No, no, I'm not asking. It's just intriguing. You have to understand that. But, to answer your question, yes, I was planning on bringing her into the fold as a Guardian. Until her breakdown, that is...."

Wolf now had his answer. He knew he could bring some mental peace to the woman after all this time. If he could just find her...
. "Well, thanks for clarifying that for me, Walt. It means a lot. And, I hope you can trust me to make things right for you. Initially you really weren't wrong about her. She has some strong...emotions... she has been working through."

Walt's eyes narrowed as he thought about Wolf's words. "Hmmm. It's intriguing that you seem to know her, even though I can only imagine how much time has passed. But, I do trust you." He walked across the room to his loyal friend to pat him on the arm. "Now if you could just go back in time and find my pearls." He paused before he resumed fixing the room, his face lighting up. "You could do that, couldn't you?"

His thoughts on Omah, Wolf stared unseeingly out the patio window. Just half-listening to his boss, his head suddenly whipped around. "Did you say pearls? Is that what you're looking for? When was the last time you saw them?"

"Now why does everyone ask that? If I knew, I would look there...."

Wolf had to smile. "No, I mean what was going on around then? And don't tell me you can't remember. You remember everything."

"Everything except where I put the pearls...." Walt quit mumbling as he thought back. "Well, that was the time of the huge Tomorrowland expansion. We were working on the Matterhorn, the Submarines, and the Monorail at the same time. I know the pearls were in this room. Why are you smiling?"

"You said the magic word: Submarines. I think I know where your pearls are, Walt."

"You know who stole them?"

"Oh, I don't think they were stolen." Wolf now had the answers to two mysteries. Not bad for a day's work. "I have to make a trip to get them back for you."

"Present or future?"

Again, only Walt could know to ask that. "Future, and, no, you can't come with me."

"You and Omah always tell me no. I don't like being told no."

"Sorry, Boss. I'll see you soon."

Walt seemed to be thinking back and he stopped Wolf from

leaving. "I had wanted to give those pearls to Lillian back when the new Tomorrowland opened. You know how the mermaids on the float threw fake gems and pearls to the guests along the parade route? I was going to have one of the girls throw Lillian my pearls. Can you arrange that?"

Wolf gave him a wide grin. "Now I know why you keep me around. I'll see what I can do. No promises except that you will get them back."

Walt said nothing. He knew Wolf.

Fullerton – Current Day

"**W**olf! It's you? Where've you been?" Peter was excited to see his friend suddenly show up in his room. "Hey, how'd you do that? Where's all the lightning and stuff?"

Wolf could see that the questions would just keep coming and held up a restraining hand. "Nice to see you, too, Peter. I, uh, learned something new. Didn't your mom mention it?"

Peter couldn't understand why Wolf turned red all of a sudden. "Mom? No, she didn't say anything. Do you want me to go get her?"

"No!" When the boy looked startled by the sharp way he was answered, Wolf had to lower his voice. "I mean, I'm sure she's busy and I don't want to bother her." *Not until we all have enough time to forget it ever happened.* "I wanted to see you."

That perked Peter right up. "Me? Cool! Oh, guess what? I've already found the answers to two of the clues! I'm working on the next one now. If I can figure it out in time, we can go back to the apartment tonight and be there in the Park it opens in the morning."

Wolf had no idea what he was talking about. "What clues? Did you find another Hidden Mickey trail?"

"Oh, that's right. We haven't seen you since you jumped out of the window. You've been gone a long time. You know that apartment Walt gave me? I found another capsule in there!"

Wolf paused as Peter went over to his desk to dig out the clues he had found so far. Since he didn't remember any clue search based in that apartment, he wondered if it was another one Walt had done without him. Well, he'd probably have time to ask Walt if he could just get Peter to focus.

When Peter came back with the yellowed papers in his hand, he was surprised when Wolf didn't seem interested in them. Disappointed, his hand dropped to his side. "Oh, I thought you'd want to see them...and help me with this latest clue that has me stumped."

Wolf could see the letdown all over Peter's face. "Sorry, buddy, I'll have to make it up to you later. I'm on a special errand for Walt. Do you remember those pearls that were on the mermaid you found in the Mansion? Where are they?"

On hearing Walt's name, Peter instantly forgot the disappointment that Wolf apparently wasn't going to help him. "Walt? Really? Did you just see him? What does he want you to do? Can I go with you?"

"Peter..."

"Does it have anything to do with Disneyland.... What?"

"The pearls. Do you know where they are?"

"That's all? Just the pearls? That's no fun."

"Peter...."

The excited look on Peter's face fell. "All right. All right. They're over.... Turn your back. It's a secret hiding place."

Wolf looked at the arm-folded stance Peter had assumed and did as he was asked. *Boys.* "Fine." He could hear rummaging under the bed and then a scraping as something was pulled out. A loud click, and then it was shoved back in place.

"Okay, you can turn around. Are these what you want?"

Wolf took the gleaming strand of pearls in his hands. "Yes, I think these are just what Walt was asking about."

"Are they real? I tried to find out, but didn't get very far."

Wolf glanced up at the boy. "What do you mean? What'd you do?"

A blush started creeping up Peter's neck. It was obvious he wished he hadn't mentioned it. "Uhm. I called a jewelry store to see if they were real or not."

"Oh? What'd they say?"

The blush got brighter. "I tried to describe what they looked like. The woman on the phone said she wouldn't be able to tell from what I was saying. So I tried again. She finally told me they'd have to see the pearls. When I told her I couldn't do that, and asked if she really couldn't just tell me, she, uh, told me to hold them up to the phone so she could see them."

Wolf bit his cheek. "And you did?"

"Hey, I didn't know she was joking. Just drop it. Are they real or not?"

Wolf let Peter off the hook. "Yes, they're real. And I need to get them back to their owner. He's been worried about them for a long time."

Peter gave a little laugh. "Considering who it is you're talking about, it's been a lot longer than he thought!"

"You're sure right about that, Pete. And, no, you can't come with me."

"Aww. Are you coming back soon? We all really miss you."

That heartfelt admission made Wolf smile. It was nice to be missed. "Yeah, I'll be back soon. You be good."

Peter made a face. "That's no fun. But, I'll try."

CHAPTER 11

Flashback – Atwater Village – 1964

Admiral Fowler entered the Tam O'Shanter Inn on Los Feliz Boulevard. It was easy to spot his boss. Walt always sat at the same table. Two drinks were already waiting as the Admiral waved off the hostess and made his way to the table.

"What's the smile for, Joe?"

"Afternoon, Walt." Joe took his chair, his chin indicating the room around them. "This room. This building. Every time I come here, the first thing I think is that it looks like you built it for Fantasyland. It's just waiting to be moved into place."

Walt nodded as he looked around the comfortable room. "Well, they did use movie studio carpenters when they built it in 1922. Great theme work. Oh, I ordered for you already. Hope you don't mind."

Joe looked mildly surprised when plates of hot food were set in front of them. After taking a sip of his drink, he waved his glass over the plate. "So, what's the special occasion?"

"I just wanted to thank you and Maurie for having Lillian and me over for that terrific steak dinner."

Joe looked at Walt over the rim of his glass. "That was up north. And ten years ago."

There was a sparkle in Walt's eye. "Was it? Time flies."

"If I remember correctly, you invited me down here for a day or two to check out the construction site. I was just supposed to be a part-time consultant. Ended up being here for three weeks."

"Well, Disneyland was set to open eleven months later. I needed you."

"Yeah, that was obvious!" Joe gave a short, humorous laugh as he wiped the condensation from the glass onto a white cloth napkin. "And I'm still here."

"Best construction chief I could've found. And, as much as I hate to admit it, you were right."

There was a long pause as Joe waited for his boss to continue. When it became obvious, he asked what was expected of him, "About what? There've been so many things."

Now it was Walt's turn to laugh as he cut into his steak. "You're probably more right than you know. But, I was thinking about Fowler's Harbor."

Joe gave a grunt between bites. "At least you quit calling it Joe's Ditch."

"Thought that had a nice ring to it. No, you were right." Walt pointed at Joe with his fork as he kept talking. "We did need a dry dock for the big boats inside the Park. It would've been very difficult to work on them without it. Look at the trouble it took just to get the *Mark Twain* to the river! Using flatcars on the railroad track was the only way."

"Well, I did learn a thing or two working in the San Francisco ship yards."

Lost in thought over the myriad of difficulties in getting Disneyland built in less than a year, Walt brought up another innovation the Admiral had conceived. "Building a wood mill on site was a good idea, too. Not many know that was how the Opera House started out."

Not one to boast of his accomplishments, Joe finished off his lunch with a smile of appreciation and changed the subject. "I see why you love coming here. Great food." He could also see that Walt was done eating, but showed no sign of leaving. His boss was usually impatient to get back to work. "Was there something else?"

Walt shoved aside his plates and leaned his arms on the tabletop. His face revealed a mixture of excitement, business, and plotting. "Yeah, Joe, there is something else." He let the moment drag on a bit longer until he could see a wariness come into the Admiral's posture. Yes, he had made a good decision in convincing Joe to stay on all these years. Now the Admiral was needed for something else coming down the line. "Tell, me, Joe. What do you know about Florida?"

Disneyland

After claiming to have the answer to the clue, Peter, Catie, Alex, Adam, and Beth were back in the hidden apartment. Arriving at Disneyland a few hours before closing time, they had made it to the room undetected. Now, in the early hours of Sunday morning, it was discovered Peter hadn't yet worked out all the bugs.

"I thought you said you knew right where to go, Peter." Feeling like he'd been had, Adam, though secretly pleased to be in the apartment again, was staring at the boy.

"You look just like Dad did when I scratched his car."

"Leave your dad out of this...unless you'd like me to let him know what's going on right now."

Peter bit back his next response. "Sorry, Uncle Adam. I think I know the general area we need to go. I thought we'd just figure it out really easily once we were here." He tried the charming smile he and his dad had perfected over the years.

Also slightly irritated, Beth had to chuckle. "That look doesn't work on us, honey. We've been around Lance way too long for that!"

Peter dropped the face. "Well, I really do think the answer is somewhere in Frontierland. Or Main Street. Or...."

"So, you really don't know."

"You can help, Uncle Adam."

Adam and Beth retook their places on the messy sofa while the silent twins watched to see what would happen next. They had learned that sometimes silence was the best protection. Let Peter sink his own ship. "I think you had better get busy on Beth's tablet again and find us the answer. Quickly."

"Yes, Uncle Adam." Peter took the tablet that Beth handed to him and brought up the search site he had been on when Uncle Wolf interrupted him. Catie came over to the table to help him while Alex plugged in some ear buds to listen to his music.

It didn't take Peter very long to find some interesting pieces of Disney history. "Hey, did you guys know there used to be a restaurant called Maurie's Lobster House?"

"Ooh, lobster sounds good just about now." Comfortable on the sofa, Adam was doing his best to stay awake. Cuddled next to him, Beth had already fallen asleep. "Where was it?"

With Catie peering over his shoulder, Peter had already moved past the small reference, and had to scroll back up. "Umm, oh, here it is. Over in Frontierland at Fowler's Harbor. She was Admiral Fowler's wife. Looks like that place is gone and the Harbour Galley is there now."

"Well, actually, that's in Critter Country, Peter."

Peter, doing what he loved, deep in the history of Disneyland, had to stop and look up at Catie. "Oh, yeah. I guess you're right. The walking area around the back is just before the canoes. Do you know the name of the street that Fowler's Harbor is on?"

Only Catie and Adam were interested in trivia that early in the morning. Alex hadn't even heard the question. Catie didn't know the answer, but Adam thought he did. "It's Mill….something."

"Mill View Lane," Peter filled in for him. "This says it was taken from the Admiral's actual address in Florida."

"Florida?" Adam had to think to make the connection. "I know he was instrumental in getting Disneyland built on time. That's right. I forgot that he was also used at Walt Disney World. Walt loved his 'Can do!' attitude. Everything that was thrown at him got a 'Can do,' response. And he did it, too!"

"Do you think this is the Admiral in the clue?" Catie hoped that was the case. Becoming drowsy, she glanced over enviously at her mom as she stifled a yawn. It would be nice to go to sleep for a little while before rushing out into the Park again.

Peter looked at Adam for confirmation. "Sounds like it to me. What do you think, Uncle Adam?"

Adam gave a slow nod as Catie came over to snuggle into his side. He wondered how long it would take her to fall asleep like her mom. "I think that might be the answer, too, Peter. Now you just have to figure out what the sign of the Admiral would be. You see any pictures there of Joe's work?"

When he narrowed his search to focus on just the Admiral, Peter let out an exasperated breath. "Oh, wow, he was involved in just about everything here. How do we go through all that?" Knowing Uncle Adam would probably tell him to figure it out, he didn't wait for an answer. Scrolling through the information again, he looked for a different angle. "Wait a minute. I think I see something. There's one picture that keeps coming up. It's dated 1961."

He held the tablet up for Catie and Adam to see.

When he saw the old photograph, a big grin spread over Adam's face. "That looks like a sign to me."

At first confused, Peter just stared at where Uncle Adam was pointing. He had merely looked at the general picture, not any specifics in it. As recognition came, a smile erased his frown lines. "And that's still there! I know it is! We see it every time we go by on the *Mark Twain* or the *Columbia*."

Peter's enthusiasm was infectious. The tiredness in Catie vanished as she looked from her dad to her friend. "Let's go see!"

"Now hold on." Adam held up a restraining hand as Peter closed the tablet and headed for the door. "First, we need to wake up Beth. Then, we need to check to see how many people are in the Park already. If it's early enough, the *Columbia* should still be berthed. She won't come out until the Park gets busy. And, if it's a slow Sunday, she might not come out at all."

Peter was almost dancing in place. "This would be the perfect time to go. There won't be any cast members on board yet."

Beth had heard the commotion and was already awake. "What happened? Did you find something?"

"We found it, Aunt Beth! We found the sign of the Admiral!"

Swinging her legs over the edge of the sofa, Beth tried to work a crick out of her neck as she sat up. "Ow. Miss my pillow.... How long have I been out?"

"Couple of hours. These two," indicating Peter and Catie, "were too excited to sleep." Adam placed a hand on his daughter's arm. "And still are, from the looks of it."

"What's the plan?"

While Beth and Adam discussed Adam's plan, Peter and Catie tried to devise the best method to get the attention of the unaware, distracted Alex. The Bucket of Cold Water plan was quickly negated by the boy's mom and dad. They had to go to the second-best plan and sneak up behind him, using a piece of fabric to tickle his nose until he jerked around and started sneezing.

"Kids." The tone in Beth's voice stopped Alex from throwing the first punch. "We have work to do. You can settle that later. Without hitting, Alex."

Alex pushed Peter away from him as they followed Adam to the exit of the apartment. "Stupid clues." Shoulders hunched, his muttering continued as they blended in with the first wave of people walking toward Sleeping Beauty Castle. "Rather be riding Splash Mountain and Big Thunder."

There was a crispness in the air that early in the morning. Mist lazily rose from the Rivers of America as the group slowly walked past the entrance to the Haunted Mansion. Most of the guests around them hurried into the entrance to the Mansion or kept going to be one of the first riders on Splash Mountain.

Adam had taken Beth's arm as they walked. "Remember when we rode Splash looking for a certain dog named Sunnee?"

She had to laugh at the reminder. "Yeah. That clue was 'Sunnee Holds the Key.' And I recall you got into a lot of trouble because we didn't have to ride Splash at all. It wasn't here in Walt's time."

"Yeah, I know. You did get a Blue Bayou dinner out of it. It was fun, though."

"Yes, that was a good time. That first clue search you and Lance went on, wow, look where it's led us." She nestled deeper into his side. "Now our kids are following clues all these years later. Who would have thought it possible?"

"Walt did." Adam still marveled at the man's vision of the future.

"Hey, look, the restaurant's still closed. That's good."

Peter's excited voice broke into Adam's and Beth's reflection. They stopped at the buildings that looked like they had been transplanted from the eastern seaboard. Nautical knickknacks, ropes, lobster cages, and ship's bells adorned the weather-beaten buildings and the dock where the silent *Columbia* was tied.

As they walked around the dock in front of the ship, their eyes all turned to the last wooden building on the dock. It was a two-story building, brown wood with crisp white trim. There was an inviting porch out front that framed the two windows and a white door. On the shingled roof that shaded the porch was a greyed wooden sign that had half a ship's wheel holding up each end. Two dusty brass lights stuck out from the sign, the dim light now extinguished in the early morning sunlight. On top was a small, matching birdhouse, also trimmed in white and shingled.

It was the words on the sign that now held their attention. Hand-painted white letters spelled out Fowler's Inn.

"It has to be behind that sign." Peter stood on tip-toes in a futile attempt to see what might be hidden out of their sight. With a glance over his shoulder, he made sure the deck of the *Columbia* was still empty. "I think I can get up there if you give me a boost, Uncle Adam."

Beth sent Alex and Beth to peer around the edge of the Harbour Galley.   "Make sure no one's coming this way. Sometimes guests like to sit here in the shade and wait for the *Columbia* to get underway."

At the all clear signal from Catie, Adam hoisted Peter up to the roof. "Hurry, Pete. We don't know how much time we have."

On his hands and knees, Peter kept himself from looking down onto the deck of the *Columbia* as he scurried over to the sign. There was always something fascinating to see from a different perspective and he knew he needed to hurry. There wouldn't be any easy way to explain why he was up on the roof of any building in the Park.

"Someone's coming!" Catie ran back to her mom, her arms waving in the air. "One of them is dressed like a chef and the others are in Frontierland clothes! I think they might work here!"

"You've got to hurry, Peter! We might have company."

"It's right here." Peter sounded surprised as he popped up from behind the sign. "It wasn't even nailed down, just like the one in Adventureland."

Adam caught the capsule as Peter dropped it and handed it off to Beth. Just as Peter put his feet over the edge to be helped down by Adam, the first cast member came around the corner.

"Hey! What are you doing up there?"

Beth pushed Catie and Alex toward the walkway that went behind the Inn and ended up at the canoe dock.

"We'll meet you at the canoes, Beth. Get out of sight."

When the two kids took off, Beth gave one last look at Adam as she hurried after the twins. Adam could handle this.

Peter got back to the dock with a little less grace than Adam had intended. Spooked by the sudden appearance of the cast member, he almost dropped the boy. Adam quickly pulled the cap off his head and hoped it hadn't been seen. "Did you get the hat, Peter?"

"What?" Behind Adam's back, Peter was surprised when a hat was suddenly rammed into his hands. "What hat? This one?"

Adam gave a fake laugh and turned to the cast member. "Kids. What can you do? His brother threw the hat up on the roof and Peter here had to get it. My wife just took off trying to catch the little boogers." He gave a lopsided smile and pointed over his shoulder at the empty dock. "I really need to help her with them. They're a handful. We good here?"

Not sure what he had really seen or was hearing, the cast member could only slowly nod his head. "Yeah, I guess. Just keep off the buildings, sir. We don't want anyone to get hurt."

"Yeah, you're right! Good policy. Well, thanks." Adam pushed Peter ahead of him and hurried out of sight around the corner. "Just keep walking."

The twins were watching the loading of a canoe as the nervous Beth fidgeted nearby. She gave a sigh of relief when Adam and Peter appeared. The capsule was pulled out from under her jacket and quickly stuffed into Adam's backpack.

"Dad! Can we ride the canoes?"

Adam looked over at Alex as he tried to get his heart-rate to slow down. About to say no, he changed his mind. "You know, that's a good idea. Let's look like normal guests on a normal day. Let's ride the canoes. Gosh, thought I was going to have a heart attack back there." The last words were mumbled quietly to Beth as they walked down the wooden ramp and grabbed paddles out of the waiting bins. "I had to shove my hat at Peter and tell the guy Alex had thrown it up on the roof. Don't know for sure if he believed me or not."

"Well, security isn't here, so I guess he let it pass."

Adam groaned. "Yeah. I wasn't looking forward to being escorted out of the Park."

Beth made a face as she took her place in the canoe. "Been there. Done that. Not fun."

"I did tell you I was sorry I got you fired, didn't I?"

"Yes, Adam. Five years after the fact, but, yes, you did."

He leaned over to give her a kiss. "You were a great Keelboat pilot, too."

"Yeah, I was."

Much to Alex's delight, the family stayed in Disneyland for the rest of the morning. The adrenaline and energy lasted until just after lunchtime. They wearily piled into the Monorail for the quick trip over the Disneyland Hotel.

"No, you're too big to carry. You're going to have to walk." Adam gave a chuckle at Catie's weak plea that she was too tired to walk all the way to the Hotel. "The car's in the Hotel parking lot. You can sleep on the way home."

"That was nice of Russ to give us a Hotel pass so we could leave the car overnight."

"Yeah, nice." Adam let out a sarcastic grunt. "We have to take him to Club 33 for dinner next week."

Wondering about Adam's tone, Beth gave a shrug. "That's fine. We haven't been there in a while."

"And three of his friends. We're paying."

"Oh."

As they exited the Disneyland Hotel's main building, valet Russ gave a jaunty salute to Adam as they passed. "Thursday works for me," he called out as Adam unlocked the car.

A slanted pair of green eyes watched from the shadows as the Jeep pulled out of the parking spot and headed for the exit. "Well, well, my little pet. You did much better this time. Much better. Now for the final blow!"

Puzzled, Russ looked over at the welcoming statues of Mickey and Minnie when an odd wisp of green smoke drifted over him. It had to have come from that direction, but there was no one there. There was an acrid smell, too, sharp and distasteful to his nose. And…old. It smelled old.

As the mist evaporated, he could only imagine he had heard a cackling laugh float by in a nonexistent breeze.

Chapter 12

Fullerton

Adam dropped Peter off at his house, honked a hello to Lance, and headed home.

Dropping his arm from a wave good-bye for the twins, Lance draped it around Peter's shoulder. "Well, I see you're carrying a canister and I didn't get a call at five a.m. this morning, so I'm assuming you were successful."

Peter did a quick glance up at his dad's face to make sure he wasn't getting blamed for that early call yesterday. "Yeah, it was good. I had to climb up on the roof of Fowler's Inn. The bad part is that we got caught."

"You don't seem too upset by that. So Adam must have been able to talk your way out of it."

"Yeah, he did." Bouncing into the house in front of Lance, Peter walked backward, one arm gesturing as he became more animated in his tale. "I was up on the roof, and this guy came around the corner, and, then Aunt Beth ran away with the twins, and I was, like, whoa! Then Uncle Adam shoved his hat into my hand, and I'm, like, what? And then he says that Alex threw it up on the roof, and I had to go get it, and then we had to go chase the twins!" He held the gray canister out in front of him as if he still couldn't believe the series of events. "And this wasn't even nailed down! I was, like, wow, here it is!"

Still trying to sort out the scattered story in his mind, Lance took the container and shook it. From the lack of sound he knew there would only be papers inside. He gave a tentative tug on the end cap. It didn't budge. "It wasn't secured to the roof? At all?"

Peter took it back and shook his head. "Nope. I thought that was kinda weird. Just like the one in Adventureland. Walt musta really been in a hurry. I don't see how they could've stayed up there for so long and not be nailed down." He held the canister up to his ear and copied his dad's movement. "Sounds empty." When he fiddled with the sealed end, it came right off in his hand.

Lance frowned at the ease with which Peter pulled off the cap. To him it had felt like it had been welded on. *Must not have turned it the right way.* "Yeah, that is odd. With all the renovations and additions to Fowler's Harbor over the years, you'd think it would have been found or fallen or something. Maybe Wolf had something to do with this one."

"I asked him, but he didn't seem to know anything about it when he stopped by."

"Wait, hold on a sec." Lance put a hand on Peter's shoulder as the boy headed for the stairs. "When did you see Wolf? I, uhm, heard he was back, but didn't see him. Your mom did, though."

Peter wondered at the expression on his dad's face. It looked like Lance was trying hard not to laugh. "He popped into my room yesterday when I was working on the last clue." Peter gave a shrug. "He didn't even have any thunder or lightning. Just *pop*, and he was there. He just took the pearls and left. I think he was taking them back to Walt."

Feeling the beginnings of a headache, Lance ran a hand over his face. "The pearls from the mermaid? How does that figure into this Hidden Mickey search?"

"It doesn't," Peter answered really slowly, unable to understand why his dad wasn't keeping up. "He just told me he wanted to take them back to Walt."

With the realization he wouldn't be getting any more answers to his many questions, Lance sent Peter up to his room. "Go get cleaned up and then head up to the War Room to say hi to your mom. She'd like to see for herself that you're okay."

Always happy to get into the War Room and pretend he was a full-fledged Guardian of Walt, Peter bounded upstairs. He would work on the next clue as soon as he explored the secret hideaway a little more. Another thought hit Peter and he leaned over the oak banister. "Hey, Dad! Can we go back to the apartment tonight if I figure out the next clue?"

As much as Lance wanted to stay there himself, he shook his head. "You've just had four days off from school. You go back to the grind tomorrow. So, no."

Unfazed by the negative answer, Peter just grinned as he headed into his room. If he found something really, really interesting in the capsule, he figured he could probably change his dad's mind.

A large raven sat outside the window of Peter's room. His body the color of midnight, his red eyes stood out like two glowing embers from a fire. Ignoring the constant barking of the frustrated Dug one story below, the bird tilted his head as he watched the boy. Ever patient, he stood at his post while Peter finished his homework and, finally, finally, pulled the canister's endcap off. As the yellowed paper was held in his hands, the raven leaned in closer, his beak accidently tapping the window. He froze when the boy looked in his direction, only to relax when Peter appeared to show no interest. When the boy's attention returned to the paper, the bird maintained his position. It had taken a couple of days, but, once the boy gave the awaited cry of discovery, the raven could finally take to flight. Before he got too far, though, he made a swooping dive at the frantic dog, pulling a long, golden hair from her tail. With a victorious, "Caw!," he took to the open sky once more, disappearing from sight as he flew straight to Disneyland.

"I'm wishing you would figure out this clue. If you get grumpy, you will find your way to your heart's desire.

"Now it is time for you to bring me <u>my</u> heart's desire. The third and last clue is: Its gold is more brilliant than the sun.

"Do not fail me."

"That has to be it. It has to be Snow White's Wishing Well." Peter leaned back from the computer screen and let out a long sigh. It had taken him three days to figure out this latest clue. "Hmph, I have no idea what Walt's heart's desire is. Wonder why he keeps saying that in all the clues. Doesn't make any sense. How can I bring Walt something?"

Peter glanced over at his bedroom window. The pesky bird that had been irritating Dug was finally gone. "I need to text Catie. She's probably still working on it."

Hey, I figured it out. Snow White Well. You think that's right?

Catie's text came back within ten minutes. *!!!!Sounds perfect!!!! Wishing is song at the Well. What about grumpy part????*

Not sure. Figure it out when we get there. Can you go Sat?

Have to ask. Text back later!!!! So excited!!!! ☺

Peter silently wondered if a phone could be worn out by using the exclamation point too much. "Oh, I'd better ask Mom and Dad, too. Forgot to tell them." After glancing at the clock, he turned to rush from his room. "Ooh, dinner time. I'm starved." At the door, though, he paused and made a wry face. "Dad's turn to cook tonight." He hurried back to his desk and quickly ate a granola bar from his hidden stash. "Better safe than sorry."

Flashback — Disneyland — 1961

"**W**ishing has long been a favorite subject of mine. Wishes have come true for many of the characters in my motion pictures… and for me, too. A wish is really the first step in the realization of a dream or goal. Down through the ages, people have used different symbols to wish for things. Sometimes they looked at the stars, and other times the symbol was something else—very often wishing wells. This international club is known throughout the world. Its work—helping needy children—is carried out through many charities in many lands. So here at Disneyland, where we have visitors from all over the world, this Disneyland-International Club Wishing Well is dedicated to youngsters everywhere. When you throw your coins into this wishing well, just remember that wishes made here at this well will really come true… for the children of the world."

On the east side of Sleeping Beauty Castle, surrounded by children from twenty-five nations, Walt finished his speech to dedicate the lovely new addition to Fantasyland. Behind them was a beautiful wooded glen where the Little Princess, Snow White, stood at the top of a rocky waterfall. Next to her, also made out of white Carrara marble, was a deer. The seven dwarves and other woodland animals were spread out over three levels, while happy fish and frogs spurted water high into the air from the pond at the bottom.

As coins were being tossed into the golden-spired well, the guests were reminded by the words painted onto the well that "Your wishes will help….children everywhere." The children who participated in the ceremony and the sponsors were dismissed and they quickly dispersed to spend the rest of the day in the Magic Kingdom.

Left alone with John, Walt looked up at Snow White, a contented smile set on his face. "You did well, John. Nobody guessed that the Little Princess was the same size as the dwarves! Forced perspective did its job on Main Street, here at the Castle, and now in this grotto."

John just nodded. It was a beautiful little spot in the Park. And, as the years passed and the trees and plants grew and filled in, it would become even lovelier. Just as his boss knew from the beginning. "It's odd that all we know about the statues is that the artist is Leonida Parma and they were fashioned after a set of bath soaps. Just wish we knew who sent them to you."

Walt dug into his pocket and then tossed another coin into the well. "Maybe now your wish will come true."

John gave a laugh as Walt turned to go. "Where you off to, Walt?"

"Back behind the Jungle Cruise. Those four electric runabouts are scheduled to start running on Main Street in two days and I want to check them out."

"You just want to drive them around first."

There was a twinkle in Walt's eye as he gave a broad smile. "Well, I have to make sure everything is well tested for our guests."

"Right. Have fun."

"Always, John, always."

Disneyland – Current Day

"Hey, Peter, do you know how many wishing wells are in Disneyland?"

"You mean besides this one and the one at Minnie's house in ToonTown?"

Catie made a face. "I can never pull one over on you! You're too smart."

"Did you know when the song was added to the Wishing Well?"

"Oh, I thought it was here from the beginning. When was it added, Peter?"

"Way back in 1984. I didn't know it ran all the time until your mom told us."

Both Peter and Catie leaned over the rim of the wishing well to look for anything obvious. The coins that littered the bottom were protected by an elaborate, scrolled grillwork. Peter tried to look into the blue shingled, peaked roof, up past the brown lintel, but it was boarded over. There was no capsule and no good place to hide one.

"I don't see anything. There isn't anything carved into the well or the wood, either. Maybe it's something else in this area. What do you think, Catie?"

Catie was looking over at the Grotto and smiling. *This is such a romantic spot.* She knew that some couples come here to get engaged. Peter's voice broke into the little, private fantasy running through her mind. "What did you say?"

"Why do you look all mushy?"

A blush crept up the girl's neck. "I'm not mushy! I...I just like this place, that's all."

Peter shrugged at her discomfort. "Whatever. I just wondered if you had any ideas on where we might look next."

"Can I see the clue? I'd like to read it myself."

"Oh, I left it at home with the others. Didn't think we'd need it. Sorry. It just said something like if we got grumpy we would find our way."

"Well, I could get grumpy, but I don't think that would help." The joke helped Catie get over her embarrassment of getting caught daydreaming about Peter. *Good thing he can't read my mind.*

"We could go ride Snow White again. I kinda think it means the dwarf Grumpy. He's in the ride a couple of times." Peter pointed toward the side entrance to Fantasyland. The walkway came out near the exit of the Castle's Sleeping Beauty Walkthrough. Snow White's Scary Adventure would be on the opposite side of the court-yard, just across from Peter Pan.

Catie didn't agree. "We rode it three times already. The ride was, like, totally redone when Fantasyland was remodeled. There were so many changes, how could a clue inside still be there? It has to be something else."

"Then, where else is Grumpy in the Park?" Peter folded his

arms as he challenged her.

Catie tilted her head at him with a 'you're kidding, right?' look on her face, and pointed over her shoulder. "You mean, besides that one?"

Grumpy was indeed in the Grotto. On the first level below Snow White, there was an arched stone bridge. On the far side to the right were Doc and a friendly squirrel. In middle was Sleepy. On the left side, nestled next to the rocky wall, was Grumpy looking, well, grumpy with his arms folded over his marble chest.

Peter walked to the edge of the walkway over the stream that flowed from the fountain to the Castle Moat. He studied the statues for a minute and broke out in a wide grin. "Notice something different about Grumpy?"

"Does he look happy?"

"He never looks happy. No, notice what's behind him?"

Catie looked at Grumpy and then at the other figures. "There's an opening behind him. It looks like the entrance to the dwarfs' diamond mine."

Peter suddenly became all excited. "I doubt that goes to a diamond mine, but it looks like it does head toward the Castle." He lowered his voice when a young couple stopped next to the kids to take a few pictures. Almost jumping up and down, he could barely contain himself until the couple slowly wandered off toward Main Street. "Look over here, Catie!" as he grabbed the girl's arm. Hauling her toward the Castle, they ran alongside the gray metal fence topped with leafy scrollwork that blocked them from the greenery. He stopped in front of four stone steps that led up to a door built into the side of the Castle. The steps were closed off by a simple metal chain draped cross the entrance. "Look down there. There's a little drop from the cement to the dirt, but then there's a series of flat rocks that lead over to the Grotto." He had to stop talking again when a family came out of the Castle and went toward the Wishing Well. Whispering, he resumed his line of reasoning. "I know I can make it over to where Grumpy is. Maybe I can squeeze in behind him to see what's inside that tunnel. I'll bet that's where the next clue is."

Catie wasn't sure. "Nobody is supposed to go in there, Peter. You know that. It has to mean something else. Besides, how are you going to get in there without being seen?" She waved an arm at the large group of people posing in front of the Grotto. "There are people here all the time. They even bring out the Evil Queen for autographs and pictures next to the Well. Then there's even more people!"

Peter grimaced. Now that he was on a scent, he didn't want to stop or be told no. "You're right about all the people. I don't know why this place is so popular. Why are you making that face at me?"

"Never mind. You wouldn't get it." *Boys. Sheesh.*

Girls. Sheesh. "Well, I still think I'm right. And I'm still going to go inside and check it out. Do you want to come with me?"

"No! There might be spiders."

Peter shrugged as he looked at all the trees and bushes around the Grotto. "More than likely. I don't mind. But, if you don't want to go, you can just stay around here. You still have your walkie-talkie?"

"Yeah, it's in my purse. How are you going to get in there and not be seen?"

Hands on his hips, Peter studied the area. "I don't know yet. It's going to be dark soon. Maybe that will help. Are there fireworks tonight?"

Catie pulled out the Park's daily schedule she had picked up when they came in. "Yes, at 9:30. But, Peter, they close off the Castle during the fireworks. You won't be able to get anywhere near here."

"Let's go have dinner at the Big Thunder Ranch Barbecue. I think I have a plan." Peter patted the master key to Disneyland that was hidden in his pants pocket as they headed across Main Street and entered the Frontierland entrance.

Not aware that he had a key that opened every door in the Park, Catie wasn't too worried. She just knew that Peter wouldn't be able to get past all the ropes and cast members who blocked off the Castle to sneak into the Grotto.

Seated in the front of the Hub, the crowd around her watching the brilliant show overhead, Catie started to worry. Eyes glued to the Grotto barely visible at the side of the Castle, she strained to see Peter, but was too far away. Once, when the green lasers bit through the sky over her, she thought she saw a blur of black against the grey stone. The shadow moved too fast and then was gone. During a lull in the booming noise, she held the walkie-talkie to her ear and pressed the call button. "Peter? Can you hear me? Peter!"

The radio crackled. "Cat....hear....dark."

"What? Say that again? Oh, shoot."

The fireworks and lasers merged in an incredible display. "Oohs" and "Aahs" were heard all around her. The music soared over the loudspeakers and images danced across the face of the Castle to vanish for a moment and then continue on the nearby Matterhorn Mountain.

As soon as the next break came, she hit the button again. "Peter? Are you all right? I couldn't hear you."

"Fine...almost..."

"Almost what?" The girl shouted into her radio, much to the annoyance of the people sitting next to her. "Sorry," she mumbled as they glared at her. The radio was put in her lap as she waited out the rest of the show. The minutes ticked by until the grand finale filled the sky with bursts of color and smoke.

As the lights came back on, the crowd around her surged to their feet, most of them headed toward the exit, happy at the end of another day. Catie, though, anxiously watched the cast members for that moment when they retracted all the ropes and barriers and opened the Castle once more. Immediately she headed for the Grotto, now, thankfully, empty of other guests. When she noticed the Grumpy figure was slightly turned, she quickly hit the button in a frantic attempt to call Peter once again.

But, all she heard was static coming from the other end.

Peter was gone.

Chapter 13

Disneyland – Current Day

Surrounded by darkness, moving slowly forward on his hands and knees, Peter held the flashlight tightly in his mouth. At every step, his backpack scraped against the ceiling. The weak beam of light indicated he should have checked the batteries before leaving the house earlier that day. One hand would occasionally wander a couple of inches to the right or to the left to check the closeness of the dirt wall. During a momentarily lapse in concentration, he wondered how he would explain the dirty stains on his jeans to his mom.

The tunnel seemed to close in on him the further he got from the small entrance. Not usually claustrophobic, the boy's anxiety level worked its way higher as he crawled around every twist and turn. The loud, booming sounds of the fireworks show were long muffled and silent. All sense of time had slowly ebbed away until he couldn't have said if he had been in the tunnel for five minutes or five hours. Even his lifeline to Catie—the walkie-talkie—had gone silent.

As he thought about the location of the Grotto, he wondered exactly where he would come out. Originally he figured it would be inside the Castle. Now, with the many turns, he thought he might come out near the restrooms built into the Castle wall across from the Matterhorn and just before the Alice in Wonderland ride. There was a tall hill back there, covered in trees and bushes. *That would be a let-down.*

When his words echoed back to him, he realized he had spoken aloud, the words mumbled around the ineffective flashlight. With a nervous laugh, Peter added that he might as well have brought Catie if anyone was going to be scared.

"There's nothing to be afraid of. I'm still in Disneyland. Somewhere...."

He arrived at a point where he felt he had to make a decision: Should he keep going? Or should he turn back? Just ahead he thought he could make out a soft, green glow. It was way ahead of him in a long, straight part of the underground passageway. "That's weird."

His indecision was now forgotten as he continued on his way. No matter how far forward he went, that glimmering, dancing light, he found, always seemed to be the same distance away. He never got any closer to it. "So much for an exit sign."

The dirt path now felt as if it had started to climb. It had actually been climbing all along, but was too subtle for the excited, half-scared boy to notice. As he took his next step, the eerie green glow suddenly stopped moving. Peter stopped in his tracks, unsure of what was happening. The light seemed to be, sort of, waiting for him.

Still on his hands and knees, Peter let out a loud sigh. "Now what?"

Just as he was about to reach his silent, unmoving vision—as he started to consider this strange phenomenon—it leaped straight up and out of sight.

Feeling an unexpected sense of loss, Peter hurried the last few yards to where it had been hovering. There he found a metal ladder built into the wall. The wall, he discovered, instead of being dirt, felt solid, like it was made out of stone or plaster. His flashlight was only able to light up the first few rungs. However, as he looked up, he could see the green sparkle floating at what he hoped was the top.

Glad to be able to stand upright, he took a chance and clicked off his one source of light. The flashlight was almost dead anyway, and he realized he might need it later to retrace his steps. After rubbing his dirty hands off on his jeans, he grabbed one of the rungs and began to climb. At each step, his green companion glowed brighter and brighter. "I must be doing the right thing, then." Peter shook his head in the darkness. "It seems, um, happy. This is getting more and more curious."

Once again, time seemed to lose all meaning. Peter continued his ascent up the ladder as each new rung presented itself. He could neither tell how high he climbed or how long it had taken him. He just climbed.

He suddenly found himself face-to-face, if it could be called that, with the bright green object. All motion stopped as he reached out with a tentative finger to touch this strange light. There was a mild sensation that traveled through his fingertips and partway up his arm. "That tickles!"

His hand still surrounded by the shimmer, it moved about an arm's length higher, taking Peter's arm with it. It was then he found the end of this part of the journey. His fingers closed around a handle to what looked like a trapdoor.

As he pushed the door upward with his hands and shoulder, the green light, its mission apparently complete, extinguished, leaving him in total darkness.

"**A**nd then the fireworks ended and I ran back to the Grotto, but Peter was gone and he hasn't been answering the radio and I don't know where it comes out and...."

"Slow down, honey. We'll figure this out."

Leaving Alex at the Brentwood's to play pool with Lance, Adam and Beth had arrived at the prearranged meeting place. At 10 p.m., both Peter and Catie were supposed to be at the pick-up zone on Harbor Boulevard, just outside the entrance. Who they found was a wide-eyed, panicked Catie, near tears and not making much sense.

Beth brought her daughter in for a comforting hug. She was surprised when the girl pushed away from her.

"No! We don't have time for that! You have to come and help me find Peter! I went all around the hill, but I can't find him!" Catie took Beth's hand and started to pull her toward the entrance. "We have to get in before it closes!"

"Okay, okay, sweetie. Just calm down. We'll find Peter. I'll take a chance and leave the car here. This is just supposed to be a drop-off zone." Adam threw a worried look at Beth over the girl's head. Peter might be impetuous sometimes, but he never left Catie alone like this. "You just take us to where you last saw him, all right?"

Moving against the flow of traffic that was heading for Disneyland's exit, it was slow going up Main Street. Smaller than her parents, Catie easily dodged and weaved through the crowd of people and strollers. Impatient, she had to wait for her parents to catch up a couple of times.

When they finally got to the empty Grotto, Catie retold her arm-waving tale.

"He went where!?" Beth looked at the statue of Grumpy and couldn't believe someone could have actually fit into that opening.

"I told you. He went in behind Grumpy. At first we were talking on the radio and then it just went out." Catie's eyes filled with tears. "I haven't talked to him since the fireworks."

"You said you went around to the other side of the Grotto? What's there again?"

"Just the bathrooms and a big hill. There's lots of trees and stuff, but Peter could have gotten down from there. And over the fence if he had to."

Adam looked up at the Castle looming over them. "Gosh, I don't know what lights are supposed to be on in those windows and which of them might be Peter. Try the radio again, honey."

After the radio only produced static, Beth ran a nervous hand against the back of her neck. "Do you think we should call Lance and Kimberly? Kimberly's been inside the Castle for various reasons. She undoubtedly knows the Castle better it than we do."

At the mention of Peter's mom, Catie tugged on Beth's arm. "Ask Aunt Kimberly to bring the clue with her. Maybe it says something we need to know. Peter said he left it in his room."

Beth made a grimace as she took the phone out of her purse. "This isn't going to go over well."

After a glance at his watch, Adam had to agree with his wife. "They won't be able to get here for at least half an hour. Lance might have to come in through the security entrance over on Disney Drive. Then there're all the boys. Do they have someone who can watch them?"

Beth didn't know. "Maybe they can leave them in the security office. I know Norm is really fond of all the boys. I think he's on the night shift."

Adam pulled Catie in for a reassuring hug. "We'll find him, honey. Don't worry."

"I could go through the tunnel and see where he is."

"That's really brave of you, honey, but let's just wait for his parents. I don't want to lose both of you in there."

"I can't just wait. I have to do something!" Not completely leaving the warmth of her dad's arms, Catie tried the walkie-talkie again and again. "Peter? Come in, Peter. Come on, pick up, Peter!"

The only response was static.

Kimberly ran into Peter's bedroom while Lance got the boys into the car. After a moment's grumble at the mess that greeted her eyes, she headed for his desk, looking for the familiar yellowed papers. Partially hidden under his schoolwork binder, she pulled out all the clues he had collected so far. The first clue she had seen. The second and third were unknown to her.

As her eyes quickly scanned the oddly worded clues, something clicked in the back of her mind. Her heart began to pound in her chest. She had to read through the words once more, slowly this time, just so she could make sure.

It wasn't the clues to the next capsules that made her blood run cold. It was the demands on what Peter was supposed to bring with him. Individually they meant nothing. But, when they were put together....

A red as deep as blood.

A heart of greater value than life itself.

Its gold more brilliant than the sun.

"Oh, gosh! What was Walt thinking? Peter's never seen it! This…this isn't right. Something's wrong." As she stuffed the clues into her purse, Kimberly ran to the garage and told Lance to get to the Park as quickly as he could. Not wanting to alarm Lance or the boys, she kept her fears to herself.

The trip to Disneyland had never been so long, so slow in her life.

"**T**he boys are in the security office. Norm promised them they could man the security channel. Didn't have the heart to tell them Disneyland was almost closed and there wouldn't be much activity."

"Were you able to get ahold of Wolf?"

Adam's question stopped Lance's recitation. "Wolf?" He glanced at his tight-lipped wife. She had been tense since they left the house and this reminder might not be the best timing for her. "Nope, haven't seen him in a while. Peter said he came by a couple of days ago, but we haven't heard from him since. Why?"

"I just thought he might be useful. Since I'm not a cast member, I'm, of course, not that familiar with the workings inside the Castle. Beth doesn't know that much, either."

Seeing she wouldn't have any private time with Lance, Kimberly tugged on his arm. "I need to talk to you. It'll just take a second. Now."

"Sure, sweetheart. Just a sec, guys." As they walked off a few steps, Lance looked into her pale face. "We'll find him, honey. I'm sure he's just out of radio range and probably having the time of his life while we worry for nothing."

"You don't understand, Lance!" Visibly upset, Kimberly pulled her hand from his grip so she could reach into her purse. "Did you ever see all three of the clues Peter found? Did you see them together?"

Lance could only shrug. "I guess not, now that you mention it. Pete always seemed to have it under control. Adam and Beth have been along most of the time. Why?" His reassurance seemed to have no effect on his wife and he was baffled by the level of her distress.

Without preamble, she thrust the notes into his hands. "Come over by the light and read them. Not the location part. Read the demand part." Kimberly couldn't stand still and began to pace while Lance read through the notes. When his breath caught, she knew she had been right. And that knowledge did nothing to still her fears.

Lance's voice was strained when he spoke. "Peter doesn't know anything about that. We never told him."

"And I've never touched it again since we returned it to our secret room. It...it scared me, Lance. How can Walt have put such a demand like that in there? How is Peter supposed to take it to him? I...I just can't figure it out."

Unable to tear his eyes off the words, Lance put a hand on her arm. "The only logical explanation I can come up with is that these clues couldn't have been written by Walt."

Kimberly's green eyes snapped back to his face. Her voice was almost a whisper. "That's what I keep thinking. He gave that...

that *thing* to us in a quest years ago. It's still where we left it. Somebody else must know about it and want it really badly to go through all of this."

Lance looked over at the Michaels as they waited for them to come back. Beth had said all along that *something* just felt wrong about the clues or the paper or the handwriting. *Something* was off. He dug his phone out of his pocket and sent a call to Wolf. It went straight to voicemail. Lance sent two more, just for emphasis. "And this leaves us with one question: If Walt didn't set up this clue search, and Wolf doesn't know anything about it, who did?"

"Do you think we need to go get the pendant? If it means saving Peter, I'll gladly give the cursed thing up."

"Do you have the master key?" At Kimberly's brief nod, he glanced back at Adam, Beth, and Catie. They knew nothing of the pendant or the secret room over the Silhouette Studio. "Then why don't you go alone to the room and grab the diamond. Both of us can't leave and not explain anything. Hide it in a pocket or something and we'll see how this plays out."

Peter shoved the wooden door with all his might. It hit the floor with a dusty *bang*. Relieved to be out of the dank tunnel, he hoisted himself up into the room. Somehow he knew he was inside the Castle. There were no windows and no decorations in the room to indicate where he was, but he just knew.

It took a moment for him to realize the room wasn't as completely dark as it should have been. There was a bright glow coming from one of the walls behind him. As he turned, his eyes opened wide with astonishment and his jaw dropped.

On the wall, lit by some unseen spotlight, was a framed animation cel. As he got closer, he could see there was no glass in the frame. From listening to Uncle Adam, he knew the glass would ruin the paints that colored the cel.

The picture was a drawing of the Castle in which he found himself. It was colored all gray, just like it looked when Disneyland first opened, and there were pink and blue spotlights hitting the turrets. Tinker Bell hovered mid-air in front of the castle, her wand raised to shower the Castle with pixie dust. There was even an arc of the sparkling dust all around the top of the Castle. Had Peter been older, he would have recognized that this was the opening scene from the weekly show Walt put on every Sunday, *The Wonderful World of Color*. What really captured Peter's interest was the fact that the cel was signed in the lower right corner by Walt himself.

"Oh, wow! This is beautiful!" Peter reached a hand toward the cel, but caught himself just before touching the fragile surface. "This has to be priceless. I'll bet no one even knows it's in here. That means it's mine now!"

He carefully took the sixteen-by-fourteen inch picture off the wall and walked closer to the light source. "It looks like the signature was done with some kind of pen and everything else is paint." Something caught his eye in the dim light as he held it closer to his face. "Wait a minute. What's this?"

He could make out small words on the left side of the cel. They appeared to run behind the paint on the Castle. "I can't see it very well. What does that say?"

Peter had to get out his flashlight to read whatever was written on the cel. "Why would someone paint over the words?" He narrowed the beam on the light and aimed it at the words.

"To find your next clue, you mu...."

"No! That can't be right. Why would Walt put the next clue under a painted cel he signed? Let me see if I can get the frame off. Maybe I can see the words from the back."

All thoughts of Catie and his parents and where he was supposed to be were gone from his mind. All Peter could think about was the next clue. Using a pen, he worked the metal ties holding the frame to the cel and its clear backing. Mindless of the damage he was causing to the wooden frame, he kept at it until the cel was loose in his hands. "Now I can hold it up to the light and see what it says."

Peter was dismayed to find that his theory didn't work. The words were not visible from the back. "Oh, great. The only way to get the next clue is to scrape the paint off the cel. That will destroy the paint and make the picture worthless. But, I need the next clue."

Torn, he held the clue out at arm's length to stare at the beauty of it. "I can't ruin this cel. It's probably one-of-a-kind. But I have to. That's the only way to continue. What am I supposed to do!? This isn't supposed to be hard!"

Behind Peter, blended into a dark corner of the room, a pair of eyes watched as the boy became more agitated. The edges of the eyes crinkled as the unseen person smugly smiled.

CHAPTER 14

Disneyland – Current Day

Peter tried hard not to panic as he vacillated back and forth. He gripped the cel so tightly that the corners curled. "I can't ruin this! Walt drew it himself…. But he painted over the clue and then left it for me to find. Why would he do that? What am I supposed to do?"

Pacing in and out of the one spotlight in the high-ceilinged room, Peter attempted to weigh his options, but was too upset to be rational. The beauty and the value of the cel warred against what might be at the end of the clue search. Was it worth ruining the one piece for what might be next? Or, should he keep the animated piece and be proud to own such a rare find?

"I can't do it." He was almost in tears now, frustrated by not knowing what Walt wanted him to do. "But I have to ruin it. I have to go on to the next clue."

With a loud *sniff*, the distraught boy dug around in the hidden pocket of his backpack until he found a small pocketknife. Blade in hand, his fingers shook as he lowered the blunt edge toward the pink and blue Castle. "I have to do it. I have to do it. I have to do it." The muttered words became a mantra as he tried to force his hand to do what he felt was his only option.

As the blade barely touched one of the sparkles over the Castle, the whole top layer of paint—the pixie-dust semicircle—fell to the ground. Realizing what he had done, Peter dropped to the hard floor, put his head on his knees, and wept bitterly.

"Aww, why the tears, my pet?"

Too upset to grasp that he wasn't alone, that someone had

been in the room with him the whole time, Peter jerked a shoulder at the intrusion. "Go away. Leave me alone."

The voice moved closer. There was an attempt to sound sympathetic, but the hard, bitter edge couldn't be masked. "Oh, I can't leave you alone. You see, you're here because of me. I led you here and you have something that belongs to me. And I want it. Now."

"What? I don't understand." Peter looked up from his position on the floor as he roughly swiped an arm across his eyes and his nose, the cel forgotten at his feet. "Who are you?"

A tall woman moved into the spotlight that had illuminated the now-ruined animation cel. "Oh, I am so sorry. Where are my manners? We haven't been formally introduced, have we?"

When an actual introduction did not come, Peter, wary now, slowly got to his feet, his eyes narrowing as he stared at the woman. She seemed vaguely familiar to him, but his tangled mind couldn't place how he might know her. Dressed in the deepest purple, she also wore a pendant with a bright green stone that caught his eye as it shimmered in the light. "Why do you look familiar? Hey, how did you get Lisa's necklace?"

Not taking her eyes off the boy, a long, slender hand rose to the metallic raven at her throat. "You don't recognize me? Oh, my. How embarrassing. Here, let me fix that."

With a graceful wave of her hand, the green light that had led Peter to this room emerged from the pendant. It wove around the woman until she was completely immersed in the glow. When it went out, Peter gasped.

After a self-conscious touch to the curved horns on her hat, she smoothed nonexistent wrinkles out of her billowing robes. The pendant that had transformed Lisa into her minion had morphed into a tall staff that she regally held in her right hand. At the top of the staff, the black raven now held a green, pulsating orb in its talons. "Is that better?"

"You're...you're Mal...." Unable to believe what was in front of his eyes, Peter could only stare.

"Yes, yes, I am known by many names. You may use that one. Or Nimue. Or Her Majesty. As you choose." When she took a step closer to Peter, the boy backed away, one hand out in front of him as if to ward off the danger. "Why do you fear me? We made a deal. You just need to hold up your end of it."

"Stay away from me! You...you can't be here. You're not real."

A pale hand went to her throat in mock surprise. "Not real? I?" She made a pretense of pinching her arm. "Why, I feel real. Would you like to pinch me, too?"

Peter backed away from her outstretched arm until he smacked into the far wall. He was trapped. "Don't touch me! I'll... I'll scream!"

"To whom?"

Peter's mouth clamped shut. He knew she was right. He was alone.

When the boy fell silent, the black-tinted lips curled into smug smile. "That's better, my pet. Now that you are finally being reasonable, we can get down to business. I want what is mine. The clues were simple enough—even for you." Her extended hand now turned palm up. "Give it to me now."

The wall pressing into his back, Peter couldn't even move an inch. "I...I don't know what you're talking about. I don't have anything of yours."

The hand in front of his face closed into a fist. As Peter tucked his head into his shoulder, expecting a blow, Nimue smirked as she returned to the center of the room. *Ah, he is afraid of me. Good. He should be.* "Oh, I'm not going to strike you, boy. But, I see you do need some....persuasion."

Peter slowly opened his eyes and immediately wished he hadn't. The staff was pointed straight at him. As he frantically tried to find another way out of the room, the green light—the same one that had formerly seemed so friendly—now snaked out from the green sphere. It was twisted and spiked like lightning. When it struck Peter, it felt like tiny pinpricks over his whole body.

Surrounded by the green glow, Peter, unable to run, madly flailed his arms as he slowly rose from the ground. Knowing it was useless to scream, he could only watch as the thick beams in the ceiling got closer and closer.

"Now," came the calm, deadly voice far below, "about my necklace...."

"I can use my security key get us into all the rooms in the Castle. I just don't know exactly where to go." Lance took the lead as they all hurried up the stairs in the Sleeping Beauty Walkthrough.

"There are lots of doors up on the third level, Uncle Lance. Most of them are in the Corridor of Goons. Peter and I saw them when we were looking around."

"Thanks, Catie. That'll help. If we have to, we can split up to check every room. Kimberly knows some storage areas where we might look, too."

Alternately pounding on the doors and listening for some reply, and then opening the thicker ones, the anxious group made their way through the closed attraction.

At the top level, across from the window of animated Goons, Lance thought he heard a chuckle. Not sure if it was part of the attraction's sound effects, he held up a hand for silence. As the others crowded around him, he pointed at one of the wooden doors. Built to look like a fortified castle gate, Lance inserted his master key into the small brass deadbolt. The door swung inward on silent hinges. The room smelled old and dank and an odd green mist swirled around their feet only to dissipate in the still air.

"Peter?" Kimberly pushed past her husband to enter the room. "Mom!"

"Honey? Where are...oh my word!" Stopped dead in her tracks, she had followed the green light up to her son. She fought back a scream when she saw Peter dangling twenty feet above their heads. Seeing what was happening, Beth stayed back in the doorway to shield Catie.

"Let go of my son!" Adrenaline kicked in as Lance and Adam rushed at the woman. But, in their mad lunge forward, they were just as suddenly knocked to the ground by some unseen force.

The tall woman, dressed in her regal robes, slowly turned to face the angry group behind her. "My, my, what have we here?" As her attention turned away from Peter, the crackling arc that held him in its grip wavered, causing him to drop half the distance to the floor.

At the women's combined scream, Nimue turned back to the boy. She was tiring, her power ebbing, but she would not let them see evidence of that fact. Peter rose again, still in her grip.

Helping Lance and Adam to their feet, they were all shocked and relieved to see Wolf suddenly appear in the open doorway.

Peter was the first to react. "Uncle....," but he cut it off when he saw Wolf make a frantic motion for him to be quiet.

Eyes wide at the scene before him, Wolf instantly recognized who held Peter captive and knew what he needed to do. Quickly and silently he pulled Adam and his family from the room with instructions for them to wait in the castle courtyard. Then he vanished from sight.

Her concentration on keeping the boy aloft, unaware of what had just happened behind her, Nimue was pleased by Peter's outburst. As the staff lowered, so did Peter until his feet finally touched the floor. "Ah, I see the boy has more intelligence than the father. You cry uncle, do you? You are wise to admit defeat." She smiled as she studied her black fingernails. "This might have gotten… ugly."

"Might have?" Kimberly couldn't help herself as she and Lance rushed to Peter and she pulled the boy into her side. "You will not touch my son again."

The sharp eyes swung toward Kimberly as if she was being seen for the first time. Kimberly was slowly scrutinized from head to toe, a look of disgust on Nimue's face. "Lovely. Another blonde. Will I ever be rid of them?"

"You seem to forget that the blondes always win."

Lance took Peter from Kimberly so he could feel all of his limbs. "Are you all right, Pete? Did she hurt you?"

"My, how insulting. Whyever would I hurt this delightful child?"

"You hung him from the ceiling!"

The same low, chilly chuckle he had heard before again came from her black-lined mouth. "Your son is the least of your worries. The boy has something that's mine. I want it back and I want it now!" The woman raised her staff high in the air as if she was going to cast another spell, her lips now moving silently. Her powers almost exhausted, she would go to any length to get her property back.

"You'll get nothing from the boy—no matter what you do." Lance could feel his son squirm in his arms and knew Peter was about to say something. He doubted it would help, so he clamped his hand lightly over Peter's mouth.

Her eyes flew open and the staff was lowered to the ground. The spell was forgotten for the moment as Nimue strode closer to the family. The green orb flashed and sparked in response to her anger. "We made a deal. He would get a clue search and I would get my necklace. Now I want to collect what is mine. He wouldn't dare come without it!"

Pulling his dad's hand away from his mouth, Peter squirmed out of his grasp so he could push past Kimberly. He waved his empty hands in front of Nimue. "See? I don't have any stupid necklace! I don't even know what you're talking about! You…you made me ruin Walt's picture!"

"You don't know about it?" A brief look of confusion crossed the Evil Fairy's face. "You must! Its…its aura, its essence, is all over you. Do not lie to me, boy." A finger extended toward Peter as she attempted to probe his mind. *There was no question, no doubt in my mind. I should have done this sooner.* Her power getting weaker, she had to move closer.

As Nimue advanced, Kimberly shoved the agitated Peter behind her so Lance could hold onto him. When Wolf suddenly reappeared in the doorway behind the witch, Kimberly forced her eyes to stay on Nimue. In Wolf's hands was an ancient sword and it took all she had not to gape at the magnificent sight.

To give Wolf the time and distraction he might need, Kimberly yelled out at Nimue, "He isn't lying to you, witch. Peter has never even seen that red diamond heart." Closing the gap between them, her hands balled into fists, Kimberly stood nose-to-nose with the Evil Fairy. "He doesn't know anything about it…but I do!"

Flashback – Disneyland – 2002

In the hidden room over the Silhouette Studio, Lance used the sleeve of his jacket to wipe the heavy layer of dust off of the glass dome. Kneeling down, he and Kimberly looked inside. Hanging off of a Y-shaped brass stand was an antique-looking gold chain with a brilliant red, heart-shaped diamond that dangled several inches above its wooden base. The gem was backed by three small circlets of gold set in a very familiar shape. The simple, yet elegant setting looked to be very old. The chain itself was heavy, but it was still beautiful with its intricate woven gold. It connected to the pendant at the top of two golden ears and the framework was in the shape of a classic Mickey figure. Lance thought perhaps they were looking at the very first 'Hidden Mickey.'

"This is incredible, Lance." Kimberly could only whisper as she looked at the piece. "I'm almost afraid to touch it."

"Let me lift the dome. Then we can see it better." Lance put both hands around the glass sides and lifted straight up, careful not to hit the exquisite piece of jewelry. The glass covering was set aside on the table and forgotten.

The two of them simply stared at the large diamond. Now free of the dome, they could see the fiery gem without the distortion of the glass and dust. Catching the light in the room, dim as it was, rainbow sparkles shimmered off of the facets of the gem.

As if it might shatter at any moment, Lance gently took hold of the chain and slowly lifted the pendant off its stand. Letting it dangle at eye level, Kimberly was now better able to examine it.

As he turned the heavy piece back and forth, he noticed the gold setting and wondered out loud. "That looks like a Hidden Mickey you'd find in the Park. Do you think Walt had this made? Wow, this red diamond is huge! Have you ever seen anything like it?" The stone looked to be about an inch wide and an inch tall.

She shook her head as she was nearly speechless. Reaching out to touch the gemstone, she let the pendant lay flat in her hand as Lance held the chain, her fingers closing over the stone. "I've never even seen a red…." Her sentence was cut short. In a split second, Kimberly felt as if fireworks had gone off in her head. The bright light expanded, engulfed her, and was followed by a vision.

In that moment, Kimberly saw herself in a wedding dress. The scene instantly shifted to a beach surrounded by blue waters and swaying palm trees. Before she could blink, she was at Disneyland, holding hands with a young, beautiful blonde girl. Her own hair, she could see, was now gray as she walked arm in arm with someone… someone who had also been seen in all the other images.

That someone was Lance.

"Kimberly, Kimberly!" Lance's worried voice sounded as if came from far away.

At the sound, her hand jerked and the diamond fell from her palm. She watched as it swayed back and forth on the chain dangling from Lance's fingertips.

"You were saying something about the pendant and then you just stopped. Are you okay?"

Kimberly licked her dry lips as she thought about his question. "Yes." If she sounded hesitant, well, there wasn't much she could do about that. She reached out a tentative finger and touched the red diamond again. The vision instantly filled her mind again, picking up where it had left off with the unknown blonde child who looked to be around five years old. Her hand jerked back as if it was burned. Her eyes flew to Lance's face, but she could only see concern there. *He didn't see it?* It was so real…"Yes, I'm fine. I… I think I just got some dust in my eyes or something. Must have blanked out for a moment. Must be allergies with all this dust."

For some reason, she was afraid to tell Lance what she thought she had just experienced. She needed some time to process all that had happened in her mind. "I think we need to leave."

His worried look was replaced by an incredulous one. "What? But I want to look around." His free arm motioned around the room filled with boxes and mementoes from Walt's life. "Look! That box says Studio and that one says Disneyland. That one says Hats. We can't leave yet."

With a silent shake of her head, Kimberly found a small velvet box under the table where the pendant had been displayed. "Here, put the pendant in this." She watched him let the pendant drop into the box, the chain spilling from his fingers link by link until it was all inside. Kimberly then snapped the lid with a decisive *click*. "This needs to come with us." Before he could even reply, the box was slid into her jacket's pocket.

As Lance looked around the room, he thought he understood what she meant, but wondered why she was acting so oddly. "You're right, I guess. This isn't our room. It's Walt's. There's nothing in here we should disturb except this pendant. I think that's what Walt wanted to reward us—well, whoever found it—with at the end of this quest."

"Yes." Kimberly was distracted, her mind still trying to grasp the visions she had just seen. While they had been just fleeting glimpses, they were the clearest 'dreams' she had ever had. They were so vivid, not abstract like her sleeping dreams. The whole episode had to have taken place in only a second or two of time. Yet, she felt as though she had seen a lifetime pass before her eyes…her lifetime.

"I think we should take the book Walt wrote and the pendant with us and leave the rest. We have the key. If we ever need to return, we can." Lance picked up the glass dome and placed it over the now empty display.

Looking around the room one last time, Lance knew that sometime in his future, he would return to this room. As he glanced over at Kimberly, he could see her blonde hair glowing in the amber light. Lance came to another realization in that moment: He also knew he wanted to spend the rest of his life with one woman.

And that woman was Kimberly.

Disneyland – Current Day

"Lance, take the boy down to the courtyard. He isn't needed here any longer."

All eyes in the room turned to the new speaker. Holding the sword upright in his hands, Wolf never took his eyes off the purple-robed figure. With his head, he motioned for Lance to do as he said. "Trust me, Lance. Go. I have this covered. Kimberly, I need you to come over here by me. Don't block my arms."

Quickly recovering from the shock, ignoring Lance and Peter as they hurried from the room, Nimue held out a welcoming hand. "Wolf. My pet. It is good to see you again."

"Don't speak to me that way. I was never your pet."

Nimue gave an amused chuckle. "My, my, you're still rather touchy about that, aren't you? You made such a good pack leader."

"That spell is broken, witch. You'll never have that power over me again."

"Meddling fairies. That may be true, but this beauty," as she nodded her head toward the wide-eyed Kimberly, "will do just fine as your replacement."

Kimberly gave a gasp and shrank back when she saw the staff point directly at her. Its head glowed and arced as a tendril of power suddenly leaped toward her.

Springing into action, moving faster than she could follow, Wolf jumped forward. With a loud *swish*, the blade of the sword sliced through the light, absorbing it. "Did you bring it?"

Kimberly barely heard his whisper. Eyes glued on the menacing green sphere, she could only nod.

"Bring it out and hold it up in front of you. You won't be harmed."

When the pendant dangled in front of Kimberly's face, the glowing orb became dull as its bright color faded. Nimue gave a triumphant smile. "Ah, that's more like it. That jewel is mine. I want it back."

"Your words are weak, just as you are." Wolf aimed the tip of Wals' ancient weapon at the Evil Fairy. The power bestowed upon it by the three Good Fairies many years ago still glowed on the blade. He could feel it hum against his palms as if it was eager for another battle. "You haven't quite recovered from our first battle, have you?" A small, taunting smile came across his lips when she hesitated to answer. "I see you remember this sword. Its power still remains."

She could feel the force emanating from the blade. It became a living, breathing thing all around her, sucking away even more of her power. Her breath labored, Nimue put on a brave face as she reached out for the red diamond. "I just want what's mine. Let me have it and you all will live."

Wolf chuckled low and deep. "You have no say in that, Nimue. You haven't enough power to do as you say. I can see we're quite safe."

The eyes glaring at him narrowed. "Then lower your sword and we shall see."

Wolf ignored her sarcastic request. "I have a question for you. Why?"

As if too heavy to hold it upright, the staff slowly lowered. "Why what, Wolf?"

"Why did you attack our mothers? Omah's and mine? What possible outcome did you foresee?"

"Omah! What does she have to do with this?"

Wolf shushed Kimberly's angry question. "Answer me, Nimue. Why did you attack them? You wanted us dead. That would have been the end result if we had just lived out our lives back then."

There was a very unmajestic snort. "You really don't get it, do you? My dear pet, I didn't want either of you dead. I wanted you for my pack! Do you know how hard it is to get good minions these days? The forces of evil just aren't what they used to be in the good old days." Agitated now, Nimue paced back and forth, gesturing with her free hand. "You saw my men! Scraggly pack of idiots. What better followers could I have than the sons and daughters of powerful leaders! Chiefs and shamans and tsars and moguls. You would have been magnificent!"

"You ruined our lives! We didn't ask for this!"

The pacing stopped as she turned to Wolf, a look of irritation obvious on her face. "And now you have squandered your gift beyond all comprehension!"

There was no point in letting the argument continue. "How many of us are there?"

Nimue waved an airy, dismissive hand. "Oh, who can keep count after all this time? I sent my best man and your father killed and skinned him." Head held high, she folded her arms imperiously over her chest as she looked down her nose at her adversary. "Perhaps I should have gone further back in time and claimed your father as my own. He had more sense than his son."

After a prolonged silence, Kimberly cast a look at Wolf who still stood beside her. He could only stare at the woman who had altered his life forever. "Wolf? My arm is getting tired."

Now that his question had been answered, there was nothing left to say. "Go back where you came from, witch. There is nothing here for you any longer. The clue search you set up for Peter was meaningless."

Kimberly gave a small gasp. "That explains it. That's why the whole thing was so odd, why nothing was secured or as it should be. Walt had nothing to do with it."

Ignoring her words, Nimue's slender finger pointed at the pendant, still slowly turning at the end of Kimberly's hand. "There we will disagree once again, Wolf. We are not finished. There is still my diamond."

"You're not as demanding as you were when you faced a defenseless boy." Wolf took a step closer, the sword that Wals had used to defeat her in the epic battle now aimed at her heart. "We can end this now, or you can go back to your castle, your time, and never bother us again. Either way, I will enjoy it."

"Or, I can summon the forces of ...."

"No, Nimue, you can do nothing. Merriweather told me your powers would be scant. I can see that's true. You might've gotten a mere boy to cower and willingly hand you the necklace, but we will not do so. Go home and do not come back."

Knowing she was defeated, the evil fairy tightly grasped her staff. Not wanting to possibly damage the precious diamond, she focused her last remaining spell on Wolf. With one final surge, a green bolt shot out at him. The sword effortlessly turned sideways to block the energy and it dropped harmlessly to the ground in front of Wolf. As he ground out the small green ember with his foot, rage filled her eyes. "I will go. For now, Wolf, you are correct. But, remember this: It will not always be thus." As she leaned toward Wolf, her voice dropped to a menacing whisper. "I will regain my strength. My power will return. And I promise you this: I will come back to get what is mine."

With a grand gesture, a regal flourish of her hand, the green mist encircled her and she was gone.

"Can I lower my arm now?"

Wolf wiped the sweat from his brow. "Yes, sorry. She's gone."

Kimberly held the necklace out to Wolf and put it into his outstretched hand. "Please make this go away." When he slid it into a pocket, she symbolically dusted off her hands and took a deep breath. She was more shaken than she would admit. A sparkle on the ground caught her eye. Forgotten in the battle, the piece of celluloid still lay where it had been dropped. "Is this what Peter had been searching for?" Kimberly picked it up and turned it front to back. "I don't understand. It's blank."

Not willing to set down the sword just yet, Wolf looked over at the clear cel. "It was all a trick to get Peter to bring her the pendant. As you realized, this was never from Walt."

Kimberly ran a shaking hand down her arm and shivered. "Let's get out of here. I need to hug my son." As they ran down the stone-like steps, past the silent displays and bejeweled storybooks, Kimberly had one last question, one she feared to ask. "Was Nimue right? Will she be back?"

His mind still on what had happened, Wolf could only nod. After a few moments of silence, he answered, "Yes, I'm afraid that part wasn't a bluff. She will regain her strength. But, I don't know if it will be in our lifetime. Well," he added with a slight grin, "at least, not in *your* lifetime."

CHAPTER 15

Fullerton

"It was a fake! The whole thing was fake."

"Peter, honey, you need to calm down." Kimberly sat next to her distraught son. After the drama in the Castle at Disneyland, when they had first come home, Peter had thrown himself on his bed. The Michaels hadn't even received a good-bye when they finally left to go home. Now, ten days later, Peter was still in that same frame of mind. "I know it was scary for you, but everyone is all right. We're just so glad that you or anyone else got hurt."

They looked up as Wolf came into the family room. He tried to act casual, but they all knew Lance had called him. Perhaps he could get through to the boy. Nodding a hello to Kimberly, he basically pushed her out of the way as he sat next to Peter. "I heard you're still having a difficult time."

Taking his broad hint, Kimberly patted him on the shoulder. "I'll let you two talk. I need to check on the other boys."

Just as Peter was about to rebuff his friend, his brave front fell. "I can't believe it anymore, Wolf."

"Can't believe what?"

Peter waved a vague arm around in the air. "Everything. I was tricked. I got so greedy I ruined a priceless picture. I was put under a spell. And it was all for nothing. I just don't get it."

Wolf wondered if he should tell Peter the animation cel was also fake, another manifestation of Nimue's to get what she wanted. He decided it might help relieve the guilt Peter seemed to be feeling. "Well, I examined what was left of the cel, and it wasn't a real one." He let that sink in for a minute as Peter mutely stared at him. "Does that make a difference? Does it help to know that you didn't ruin anything from Walt?"

Peter raised one listless shoulder. "I guess. I don't know. It's…it's just more of the same thing. It was all fake. It was just like the Kobayashi Maru. How was I supposed to know what to do against that?"

A look of confusion came over Wolf's face. "The what?"

"You're kidding. You don't know what the Kobayashi Maru is?"

"Don't talk to me as if I'm an idiot. Explain."

Peter knew his attitude had gone too far. "Sorry. How could anyone not know…. It's from *Star Trek*. It was the ultimate test for captains. But what they didn't know was that it was rigged. There was no way to win. That's just what I feel like. No matter what choice I made, it was wrong because it was all bogus! How do I know if *anything* I've done was real? What if all of it was fake and it was all for nothing?"

Wolf decided to let the *Star Trek* reference slide. Even with his special ability and all he had seen during his long life, he still wasn't a fan of science fiction. "Do you trust me, Peter?"

Wolf's question caught Peter off-guard. "Of course I trust you. You're always there. You never lie. You got rid of Nimue. Of course I do."

"Then believe me when I tell you that everything else you've done—up to this last quest—was real. Do you believe that?"

Again Peter merely shrugged. "But this one felt the same as the other ones. It just felt real, Wolf! How…how am I supposed to know? If I can't tell the difference, what kind of Guardian am I going to make?" Peter lurched up from the sofa as he became more agitated. "I'll tell you what kind…I won't be a Guardian! How can I protect Walt's legacy if I make stupid mistakes like that?"

Wolf thought he saw what was behind the drama. "Is that what's bothering you? You feel you won't be a good Guardian?"

Peter turned from playing with the pulls of the blinds covering the windows. He had to do something with his hands. "Of course that's what's bothering me! I failed, Wolf! Fake or not, I destroyed something just so I could get more clues. That's…that's not what Mom and Dad…or you…would've done."

Wolf went over to where Peter stood and glanced out the window. Kimberly was outside with the boys and Lance as they all played with Dug. Despite the worry they had for Peter, they still showed what they were: A happy family. He gave an inward sigh. Having been around the Brentwood family from the very beginning, the warmth and the closeness never bothered him before. Now it did. It just magnified what he hoped might have happened, what he thought had started to happen, with Omah. But now, traveling back and forth through time until he was dizzy, there was still no trace of her.

"Are you all right, Uncle Wolf?"

The sharp blue eyes jerked back to the boy's worried face. *How long have I been standing here mooning?* "Yeah, sorry." He had to think back on their conversation. "I don't know what I would've done, Pete. Who knows until they actually find themselves in that position?" He thought back to the missing Omah and all that she had gone through. "People make mistakes all the time. Sometimes it's not their fault. Sometimes it's just the circumstances that happen after other people mess things up."

"I don't think I want to be a Guardian."

Only Wolf's sharp hearing could have picked up Peter's last, mumbled remark. "Well, it's a big responsibility. And, you're only thirteen right now. But, Pete, remember that you've been working toward that goal for a long time. You love Disneyland, and you even got to meet Walt! Your dad can't even say that." When he saw that his words didn't have much effect on the boy, Wolf put an arm around Peter's slim shoulders. "You have a few years to go before you'll have to make any decision."

"But what if Catie had gotten hurt? What if she had been lifted up to the ceiling like that, thinking she was going to drop at any minute?"

Ah, I wondered if that was part of it. Wolf gave him a kind smile. "You know something? Worry isn't a bad thing. I worry about you and Catie all the time. When I was gone…."

Peter let out a disgusted snort. "Chasing that horrible Omah?"

Wolf had to keep himself from getting angry at the crack. "She isn't what you think, Peter. You, of all people, know how much strain she was under. You know why she was upset."

"You're defending her?" Peter jerked away from Wolf, a look of disbelief on his face. "She pulled a knife on me!"

A blank look came over Wolf. Earlier Peter had said how she only wanted to get the mermaid back to Walt. *He* had defended her to his parents. *He must be more troubled than I realized. Sheesh, how do parents deal with this every day?* He took a deep, calming breath. "Okay, let's leave Omah out of this right now. What was I saying? Oh, that I worry about you. Peter, I worry about you every day. Things happen. Good things. And bad things. That's just the way of life. But we can't let the *possibility* of getting hurt paralyze us. All we can do is our best. Did you know Catie wanted to go into that little cave after you?"

Peter hadn't heard about that. "She did? But she's afraid of spiders and stuff."

"But she *still* wanted to find you to see if you were all right. How brave is that?"

The hard edge on Peter's face softened a little. "That's pretty cool. I'm glad she didn't have to."

"Me, too." Wolf pulled Peter back for a hug whether he wanted one or not. "I'm very proud of you, Peter. So are your parents and so is Catie and her family. I think you'd make a great Guardian."

Peter made a noise just to say something. He wasn't going to say yes or no at this point.

"Your dad invited me to stay for dinner, so let's just go outside and play with Dug with the rest of your family until we eat. I don't think she gets enough attention around here."

"What? Are you kidding? She….Oh, you're trying to change the subject. I get it. Yeah, let's go outside."

"You know, you're way too smart for a thirteen-year-old."

A small smile played over Peter's lips. "What am I supposed to be like?"

Wolf pulled his face into a stupid grin. "You know, like, you know, duh, for sure, I dunno, what, like, sure!"

Peter just slowly shook his head. "That sounds so bad when old people do it."

"Old!?"

Peter hit the back door running.

Mikey and Andrew were sitting in Wolf's Mustang as they played with the steering wheel and making *Vroom Vroom* noises. Watching from the porch, Kimberly stood next to Wolf. "Just make sure you don't give them your keys. I wouldn't put it past Michael to take off down the driveway."

Wolf held up the keys and jingled them. "Not that stupid, but thanks for the warning."

When Kimberly said nothing else, Wolf glanced at her face. It was obvious she had a question for him, but wasn't sure if she should ask. "Was there something else?"

"Uhm, yeah, there is. I didn't have a chance to ask before, but it was about something you said in the Castle. About Omah."

Wolf remembered he had shushed her at the time. "What is it?"

"Did Omah have anything to do with Peter's…incident?"

Wolf had to let a moment pass just so he didn't answer with any anger. "No, Kimberly. Omah didn't have anything to do with Nimue." He found his voice getting a bitter edge and hesitated again. "She…you haven't gotten to know her like I have. She isn't what you all think."

"You were gone a long time, Wolf. We didn't know where you went, or with whom."

"I know that. I'm still working through something and…you need to trust me."

Kimberly put a hand on his arm and could feel how tense he was. "We do trust you. Always have. But, you know what our impressions of Omah are and why we have them. If you want to explain something different to us, we'd be glad to hear it."

Wolf looked off into the distance. Not seeing his bright red car, he saw, instead, the dusty encampment of the Blackfoot tribe and the wolf Omah rolling and playing with the children who shrieked with delight. That was when he had begun to change his opinion of her. It was then that their relationship had begun to alter.

Thinking she was not going to get a response, unaware of his inner turmoil, Kimberly decided to change the subject. "Glad you could stay for dinner, Wolf. And, thanks for trying to help with Peter. He's been so inconsolable since Nimue cornered him in the Castle. We just weren't getting through to him."

Relieved not to have to explain himself just yet, Wolf gave her a small smile. "Well, I don't know if I succeeded, but time will tell. He's young. Hopefully he'll find another real clue and forget all about this."

Kimberly shrugged. "We both know more are out there.

They're lit up on the holographic map of Disneyland, but he doesn't even want to go in the War Room any more. I mentioned the same thing about another clue. You know what he told me? That he wasn't going to look any more. He said he's done with it. And, if he did find one, he'd turn it over to you. Now that's sad."

"He had more enthusiasm for the treasure hunts than even Lance."

"Did I hear my name? Okay, Wolf, you're not teaching Mikey how to drive yet, are you?" Lance planted a kiss on his wife's cheek as he came out to join them.

"No, not yet. I'd rather borrow your Jaguar for that."

"No chance, buddy, no chance. So, what momentous decisions have been made since you left the dining room?"

Hoping Kimberly wouldn't bring up her question regarding Omah, Wolf made the first comment. "Only that I need to get home. Some of us have to work tomorrow."

"Yeah, the poor slobs." Lance wasn't going to take the bait. He had a week off and was determined to enjoy it.

Kimberly did have one more thing she wanted to run by Wolf. "So, Wolf, are you sure you don't want to come to Walt Disney World with us and the Michaels? We were going to wait until summer, but, with what happened to Peter, decided the winter break would be better. I think you'd have a good time. You always seem to enjoy being around our families." As she waited for a response, she saw an expression quickly pass over Wolf's face. It was gone so fast she couldn't tell if was wistful or I'd-rather-be-dead. She decided to see if it had been wistful. "You could even bring someone...."

Wolf suddenly strode off the porch and pulled the laughing, protesting boys out of his car. With a silent wave, the Mustang tore down the driveway and he was gone.

"Wow, you really know how to clear a room, Kimberly." Lance flung the six-year-old Andrew over his shoulder and swung around in a full circle before heading back into the house.

Slightly stunned by the speedy exit of their guest, she just stood in the driveway as the churned-up dust settled around her. "What'd I say?"

Bothered more than he would admit, Wolf turned the radio on full blast as his car sped down the freeway. The distraction didn't work. Yes, he would love to go with the two families to Disney World. And, yes, he would love to bring someone. Someone with bright red hair and biting sarcasm.

He hit the steering wheel with a clenched fist. "I'm not going to give up. I have to find her…or at least find out if she changed her past."

As the car skidded to a stop in his parking space, he turned off the engine and pocketed the keys.

He pulled the snapshot of Omah out of his jacket pocket, his intense eyes boring into it, his face in deep concentration.

The Mustang was empty before the roar of the engine had stopped echoing through the parking lot.

EPILOGUE

Flashback – Vancouver – 1966

Wolf appeared soundlessly on the 140-foot yacht. The view of the coast of Vancouver was beautiful, but the object of his search had his nose deep in the script of *The Jungle Book*. Seated on the top deck, Walt relaxed in a deck chair as the bright July sun beat down on him.

"Nice hat, boss. Oh, and happy 40th anniversary."

Startled by both the interruption and who it was who made it, Walt dropped the script and tried to get to his feet. "Wolf? You like my captain's hat, hey? Well, I certainly didn't expect to see you here." Not feeling well, Walt dropped back into the lounge with a grunt of disgust. "You'll excuse me if I don't get up. Must be the sun."

Wolf looked at the grayed hair and the dark circles under Walt's eyes. His heart made a lurch at what was to come—sooner than anyone expected. Lips forced into a smile, he sat in a chair next to the ailing man. "That's probably it, boss. Where is everyone?"

Walt waved a hand toward the shoreline. "I think the girls have probably gone fishing or are taking an afternoon nap. I don't know. Been up here for a couple of hours. No one disturbs me." He gave Wolf a pointed look with the last words. If Wolf traveled to see him, it must be important. "What can I do for you?"

"Can't I just come by to say hello?"

Walt's chuckle was cut short by a racking cough. "Well, if we were back in California, I'd say yes." He indicated British Columbia with a tilt of his chin. "We're a long ways from home."

"Never could pull one over on you."

As his boss studied Wolf's security uniform and the differences in what was currently being worn in Disneyland, he knew this was a business trip from the future.

"I have a favor to ask of you, Walt. You remember the boy, Peter, the one who climbed the mast of the Chicken of the Sea Pirate Ship to retrieve that one clue?"

At the memory of the young boy up in the rigging, Walt grimaced. "Yeah. I guess I never figured a young one would find my hidden clues. I remember the look of fear on his mom's face. I'm going make sure the coming clues aren't so dangerous." He glanced at Wolf's passive face and gave a laugh. "But, you know that already, don't you?"

Wolf could only shrug. "Yeah. I know you'll also remember that Peter's the grandson of your right-hand-man." At Walt's nod, he continued. "Well, Peter is only thirteen right now, but I think he'll continue his grandfather's legacy as a Guardian. He's done really well with the quests he's found, and is pretty keen on the subject."

"I see the word 'but' written all over your face."

Wolf nodded. "Something happened that none of us could've foreseen and it has made Peter a little gun-shy."

"Anything you care to share, or can share? I keep asking and you usually don't tell me much."

Wolf looked out in the distance. They were anchored in a lovely spot. "It had to do with a special, um, artifact you put into place, something unexpected. It's changed hands quite a few times and caused some problems."

A worried frown spread over Walt's face as he glanced over at the ladder that lead up to his little hideaway. None of his family was in sight, and he couldn't hear anyone talking. Knowing no one else would see it, he reached into the pocket of his slacks and pulled out the heart-shaped red diamond Hidden Mickey pendant. As the sun hit the stone, a rainbow of facets spun and danced over every surface. Still mesmerized by the mysterious piece of jewelry he had received in 1940, Walt reluctantly tore his eyes from it and turned back to Wolf. "You don't seem surprised to see this."

"I know what you're planning to do with it."

Walt stared at him for a moment longer, his arm dropping from the strain of holding it upright. "Yes, I suppose you would." He looked at the pendant in his lap, the diamond now hidden in folds of his pants. The familiar Mickey-shaped gold work that held the stone in place was almost too bright in the sunlight. His fingers hovered over the stone, knowing what would happen if he touched it again. But, he was just too tired right then to see whatever the stone would show him and his hand dropped listlessly to the side. "Do you believe in destiny, Wolf?"

The question surprised him. He should have realized that he never could guess what his boss would say next. "No, not really, Walt. I think things happen because of the choices we make." When he thought about his ability to travel through time, he added, "And, sometimes, the choices that others make for us."

"Same here." Walt lifted the necklace a few inches off his lap, the diamond spinning back and forth at the end of the fine gold chain. "Some of the things this diamond showed me when I touched it were wonderful. It gave me hope to continue when things looked the bleakest. It showed me things that would happen in the future—probably some of it in your time—that gave me great pleasure." His mind turned from the visions of Disneyland to a hidden cavern deep beneath Pirates of the Caribbean. "And some of the things it showed me will *never* happen. I'll make sure they don't happen." At Wolf's understanding nod, he continued. "Some things I saw didn't make sense to me, but I have confidence that you— and the other Guardians—will make the best decisions. Some things that were shown made a lot of sense, like the treasure hunt." He patted a thick manila envelope on top of a pile of scripts. "You know what this is, obviously."

"Two good friends of mine will find it. They'll do you proud."

Walt studied him a moment. After a cough left him winded, he laid his head back on the lounge. "After what you just told me, I'm worried about this pendant. I never wanted to cause anyone distress. You know that."

"We all know that, Walt."

Visibly relieved to hear that, Walt relaxed his tense posture. "Good. Wolf, I know you came here for a favor, but I'm going to ask one of you first."

"Anything, boss."

"Take this diamond back to Merlin."

His mouth slightly open, Wolf couldn't reply right away. "But, Walt...."

"Don't 'but, Walt' me, son. I don't mean right now. When the time is right, when its use is over, then take it away. I don't want anyone to get hurt. You, better than anyone, will know exactly when to do it." He studied the look on Wolf's face but couldn't read it. "Will you promise?"

Wolf snapped his mouth shut. Perhaps it would be for the best. He nodded his promise.

"Good man. I can always count on you." The pendant was carefully returned to his pocket. "Now that we have been sufficiently distracted, what did you need from me? What about Peter?"

Wolf looked at the loved face, now covered with deep lines. *I'm going to miss you, Walt.* "You always did have a good memory. I was hoping you could do something special just for Peter. I'd like him to have his own, personal Hidden Mickey treasure hunt that will seal him as a Guardian. He's too young right now, but he's growing fast. Could you do that for me?"

Walt glanced at the yellow envelope. "Won't that one do?"

"No, it's good the way it is. It starts a wonderful chain of events."

Silent for a moment, grateful for the knowledge, Walt nodded. "Well, I'll be back home in another week. Can you give me a month? Anything specific you want in it?"

"No, you know what to do." Wolf put a hand on the manila envelope. "You know exactly what to do."

Walt gave him a big smile. "Yeah, I think this one's pretty good, too. Been working on it for a lot of years." He put his head back as he thought, but turned to face Wolf. "Are you sure you can't give me any details? What to use and what not to use?"

"I can't tell you that, Walt. Just pick what you think will last forever."

"I like the sound of that. Forever! Well, that pretty much includes the whole Park. Nothing changes!"

"'Disneyland will never be completed, as long as there is imagination left in the world'"

Walt made a sour face. "I hate it when you quote me. I said it will never be complete. That doesn't mean anything has to be taken away."

"Oh? Let's see?" Wolf made a show of thinking back and then he started to count off on his fingers. "Phantom Boats. The Viewliner. Wizard of Bras. Hall of Chemistry. The Conestoga Wagons. Flying Saucers."

"Okay, okay." Walt held up a hand in defeat. "I get your point. Don't worry. Peter will have the time of his life!" Walt struggled to his feet and walked over to the handrail to lean heavily against it. "Are you going now? You could stay for dinner, you know."

"I don't want to interrupt your family vacation."

"You are family, Wolf."

Wolf looked at Walt and held out his hand. "Thanks. That means a lot."

Walt looked at the hand and, instead, pulled Wolf in for a hug. They had never hugged before, but it just felt right. When he felt, rather than hear, Wolf's breath catch, he patted his friend's back. "You're a good man, Wolf. I'm lucky to have known you."

Wolf pulled away so he could look into Walt's eyes. There was a sadness there, and an understanding. With a silent nod, Wolf vanished from sight.

Disneyland – Current Day

Sitting on the edge of the Friendly Village, Wolf's feet were only inches from the gently lapping, green water. The emergency canoe that docked below the Hungry Bear Restaurant had been 'borrowed' and he had paddled over to the well-known break in the trees. Behind him, the voice of the Shaman could be heard as he told his tale to the seated warriors. Lights around the camp flickered as they lit the familiar scene.

But Wolf wasn't there for reflection on his family. He was there for the solitude to reflect on his last visit with Walt. The end had come quickly for one of the most famous men in the world. And the world had mourned his death.

No one mourned more than Wolf. Even now, decades later, he still missed his mentor, his boss, his friend.

He felt alone.

Wolf knew he had good friends. There was Lance and Kimberly, Peter, Adam and Beth. Catie had won a special place in his heart with her kind spirit and loving heart. He knew he could always count on his good buddy Wals. There were others, too, but, they were friends. Not family.

Walt had almost felt like a father to him. Sure, he could visit his real father any time he wanted to travel back to their village. But, now, in the darkness of the night, he sat there all alone. No one waited for him to come home.

The opportunity had been there—was still there—to go back and alter his past by saving his mother. What would it have been like if he hadn't received his powers but had lived on as a normal human? Marriage to one of the village girls would have been assured. A wife. Children. Growing old together. Grandchildren. Dying together.

But he just couldn't do it. Had he been selfish? He asked himself that question over and over. Was it selfish to want to keep the life—lonely as it was—that he had created for himself in the now? Would it always be lonely? He had to keep holding onto the hope that it wouldn't always be this way. There was the wonder, the hope that perhaps….

No, she's been gone for a long time. But his memory of her was still sharp. What did that mean? Was she still out there somewhere or did she go back to save her mother? *Why do I still remember her? And, why can't I find her anywhere? Where else could I possibly search, and how?*

Letting out an uncharacteristic sigh, he shook his head slowly side to side. *Good thing Lance wasn't around. I'd never hear the end of it if he caught me mooning over someone.* At the thought of his sarcastic friend, Wolf gave a low chuckle.

"My, aren't we all over the place? First you give a wistful sigh. And then you laugh at your own joke. Care to share with the class?"

Wolf sprang to his feet and wheeled around, surprise and happiness mixed on his face. "Omah!"

"Well, at least your eyesight is still good."

His arms reached out for her, but, then, suddenly dropped to his side. The broad grin on his face began to fade. Why was she here? What did it mean? "I'm glad to see you."

When she saw his welcoming gesture abruptly end, she began to doubt of the wisdom of her return. His words, though, seemed to be what she needed to hear. The wary look on her face turned into one of cautious joy. Not sure what to do next, she licked her dry lips. "I…I couldn't do it, Wolf. I couldn't go back and save my mother. I didn't want…."

Wolf took a step closer. He could see the unshed tears in her blue eyes as they shimmered in the moonlight. "You didn't want to what?"

One side of her lips turned up in a small grin. "I've never heard you speak softly like that, Wolf. I like it. I couldn't take the chance that…I'd never see you again." She took one step closer.

"Me, either." Wolf held his arms out again.

Omah didn't even hesitate as she rushed into his embrace.

Before he kissed her, before they sealed their futures, Wolf looked deep into her eyes. "We don't age, you and I. You know this means forever."

"I do."

Arm in arm, heads together, they quietly chatted about their future together. Wolf told Omah what Nimue/the Evil Fairy had done to them and what she had tried to do to Peter. Her plans completely ruined, she had gone back to her own time to wait and plot and scheme.

Deep in his heart, Wolf knew she would be back someday. His mind still churned with unanswered questions. Had he done enough? Could he have done anything else?

"What are you thinking? You look a million miles away. Are you thinking about me?"

"I was just thinking about Nimue."

The coy, womanly look fell. "Oh."

"I always wanted revenge for what she did to me all those years ago, how she put me under her spell and stripped everything from me." His voice dropped to almost a whisper. "It took a long time to recover my health and…my dignity.   And, now we know what she did to our mothers and why," he added, as Omah leaned back against his arm.

"I think we got the best revenge of all, Wolf. I can't think of anything else that would make her more miserable."

Wolf leaned away from her to look into her face. Her smile was smug and assured. "What do you mean? She didn't get the pendant, and she's still alive."

Omah didn't know what he meant by a pendant. Wolf hadn't told her that part of the story yet. That explanation could wait for a later time. "Oh, I think we both came out on top."

"Explain."

Omah cuddled into his warm side. She knew they would be together from this moment forward. "Sometimes love is the best revenge of all."

—THE END—

Next book...

HIDDEN MICKEY
ADVENTURES 5
When You Wish
NANCY TEMPLE RODRIGUE

ABOUT THE AUTHOR

NANCY TEMPLE RODRIGUE

Nancy lives in the small town of Lompoc, California. Her work shows her admiration and respect for the man who started it all–Walt Disney.

Her love of all things Disney was shown in her first four *Hidden Mickey* novels. This *Hidden Mickey Adventures* series features even more action-adventure Mystery starring Wolf and the next generation of clue-solvers.

Nancy's novels are written for readers of all ages, from Adult to Tweens, ages 9 to 90. She loves leaving you with a cliffhanger ending, so where the last novel *Hidden Mickey Adventures 3: The Mermaid's Tale* ends, this novel *Hidden Mickey Adventures 4: Revenge of the Wolf* picks right up. She gives you just enough to answer those lingering questions you were left with, yet leaving you with even more that remain unanswered for now.

See your favorite Disney Parks in a whole new way with Nancy's *Hidden Mickey Quests* series. Designed to be played inside the Parks, these games and quests take readers on a new, exciting journey.

Nancy actively holds book signings and speaking events. Visit blog.hiddenmickeybook.com to follow the author's blog and learn the locations and dates of her book signing events, or follow her at Facebook.com/HiddenMickeyFanClub.

9 781938 319334